# PARADISA

# PARADISA

MICHELLE IANNANTUONO

Charlotte, NC

FALSTAFF
BOOKS

WWW.FALSTAFFBOOKS.COM

---

Connor Bishara shoved his hands into his pockets, ducking his head against the saffron-scented wind. Tunis could be a sweltering bitch in the summer, but on November nights, the chill sunk in. Hordes of people bustled around the Avenue de France, providing some kind of distant, intangible warmth that slipped right past him.

His previous tours of the Middle East were numerous, but this dissonant love child of France and the Sahara remained a stranger. He was used to seeing his heritage through the scope of a US rifle. But as the city bounced back from its Maghrib prayer hour, it felt…cathartic. Just moments before, hundreds of people were stopped in their tracks, lowering themselves to their knees, unified in one thought. Perhaps it wasn't all that different from his years in the service.

He shouldered his way through the crowd, careful to keep Clara in the corner of his vision. She was a head shorter than him, easy to get lost in the sea of people, but her constant idle chatter provided an anchor. As long as he could hear her, she was safe.

They stopped at a crosswalk one block away from their hotel, where Mam undoubtedly paced and checked her watch every thirty seconds. It was near dinner time, and "hungry" was one of two moods Connor never enjoyed catching their mother in.

He'd need to shower anyway, once they got back to the hotel. His sweaty, salmon-colored, twenty-year-old Flaming Lips shirt hung pathetically loose after years of spin cycles. Beneath it his shoulders slumped with a less-than-royal posture, because that's what standing over a restaurant stove for a decade did to a person.

And boy, did everything hurt. His body hardly resembled the one that could run four-minute miles, tread water for hours, or stand at attention from twilight to dawn. That skin had been shed years ago, leaving him with this new body—this tired, pushing forty, the-mind-is-willing-but-joke's-on-you body that surely belonged to someone else.

Clara looped a hand into the crook of his arm as they crossed the street. A few strangers glanced at them, some with questionable looks, others with fondness. Connor had heard it all, by this point. "Is she your girlfriend?" often came from fifty-year-old sleezebags who habitually courted women half their age. "Your daughter is so smart," came more often from older women.

Men with younger sisters were the only ones who guessed correctly, because they *knew.* They understood the odd combination of expressions—the protectiveness of a parent without the possessiveness. The urge to guide and control without the authority to do so. And the low roar of competitive jealousy, just below the surface, that made him feel like a piece of shit.

Once across the street, Clara untangled from him. With a glance at her lock screen, she said, "It's almost six. Dinner's at seven so...guess we've got an hour to get ready for it."

Connor slid both hands back into his jacket. "Guess I'll let you shower first. You always take so long on your hair."

"Pfft. Please. I think I've learned to be a *little* more efficient in the past couple years."

Oh, he knew—didn't stop him from making fun of her anyway. They lived together back in Charleston, in a two-story townhome near the crosstown. But for the entire first year of Clara's term at The

Citadel, cadets were required to stay on campus. Military college didn't have much tolerance for beauty standards. Show up, look clean, have your belt polished.

Clara was a junior now, but the utilitarian habits of freshman year still stuck. Hell, it'd been ten years since Connor had stepped foot on a Navy base, and he still folded his underwear and cropped his hair the same way. There was something to be said for mindless efficiency.

Their four-story hotel came into view. Pretty hard to miss—a marble behemoth hogging an entire street corner. Connor held open the door for his sister and followed her inside. The warmth of the lobby brushed away some of the outside chill.

He jerked his chin toward the elevator. "You go ahead. I'm gonna grab a drink."

"Pre-gaming already?"

"Five nights straight with Mam and Dad requires a bit of social lubricant."

She sighed, losing the judgement. "Can't blame you. I'll probably get an amaretto sour with dinner."

"Gross."

Oh, to be twenty-one years old and need three types of sweetener and ice to handle alcohol. Maybe getting older gave him an appreciation for simplicity, but for Connor, it was whiskey neat or nothing.

Clara waved a hand, walking away from him. "I'll text you when the shower's free."

He gave a two-finger salute to her back and walked in the opposite direction.

The bar was a gaudy thing—red carpet and mahogany paneling, like a cigar room in a rich white dude's house. The whole hotel was a little gaudy, honestly. Probably the French influence all over the damn place. Would have been nice to see what Tunisia looked like without the French invasion, but as the colonizers would say, *c'est la vie*.

Although six o'clock was cocktail hour in America, it was pretty early for dinner on this side of the world. Only one other patron occupied the bar, his fingers delicately stroking the stem of his wine glass. Something deep and red lingered within.

The stranger looked out of place in Tunis. His dark hair contrasted starkly against his ivory skin. His pale blue eyes reflected the mood lighting of the bar, both earnest and soulful at once. Connor's throat clenched. If Eric's wallet-sized photo hadn't burned into his brain, he'd have sworn…

As soon as Connor approached, the familiarity vanished. Up close, the man hardly resembled Eric at all. Connor's memories were clear enough—sparkling eyes and roguish brown hair, ashen complexion, and a lanky frame Connor used to tackle into the grass. Eric's soft lips ghosting the back of his neck during their one vacation together. The mountains, a quiet cabin, and tossing M&M's to each other in bed, laughing when they missed each other's mouths. Pictures could fill in the gaps, but they were a ghost of the person he'd loved.

The man in front of him was real.

Connor moseyed up to the bar and took a seat, leaving one stool empty between them. The stranger spoke first, nodding to him.

"Good evening." An English accent. Relief immediately replaced Connor's déjà vu just from hearing something as familiar as his native language.

"Hey there." Connor glanced to the bartender—a young man with brown skin and thick black hair who could have looked, if you rolled back fifteen years and squinted, somewhat similar to Connor himself. "Just a shot of Jameson, thanks. No ice."

When he looked back at the stranger, the man was already watching him. Connor purposefully made eye contact, and nearly missed the man's hand extended toward him.

"I'm Raphael."

"Connor." He shook Raphael's hand lightly. The bartender slid a whiskey tumbler toward him, giving him an excuse to tear his gaze away.

"So, what is an American doing in Tunis, Connor?" Raphael offered a polite smile. Although handsome in an angular, androgynous model sort of way, he somehow looked young and old at the same time.

"Family trip. My dad's from here. Figured we'd do things a little different for Thanksgiving this year." He tilted his glass to Raphael. "What about you?"

"I'm looking after someone in the hotel."

"Ah. Caregiver?"

"More like bodyguard, I suppose."

Connor had to snort, even if it was a bit rude. But how could he not? Raphael didn't have much meat on his bones. He'd be pretty shocked if the guy could lift a barbell.

"Let me know if you need any help with that," he said, smirking. "I was a SEAL for six years. Come to room 305, and I'll punch out any bad guys you want."

That was the slight buzz of whiskey talking, of course. And maybe the high of no-strings-attached flirtation, where he could casually bullshit about how much close quarters combat he actually remembered. Raphael didn't need to know that it had been years since he'd even clocked a punching bag. Or that his abs were more washcloth than washboard, lately.

Raphael watched him a little too long, enough for the hair to prickle on the back of Connor's neck. It had been a long time since another man looked at him that way. And he suddenly wished that he'd come down here *after* getting ready for dinner, instead of covered in a day's worth of tourism grime and dressed in a band tee he should have thrown out years ago.

He didn't do this back home—cruising for the mystery and attention of a casual fling. Close quarters with other men used to be an inconsequential occurrence. After a while, the other SEALs had felt like brothers to him, and he didn't care for the muscular types anyway.

Raphael, however, was something new and anonymous. And he definitely didn't look like an overbuilt meathead.

Connor planned to leave Tunis in two days. Whatever happened wouldn't matter.

"So, who are you a bodyguard for? Or if you tell me, do you have to kill me?"

A soft laugh. He couldn't remember the last time he'd made a guy laugh.

"It's nothing like that. But you're right, I'm probably not at liberty to say much."

Connor turned his knees a little, more in Raphael's direction. He looked down at his tumbler and took another swig.

"What *can* you tell me about yourself?"

Raphael paused thoughtfully. He lifted the wine glass with three slender fingers. "I can tell you that this is the first drink I've had in eighty-seven years."

"Heh. Feels like it's been awhile for me, too. My sister—she's in college and lives with me, so I don't go out much."

"Ah. What's your sister's name?"

"Clara."

"Oh. Both your names are Irish?"

"Yeah, Mam fought tooth and nail for it. She was like, if Dad gets to give us our last name, she'd better give us our firsts."

The more they talked, the more Connor lost sense of time. It was probably getting late. His phone was probably blowing up, and maybe he'd missed his chance at a good shower. But none of that really seemed to matter. What had started out as the casual practice of flirting with a nonthreatening stranger had somehow turned into forty-five minutes of actual conversation, laughter, smiles. Raphael kept *looking* at him—really *looking* at him, in ways that made him both beam and bow his head at the same time.

Near the end of the hour, Raphael downed the last of his wine and pushed the empty glass away from him. The bartender stepped over to bus it, as Raphael spouted out a stream of flawless Arabic. Connor blinked. Once upon a time, he'd have been able to translate more than *"thank you"* and the verb for *"receive"* thrown in there. Now, years out of practice, the foreign words slipped through the cracks in his brain like sand.

The bartender slid a check across the bar. Raphael threw down a handful of dinar—probably far more than a glass of wine cost—and told him to keep the change.

"Heading back up?" Connor asked.

Raphael rose from the stool and slid his wallet back into his black bomber jacket.

"Mm. I'm needed upstairs, most likely. But thank you for your company, Connor."

That eye contact again, unabashed. An invitation, maybe.

Connor threw some dinar on the bar and shot the last of his whiskey in one burning gulp. "May as well share the ride back up, eh?"

2

———————

Connor was late. Connor was *never* late.

By the time Clara blew her hair dry and finished applying a light dusting of makeup, Connor still hadn't returned from his jaunt to the bar.

"Where the hell are you?" She picked her phone off the counter and scrolled through their text history, but the most recent messages were all her own.

*Me (6:17 PM) – shower's yours*
*Me (6:27 PM) – helllloooooo*
*Me (6:39 PM) – don't make me come get you*

It was 6:51 now, and she'd have to make good on the threat. She could see Mam and Dad in the bathroom mirror, both of them pacing and muttering to each other. Dad's stomach growled, loud enough to hear from across the room. Clara set her phone down, shaking her head. Whatever had distracted Connor long enough to keep their father waiting could never be a good excuse.

Because, frankly, Malik Bishara was not to be fucked with. The mere squint of his eyes could turn Clara's blood cold back when she was a misbehaving child. A short grunt from the back of Dad's throat equaled "You're in trouble." Adding a tap of his toe meant "You're in *big* trouble." And utter silence, Clara had learned too often, meant "I'm disappointed."

"We need to leave," Dad muttered, leaning against the divider between the bathroom and the sleeping area. "Where on Earth is your brother?"

"Uh...downstairs at the bar. He's not answering my messages, so I guess I'll go get him." *And he's just gonna have to deal with feeling like a grease trap at dinner 'cause I am not waiting on him to shower.*

Mam waved a hand to the door, gesturing for Clara to go. She stuck her phone in her back pocket and grabbed her jacket from the table by the door. Hopefully she wouldn't have to actually *leave* the hotel to go find her asshole brother, but, just in case.

She closed the door behind her and headed down the musky-smelling hallway. The entire building had that *old* smell going on. Some combination of dust, old brick, and paint layered upon paint. They covered the hotel's age with a lot of gold leaf and wainscoting, but it almost felt like overcompensation for a crappy HVAC system and the constant dank odor. Tunis was a modern city. They could easily have chosen a chic loft hotel right up the road, but Mam and Dad insisted on something *historic.*

The elevator opened as she reached it, but there was no need to enter. Connor was already there, standing beside a handsome, slender man with wavy, dark hair.

She tried not to smirk. She *really* tried. But her brother had a Type, and it was right there in skinny, pretty boy glory.

Connor stepped out of the lift, his gaze never leaving the other man. And Clara knew she wasn't going to have fun trying to explain to Mam and Dad why Connor *might* not be coming back to their room tonight.

As the metal doors started to close, Connor bellowed, "For real, Raphael. Room 305. If you need some extra muscle, give me a call."

The doors slid shut as Raphael returned a shy smirk.

Clara snorted, punching her brother in the arm. "Yeah, right. You couldn't beat up a sloth right now."

"Oh, shut up."

They turned away from the elevator and headed down the opulent-ass hallway, shoulder to shoulder. Connor's posture seemed even more slumped than usual, his hands buried in his pockets and his brown eyes downcast. Clara sighed, pulling back some of her teasing.

"Why do you want to hang with that guy so bad, anyway? I mean, he's cute, but you haven't dated anyone in *years...*" The *eek* was conveyed by tone alone, and Connor matched it with an annoyed grunt.

"Come on, I'm not that rusty. Jesus. I just liked the look of him. And we're about to leave the country, so it's not like I'd *date* him. He barely even needed to know my name." Connor waved a hand. "And I didn't learn anything worth a damn about him either. He said he's here on some kind of secret bodyguard bullshit."

"Ooh." Now that was a little more intriguing than a pretty face. "The SEAL and the Spy. It's like a gay James Bond novel."

Connor groaned, shoving her with a weak hand. "You're the worst."

"Hey, I'm not getting any, so may as well live vicariously through you."

Relationships and sex weren't interesting to her—no matter how many times Mam told her she'd fall for someone someday, and no matter how many times Ryan from Delta Company told her she'd want dick once she got his—but it was somehow gratifying to root for others. It was about time for Connor to find something good in his life. She would graduate soon, probably move out, and...then what?

It wasn't fun to think about that.

As they approached room 305, a man in a hooded denim jacket walked toward them on the other side of the hall. His head was bowed, the hood obscuring his face, and both of his arms were wrapped around himself. As he drew closer, so did the *stench*. Something like sweaty clothes and meat. Clara held her breath, nose scrunching up as the smelly guy approached.

A normal person would have gone around Connor and Clara. With his head bowed and his voice muttering nonsense under his breath, perhaps he was in too much of his own world to see them. He barreled through them, bumping Clara's side harshly as he passed, without so much as looking back to apologize.

"Hey, watch it!" Connor called after the guy, one of his hands falling to Clara's shoulder.

The hooded creep continued to ignore them, making a beeline for the stairwell. He shouldered roughly into the door, and started up the stairs before the door slammed behind him. Clara glanced up, giving Connor one of those WTF looks. He didn't look back—instead staring at the stairwell door with a furrowed brow.

"Stay here."

"Connor!" She lowered her voice to a whisper, just so Mam wouldn't come running out of their room. "Where the hell are you going?"

"That guy's up to something, Clara. I'll be right back."

"What, are you profiling now or something? Let's just go to dinner."

He narrowed his eyes. "Yeah, I'm profiling. White dude runs around a five-star Tunisian hotel smelling like garbage and wearing a hoodie over his head. What could possibly be normal about that?"

He walked away, probably thinking that would put her in her place. Funny how they'd known each other for twenty-one years, and he still didn't know jack shit about her.

Which is to say, she followed him.

"Assuming you're right, what exactly are you gonna do about it? What if he's got a gun? I'd rather not have to go to Mam and Dad and explain how you got shot by some tweaker."

Connor didn't reply, maybe because he didn't have one. Her brother's dumb bravado and paranoia couldn't hold a candle to her logic. If there were two types of people in the world—those who run away from danger and those who run headfirst into it—Connor was firmly in category two. It was honestly a miracle that she'd seen him make it to thirty-nine.

And since he was probably out of miracles by now, Clara trailed him into the stairwell.

---

When Connor reached the fourth floor, shit had already hit the fan.

At the far end of the hall, Hoodie Guy bashed his shoulder into one of the doors over and over, rattling the entire hallway with the force.

It was, quite obviously, not his room.

Connor moved quickly into a run, as the door to room 417 splintered into a spray of wood. A lot of things hit him at once—Clara's shriek piercing his ears, the scattering thump of door pieces hitting the carpet, and the swell of sawdust floating near Connor's nose and eyes. Time seemed to slow around him as he waved the fog of debris out of his face and shook the dust off his neurons.

Voices and thumping emerged from room 417. Connor crept to the doorway, craned his neck around the corner. And what was waiting in the room was…well, it was a hell of a thing.

In one corner of the room stood Raphael, and that's about where reality ended. Because in one hand, Raphael held a sword made of ivory and fire, its blade clashing with the hooded man's black dagger.

But they weren't alone. A middle-aged brunette woman in a sleeveless dress carried an equally menacing weapon—a sword so lumbering it would take most men two hands to carry it. She managed to wield it with one hand, her bare biceps rippling with the strain.

Despite Raphael's swift strikes and the woman's raw strength, the hooded man eluded them like a snake. Every time either of them got a hand near him, their touch seemed to phase right through him.

Swords. Fire. A weird-looking creep with a dagger. Connor blinked, as if that would make sense of all this, but the world remained the same.

So, instinct kicked in, as it did in all the moments when his brain went offline. He slid a hand against his ribcage, searching for a sidearm, but there was nothing but sweaty fabric. *Damn. Habit.*

Clara tugged on his other arm. "This is crazy! Let's get out of here!"

Before he could argue, a female scream drew him back to room 417. It wasn't shrill; more like the opposite of shrill. An Amazonian growl.

As he turned back to the doorway, the hooded man pushed past him, bumping his shoulder on the way. Connor leaned forward, reaching out a hand to grab him by the jacket, but the cloth eluded him.

His vision split down the middle. On his left, the hallway where the hooded man swept away faster and faster with limping steps. And on his right, the hotel room where the woman laid on the floor, her back supported by the edge of the bed. She screamed and writhed, the hooded man's dagger buried hilt-deep in her stomach. Raphael fell to his knees beside her, his flaming weapon abandoned on the other side of the room.

Connor looked back at Clara. "Stay with them! Make sure she's okay!"

"But—"

He ran away before he could entertain her protests. His gaze darted around, quickly landing on the stumbling attacker attempting to flee to the staircase. Connor sucked in a breath and boosted to full sprint, closing the distance between them with ease.

"Hey!" Connor reached out, grasping the back of the guy's hoodie by the barest tips of his fingers. It was enough force to pull the hood off the man's head and to get his attention. He whipped around, and when Connor finally got a good look at him—

*Holy shit.*

To continue thinking of Hoodie Guy as a *guy* probably wasn't accurate. Close up, it was obvious what the hood had been hiding. The man's eyes had no irises. Tiny pinpoint-sized pupils floated in milky white orbs. Pale skin stretched unnaturally across his bones: malnourished, paper-thin, like it could flake off with a scratch.

He screeched in Connor's face, spraying warm red spittle across his own chin and Connor's cheek. Blood.

Either Hoodie Guy was real sick, or he wasn't *human* at all.

Connor's hands balled into fists. *Fight or flight, motherfucker.*

He darted forward, wrapping both arms around the man's torso. They slammed into the nearest wall together, but Connor's body rattled with most of the force. The other man barely responded to it, instead digging his hand into Connor's jacket and effortlessly tossing him six feet.

Connor hit the carpet, the wind rushing out of his lungs. With a gurgled noise, he rolled onto his stomach, overwhelmed by a tsunami of pins and needles. *That was...way stronger than a guy that size should be.* He forced himself to a crouched position with a fist buried in his side.

He ran on nothing but adrenaline and fury, propelling himself up at his deceptively strong foe. It had been so long since he laid a fist on anybody, and his out-of-shape muscles protested as he swung. While he threw punches like it was yesterday, they barely landed at all. For every hand he managed to get on the freak, another fist shot right through him, pushing out a burst of black smoke in its wake. Like fighting a fucking ghost.

How could he take down something he could barely touch?

The hooded monster didn't give him the chance. It exploded into a swarm of smoke, knocking Connor into the wall and rattling every door in the hallway. The remaining smoke expanded into a gentle tide until it dissipated, coating Connor with the stench of cauterized failure.

# 3

When Connor returned to room 417, things were much the way he'd left them, other than the addition of Clara. Against the foot of the bed, the muscled woman lay with a dagger sticking out of her gut. Raphael and Clara were knelt on either side of her, their words toppling over each other into indecipherable noise.

As Connor took his first step into the room, something small and dense bumped against his foot—something hard enough to send a throb through his toe but light enough to roll away when he nearly tripped over it.

He knelt, reaching for the item. It was a smooth piece of ivory, polished with gold leaf filigree, approximately seven inches long. The same as the weapon Raphael held, although it now lacked the fire and blade…

As soon as his fingers closed around it, searing heat ripped across the inside of his palm.

"Shit!" He released—no, practically flung away—the offending hilt. His hand automatically clenched into a fist to quell the phantom burn. The bitch throbbed worse than grabbing a cast iron pan after it'd been in the oven (something that had happened more at work than he was willing to admit aloud, but hey, late nights working in a bar kitchen didn't bring out his sharpest brain cells).

He couldn't dwell on the pain, or on the mystery of why a piece of ivory stung like fire. There was one person in this room who was a lot worse off than he was.

When he finally stepped over to where Clara helped Raphael and the injured woman, they barely acknowledged his presence. They were far too occupied with the woman spitting out pained curses and Raphael's delicate attempt to remove the dagger from her waist.

Now only a few feet away, the woman's features were more distinct. While beautiful, a few wrinkles and pock marks of age marred her face. Even more peculiar were the long scars twisting over her left eyebrow and her chin—too jagged and deep to be from anything other than battle. Her hawkish amber eyes narrowed in pain, light brown eyebrows knitted together. Some kind of metal clamp hung halfway out her hair, but it no longer did its job pinning her curls back.

But what was gushing out of her wound was *far* more interesting than her face.

Shimmering golden fluid soaked her entire side. It coated her hands, slicked up Raphael and Clara's hands too, and dribbled down her chin over pale lips. The whole floor around her shined with it. A puddle of gold haloing a woman made of steel.

"What the hell is this stuff?" Connor muttered. He took a step back, avoiding the golden liquid. But Clara was already soaked in it, so God forbid it was something toxic.

"My blood..." the injured woman replied through gritted teeth. "... that I wouldn't be bleeding if you would get this dagger out of my gut!"

"This is a sacrificial blade," Raphael said. "If we remove it, your wound may not heal."

"It's certainly not healing so long as it's in me, you fool!"

Connor took a deep breath, closing his eyes. Golden blood, flaming swords, and zombies who turned to smoke. It just kept getting weirder. Maybe Raphael had drugged him at the bar, and this was some strange, terrible trip. That'd teach him not to flirt with strangers anymore.

But there was Clara at his feet, in the mix of it all. She was real, and she could see the rest of this. So, did that make this…?

"If you won't take it out, I will," the woman groused, one hand wrapped around the hilt of the dagger. As Raphael and Clara both shouted for her to stop, she ripped the blade out of her own gut with one smooth movement. Raphael's hands fell upon the wound immediately, golden blood overflowing between his fingers. Connor took a step back, tugging on Clara's shoulder.

Blue light glowed from Raphael's hands, casting a sickly shade over the woman's golden blood. After a few moments, the light faded, and Raphael slowly removed his palms.

"It's healed," the woman muttered, her nose wrinkling. "But it…I can still feel it…"

"I thought that might happen. The damage can be healed physically, but there's more that we can't see. This is beyond my scope, Athena. We need to take you to someone who can mend souls."

Athena remained silent. Connor reached down for Clara's shoulder, squeezing it, anchoring himself to it. Women weren't typically named Athena, unless they were born in a gated community and grew up in an elitist private school for "the gifted." Athena was the name of a goddess, and judging from her golden fucking blood…

This couldn't be real, this couldn't be real, this couldn't be—

"Connor."

Raphael watched him with those cool blue eyes. Unlike the charm they'd held down at the bar, they were now filled with worry.

"Uh…wha…yeah?"

"I saw you went after the spectre. Did you manage to apprehend it?"

Connor blinked at the term—*spectre*. A ghost of darkness, a trick of light. Far too elegant a term for a half-zombified crazy man. And if Raphael knew what that creature was, and was fully prepared to fight it, what the hell did that make Raphael?

He shoved that question into a box along with the overflowing pile of *what the fuck* he'd accumulated in the last ten minutes.

"N-no. I didn't get it. It turned to smoke and vanished, I guess."

*I failed.*

Raphael nodded, his shoulders loose and his expression grateful. "That's alright. I'm just glad you weren't killed in the fight."

A small smile traced the corner of his mouth, just for a second. Not anything joyful or charming, but a small token of relief. A lump worked its way into Connor's throat.

"I guess I wasn't really afraid of it," Connor said. "It was too crazy to believe it was real, even when I was fighting it."

It also summoned something too crazy to admit—that for a few moments, with his senses igniting and his muscles cranking up in combat, Connor had felt alive again. He'd been teleported back ten years, eyes darting around and poised on the balls of his feet, his mind finely tuned for battle.

So quickly, it was over. The enemy had slipped through his fingers…his sister was out of his sight and unprotected…he was so out-of-shape and out-of-place. Even in his wildest dreams, if he hoped to be some kind of gun-toting commando again, was that even possible?

Athena forced herself to her feet, a hand covering her injured side. Although the unblemished skin peeked out between her fingers, she moved as if she still had a dagger buried in her.

"I know a soul healer," she said. "But I doubt she'll want much to do with me."

Raphael leaned into the wall, arms crossed over his chest. "Why wouldn't she help you? The only enemies of yours I'm aware of were just in this room."

Athena spit out a breath. "We're not enemies, you Edenite. She just…she's always been a spiteful *kun* to me, and I never figured out why. I suppose I'm one of her husband's closest friends, and she doesn't take kindly to that… But…" There was a heavy sigh, and a scowl Connor recognized as a cover-up for pain. "But nothing has ever told me that she's cruel. She might save my life kicking and screaming, but I doubt she'd let me die in front of her."

"Die?" Clara spoke up, barely above a whisper. "How long do we have until that happens?"

"Two days, maybe three," Raphael murmured. "But there is no 'we,' Clara. This problem is mine and Athena's to sort out. We appreciate your help, both of you, but it's time we parted ways. This isn't your fight and...well, you've already seen more than I would have hoped."

Connor's right palm still throbbed, pulling half of his focus away from all this conversation. He put the pain in a mental box and buried it. At least that was one thing he still remembered how to do. His body might have been old and worn, but he still had the mind of a SEAL. Willpower was half the battle.

Clara nudged his arm with her shoulder. "Maybe Raphael's right. I don't know about any of this." She offered Athena, and then Raphael, a bewildered smile. "I...you guys be safe, okay?"

Raphael nodded, answering her lost expression with one of his own. His gaze rose to Connor next, softening around the edges. Connor clenched his injured hand, letting the memories of the bar wash away the pain.

"Sorry we couldn't have had another drink," he joked.

A spark rose to the Raphael's eyes, and his voice grew soft. "Agreed."

The other man patted down his waist, as if searching for a phone or his car keys. "I just need to find..."

Of course. The sword. Or, the hilt of one. Whatever the hell it was. Connor gestured to where he'd tossed it, somewhere near the foyer of the room.

"It's over by the door. I tried to grab it for you, but it burned the hell out of my hand."

He opened his palm, revealing gnarly, inflamed flesh. There went his love line, maybe his life line too. Now that he actually got an eyeful of it, maybe this was something worth worrying about. Maybe it wasn't just something he could shove into the Don't Ask Questions box.

Raphael's smile melted into a deep frown. The effect was so sudden, the temperature seemed to drop twenty degrees in their tiny hotel room.

"You touched my sword?"

Connor closed his hand back into a fist, and pulled it close to his chest. "Yeah…"

Raphael rocked back and forth on the balls of his feet. He had something he wanted to say, but was clearly biting his tongue.

Finally, he looked up from the floor, straight into Connor's eyes, and said, "Oh, Connor. I really wish you hadn't done that."

# 4

"You need to come with me, Connor."

No. Reality had been put in a blender set to puree. His feet were rooted into the carpet, his bones locked up.

For many years, other people told him what to do, and he did it. That was okay. It was his job. It was what he'd been *trained* to do, and maybe even what he'd devoted his life to. Let people with more intel and more experience tell you where you need to be, and they all worked together like a well-oiled machine.

This was not that. This made no sense at all.

"Listen very carefully to me."

He closed his eyes, honing in on Raphael's voice. The world around him had already shrunk to something so small, so suffocating. Squeezing his eyes shut brought fireworks of color behind his eyelids, but anything other than darkness made it easier to breathe.

Raphael's voice continued. "I can't explain everything right now. But I can tell you that by touching my sword, you have now begun the process of binding yourself to me. The process must be completed, but we don't have time to do it here. This place is not safe, and I must take Athena to her healer now."

A shaky breath rose through Connor's nose. *One. Two. Three. Four.*

Release. *One. Two. Three. Four.*

Inhale.

Fucking A, he had not signed up for this when he went down to the bar. Why hadn't he just gone upstairs with Clara? Why hadn't he just showered, gone to dinner with Mam and Dad and listened to their combo pack of incessant nagging and stoic grunts? It seemed so unappealing a couple hours ago, but now, he'd give anything to be there instead.

Inhale.

He needed to say something. Even with his eyes closed, he could feel Raphael's stare boring into him.

Release.

Connor opened his eyes, and moistened his lips.

"I don't understand," is what finally tumbled out of his mouth. He wasn't going to win any awards for orator of the year, but at least he was honest.

"Connor, please." Raphael seized his arm. "Just trust me. Can you do that? Can you trust me until I get you somewhere safe?"

Connor stared at Raphael's hand on his elbow, barely feeling the touch. His gaze traveled up the arm and to Raphael's face inches from his. He was close enough for Connor to see the starburst patterns around his blue irises...at least, until Connor's face burned too much, and he had to look away.

Trust, Raphael asked of him. The hardest thing to give.

His ears roared with muffled noise before the sound tapered into a single piercing note. *Make a decision. It might be wrong, it might be right, but it needs to be now.*

Connor took stock of what he had to lose. His career was dead and buried. His home was a heartless shell housing a sister long past hero worship. Mam and Dad were downstairs, probably wondering he was, but maybe he needed to put as much real estate between them as possible. If this turned out to be nothing, he would see them again. If this turned out to be real danger, he could prevent it. Whatever this process was that Raphael referred to, maybe they just had to complete it. And then he could get on with his life.

"Okay," he said, holding his own hand behind his back, fingers cold and numb. "I trust you."

He didn't, not really, but he chose to pretend. He chose to let himself believe in Raphael for this moment, and if it turned out to bite him, he'd just have to live with that.

Athena broke through his mental miasma with barked words. "Now that your ward nonsense is sorted out, how best should we get to Sicily?"

"Is that where your healer is?" Raphael frowned. "Well, luckily that's not far. A ferryboat south should get us there the fastest. It would also be the safest route. I doubt spectres can pursue you further on water."

"Brilliant," the woman deadpanned. "Let's leave this place before they come crawling back."

Connor watched the rest of the room as if through glass. Athena slung a bag of belongings over her shoulder and headed out the room. Raphael moved to follow her, but kept his eyes trained on Connor. Clara tugged on his jacket, breaking him out of his reverie.

"What about Mam and Dad?" she whispered. Connor's face went numb at the thought of leaving their parents without giving them some indication of what had happened. Mam would never let them out of her sight again if they scared her like that.

His mission manifested before his eyes, bold as permanent marker. "Find them and stay behind. I have to go with Raphael. Make up something, tell them I had to go home suddenly."

"I'm not letting you go with them alone! We don't *know* them. What if you go off somewhere, and I don't ever see you again? No one will ever know what happened to you."

He sputtered after her as she moved past Raphael and out the door. Connor shook his head, as the burn in his chest spread to the tips of his fingers. This situation was his fight, not hers. What the hell was she thinking, coming along? If he could physically push her back into Mam's arms, he would, but...well, goddammit, she was an adult. Besides, in a day or two, she'd decide the danger was too much. She'd ask to go home.

"She shouldn't come," Raphael said. "It's unfortunate enough that you've been pulled into this against your will."

"Just try stopping her," Connor grumbled, joining him in the doorway. "She's from military school, you know. Could probably put either of us in a chokehold if she wanted."

"I believe I know where Athena is taking us. If I'm correct, it should be an exceptionally safe location. No harm should come to Clara there. Or to you, for that matter."

"You'd tell me if that wasn't the case, right?" He tilted his head, studying the other man for signs of falsehood. But Raphael maintained eye contact, unwavering.

"I can't lie to you, Connor, even if I wanted to. Your safety is my top priority. I sometimes...well, I can't promise that I won't fail, as I clearly failed to protect Athena. But I am not motivated to deceive you."

Connor nodded, staring at his gold-stained shoes. Failure. At least they had that in common.

---

All the way to the ferry station, Connor's gaze constantly flitted between Clara sitting in the back, Athena curled away from her, and the empty road ahead of them. On rare occasion, he glanced leftward toward Raphael to observe him in profile, but Raphael never returned it. Every time he looked at the other man, part of him returned to Eric. Eric's blue eyes. Eric's shy smile. But there was something more.

The sharp line of his nose sloped upward to his deeply sunken eyes. A few tufts of black locks curled near the corners of his eyes, but his hair was largely brushed away from his forehead. There could have been golden blood running beneath those pale, sharp cheeks too. Or was that trait unique to Athena?

Connor forced himself to stare at the road instead, and refocus his mind on something far less beautiful. "What the hell was that thing back in the hotel? You called it a spectre—fine—but that tells me next to nothing."

"I don't know. No one knows much more than that."

*Great. Even our mysterious savior with a fire sword doesn't know what these bastards are.*

Clara's phone buzzed to life in the backseat. In the rearview mirror, she raised the phone to her ear. "Mam? Mam, it's okay."

Connor twisted, peering around the headrest. "You can't tell her where we're going," he said quietly enough to go undetected by Mam.

*What should we say,* she mouthed, her eyes wide and frozen. Instead of giving her a chance to fuck up, Connor plucked the phone from her hand and leaned into it, hearing Mam's steady breath on the other side.

"Mam?"

Mam replied with his name in an Irish accent long subdued after decades in America. She had been much more Irish when he was a kid —a young redhead who left her homeland to follow a handsome Tunisian across the pond. Nearly forty years would pass before they would return to Ireland, together, to take care of dementia-ravaged Gran.

"Connor Killian Bishara, you come back to this hotel right now. We have been waiting nearly two hours for you now, and you go running off without telling us? What is going on?"

"We're...we got a call from Clara's school, is all. They moved one of her finals up to Monday, and we need to go home earlier so she can get over the jet lag."

"We came to this country as a family, and we should leave as one. You don't even speak Arabic. How are you supposed to get around without your father?"

"I'm a SEAL, Mam. Or, I was. I think we'll be fine. I would never let anything happen to Clara." His tongue felt heavy with subtext. Mam's concerns were silly helicopter parenting. Reality was a lot more dangerous. But his words—his *promise*—still stood.

Silence. She didn't believe him. Of course she wouldn't. She knew of his townhome with the dishes piling up, and his stack of third notice bills on the coffee table. Last Christmas, she even bought him a fitness tracker to vanquish the paunch he hid under vintage t-shirts. But Raphael was not stopping the car, and nothing Mam said would change the facts. If she didn't accept them before he said goodbye, she'd have to live with it.

"Don't get killed," she deadpanned—the exact same thing she said every time he stepped onto an aircraft carrier. Except this time, she added, "And keep your sister safe."

"I promise."

Reluctantly, he passed the phone back to Clara. When Raphael pulled into a darkened dock and shut off the car, Clara's murmured *I love you, Mam* ended their conversation.

When the car stopped, Connor stepped out of it, sucking in the warm, humid air. This close to the Tyrrhenian Sea, there was salt in the breeze. A curved metal sign hung over the chain length gate, reading *La Goulette Village Harbor* beneath a much larger Arabic scrawl. On the gate, a list of operating times started each day at 7:00 a.m. Ferries to Sicily started at 7:30.

He rubbed his cheek, where a sliver of blood had dried. Shit. He hadn't even realized. Must have happened sometime during the scuffle with the spectre...

"That looks painful. I could help you with it." Raphael had emerged from the driver's side. He gestured toward his own jawline.

"How?" The word came out harsh, too harsh. But he'd seen Raphael's hands glow blue over Athena's wound. He knew what this other man was capable of, however wild, and there was no way for Raphael to dance around it. He just wanted to hear Raphael say it aloud.

Raphael's shoulders turned inward, almost shyly. "Just let me help you, Connor."

Connor made a disappointed noise in the back of his throat. "Sure."

He half-expected Raphael to rifle through his glove compartment and find butterfly bandages, to still commit to the illusion that he was normal and that every supernatural bit of nonsense Connor saw was some fever dream acid trip. Instead, Raphael approached, a hand raised for Connor's cheek.In the blurry corner of Connor's vision, blue light sparked from Raphael's hand as it brushed his wounded skin. With it came the squishy, indescribable sound of skin knitting back together. Pain spiked across his cheekbone once, then ebbed into nothing.

Raphael lowered his hand, avoiding Connor's gaze. "Should be good as new."

He walked past Connor and returned to the sedan, leaving Connor a teetering, puzzled man with nothing but his confusion. Connor touched his broken face, but no blood smeared his fingertips. The skin felt smooth and unblemished, freshly born.

With butterflies churning in his stomach and the tingle of new skin across his cheek, all Connor could think to mutter was, "Shit."

# 5

The first ferry departed at 7:30 a.m. for its eight-hour transit to Sicily. At the head of the boat, Clara watched the morning sun paint the sea gold.

On a bench nearby, Athena sat half-hunched, a heavy deerskin coat wrapped around her shoulders. Every few moments, she fidgeted. One hand grabbed perpetually at her side, and despite her refusal to make a pained sound, the clammy sweat on her brow betrayed her declining health.

It was quite a miracle the ferry people let her on the boat at all—she easily looked like Patient Zero for some crazy new epidemic.

Clara meandered over to the bench, sliding hands into her jacket pockets. Athena hadn't confirmed or denied anything of her nature, but it was hard not to connect the dots with her golden blood, her unnatural healing, her *name...*

Of course, Clara had seen enough blockbuster movies and high school PowerPoints about the Greek gods. Their intricacies escaped her, but she recalled the major players. Zeus, Hera, Hermes, Poseidon. And Athena—goddess of wisdom and war.

Athena's appearance lived up to the moniker. Her muscles were as toned as her eyes were sharp. But could she really be a goddess? That certainly changed some of Clara's perceptions about the world.

If this was *the* Athena, what was her God? Her God was a loose amalgamation of Dad's Allah and Mam's Yahweh. It was not the God of one book, or one tongue, or one church. She was never conditioned to believe that one group of people had all the answers—if anything, her upbringing introduced universal truths that spoke in several languages, through several books and prophets.

But Athena? How deep did truth go?

She sat beside Athena on the bench, careful to keep some distance between them. The woman was pained at best, prickly at worst.

"Who are we going to see in Sicily?" That seemed safe to ask. Something impersonal and unemotional.

Athena frowned, highlighting the chin scar that crept across her bottom lip. While one hand stayed buried in her side, the other rested on her knee, the fingers drumming against it.

"Aphrodite," she admitted after the silence. "I imagine you've heard of her. Humans were certainly fond of carving her out of marble."

"Yeah, we uh…we did name a planet after her."

Athena's snort filled Clara with warmth. At least the injured woman had a sense of humor, however buried beneath agony and armor.

Clara tilted her head, her ponytail brushing against her shoulder. "So, I guess that does make you…a goddess, right?"

"Barely anymore, by our own definition. But that's the term humans prefer, yes." Athena sighed, tugging the coat closer around her shoulders. Her gaze reached out to the warming horizon. "Since the unity, we're all called Sanctines—even Edenites like Raphael. I used to think it was unity nonsense, wiping away our culture. But it grew on me. Goddess was always a heavy word."

Clara rubbed the tops of her jeans, the friction sending rough, welcome warmth across her palms.

"I hope Aphrodite agrees to help you."

Athena made a less-than-happy noise. "Perhaps if she refuses to, I could always challenge her to a fight. She's a fragile thing. It would be no challenge, even if Ares taught her to fight all those years ago."

"Why would she refuse?"

"Hades, I don't know," she scoffed. "I suppose it must be jealousy. That's what it always is with her. Either jealousy for Zeus's fondness for me, or jealous of the time I spend with her husband. But she should know better—I have never needed the touch of men. Or women, for that matter."

Right. Athena and Artemis were the virgin goddesses—no interest in sex. Clara's cheeks warmed. Truth be told, something in that knowledge always spoke to her. It just took her to college to connect the dots. To find out that it had a word.

"Me neither," she piped, her voice cracking. "I mean I'm not into being with people, that is."

"Really?" Athena snorted again, but this time without malice. She arched a brow, tilting her head like a curious animal. "Hard to be a human who feels that way—most of you are hedonists. But I've been plenty aware of those who preferred celibacy. I had thousands of priestesses who preferred that life as well."

Clara didn't need to rub her palms together anymore. Athena's affirmation was warming enough.

---

S o, an angel, huh? Got any other secrets you want to tell me about? Hiding a pair of wings under that shirt?"

Raphael smiled, tilting his head. "No, Connor. That part's just a myth."

Connor snorted good-naturedly, reclining in the dining hall booth, resting his back against the dewy window. The truth was enough to make him dissolve through the cushion in a combination of futility and awe. This kind of truth could make a man's fruitless existence vaporize.

Now the pieces were clear, and Mam would have whopped him on the head for not recognizing the obvious. Angel statues occupied every corner of their home. Mostly Michael, patron saint of soldiers, but Connor remembered plenty about the lesser spirits. Like Raphael, archangel of healing and travel. The one that walked among men.

And of course, the first man he'd cozy up to in years would turn out to be a fucking archangel. His social life was clearly cursed. Scorch it, salt the earth, spit on it. Done.

"I thought a lot of this was just a myth," he said, admittedly not sure where his belief stopped and folklore began.

"Ah, I don't believe that. You're wearing a saint's medal. Surely that means you believe in something."

Connor's hand automatically encircled the quarter-sized silver pendant hanging from his neck. Most of the time, it remained tucked under his shirt collar. Now, the low hanging collar of his over-washed concert tee exposed it against his dark chest.

The token wasn't anything important from a religious standpoint. It was a medal for Saint Olivia, a well-respected saint in Tunisia. Initially, the medal had been a gift from Dad to Mam on their wedding day—perhaps an olive branch uniting their disparate back-grounds. At his confirmation ceremony, the medal had made its way around Connor's neck as a family heirloom.

Raphael sat across him so earnestly, so unassuming. His shoulders slumped slightly with the still-lingering weight of failing his mission. In the bar, he'd been a charming siren of a man, mysterious and fasci-nating. Almost more sublime back then, pretending to be a human, than now.

Now, he just seemed tired. Older. Desperate to keep their situation afloat.

Connor rubbed a hand over his face, letting it drag down some aging skin. "So, I guess you had some bad luck, running into one of those spectres out here, huh?"

"It wasn't coincidence. The spectres have been actively seeking Athena. It's why I was assigned to be her guard, by my brother Michael."

"Huh. And what the hell do they want with her?"

"I'm not privy to the information." Raphael's expression sunk inward, his gaze flitting toward the cheap linoleum table. "The spectres are...new, relatively speaking. No one knows where they come from or what they want. I believe Athena knows why they might be pursuing her, but she hasn't told me why."

Connor crossed his arms. That seemed like a detail that shouldn't have been left out. If they were all on the same side, why would they keep secrets from each other?

"How do you know they aren't chasing her for a good reason?"

"I..." Raphael paused, drumming his fingers on the table. Another idle motion. Why would an angel need to do such a thing? Was it just to make himself seem more human, more *real?* Or was there a free soul inside of him, something beyond duty and the divine? Connor supposed there was no reason to suspect there wasn't. He didn't know jack shit about the reality of angels, or gods, or any of this. But everything he'd read in Sunday school suggested that angels were less free than men. It's what made them so fucking perfect, at least in the eyes of God.

Finally, Raphael gathered his response. "I have faith in Michael. He probably knows why the spectres have taken a morbid interest in Athena. If he doesn't take issue with whatever she's done, then I have no reason to either. She is a victim in this situation, and I have sworn to look after her."

"I guess that's promising." Connor sighed, averting his gaze. Raphael was hard to look at for longer than a few seconds. He was too intense, almost glowing. Like if Connor held his stare too long, the other man would see inside of him.

Pain shot across the inside of his palm. His fist—he'd started clenching it at some point. Slightly overgrown fingernails dug into the gauze wrapped around his hand.

"What about, *this?*" He flexed his fingers, shaking away the sting. "Where does this leave me?"

Raphael withdrew the ivory handle from his belt, twirling it in his fingers. "This is called an Icon. I carry it as the source of my abilities and immortality. But in the older days, we used to hide Icons on Earth, and wait for humans to find them. Whoever found them first was branded for wardship. That's not our tradition anymore—we value the free will of humanity too much to trap them into serving us. But Icons unfortunately still behave the same way when a human touches them."

He hooked the hilt back onto his side. His shiny white teeth chewed slightly at his bottom lip, a ridiculously *human* mannerism for someone so divine. Connor swallowed thickly, unable to look away from it.

Raphael met his eyes again, breaking apart his wandering thoughts. "I'm sorry, Connor. I didn't mean for this to happen to you. I should have been more careful..."

"You make it sound like this is really gonna suck for me."

"It can be a mixed blessing. Mostly, I'm sorry that you weren't given a *choice*. Becoming a ward is a lifetime commitment. I suppose the most human analogy is that it's like forcing you to marry me."

Blood rushed into Connor's cheeks. "Well, uh...I guess it could be worse. You had me thinking it was gonna be an eternity in hell or something."

That earned him a small, somber smile from Raphael. Probably as good as he was going to get, today.

"I'm grateful for your optimism, Connor."

"So what's a ward? What's this binding you're talking about? Are we gonna be literally attached at the hip?"

"Our proximity is already connected, but our souls are not. To finish the binding ceremony is to merge our souls into one. The purpose, originally, was to have humans who could accurately prophesize on our behalf. So, many wards went on to become saints or spiritual leaders. But many also became champions or warriors. You could talk to Athena about some of that—I believe the Olympians had more heroes than prophets among their wards."

"How much time do I have until we have to make this permanent?"

"It's not really based on time. But I have a lot of responsibilities. I have to travel between your world and mine. So, while I'd like to give you time to prepare...I probably need your commitment in the next couple of days. Once we take care of Athena's injury, of course."

Images swirled onto the white linoleum in front of him: his parents' faces, the inside of the dingy kitchen at Saffron Flavor Grill that he'd called home for nearly a decade, the peeling wallpaper of the James Island townhome he shared with Clara. All of it dissolved. He should have known from the moment he saw that spectre that he would be enrolled in a holy witness protection program, cursed to become a god's gopher.

Granted, he had said *champions,* hadn't he? Some wards might have been scribes or loons shouting on street corners, but some were obviously fighters. If he couldn't fight for his country anymore, about the only place left to go was to fight for the gods.

---

The sun lowered into a dim sliver as their four-door European rental meandered up the side of Mount Etna. Snow draped the volcano like icing, bright beneath the full moon. In the farthest reach of the horizon, a scatter of twinkling lights shone from all the villages surrounding the great mountain.

In the passenger seat, Connor shivered beneath the hoodie that he'd strewn across himself like a blanket. For hours, he'd hoped that feigning sleep would reward him with the real thing, but his brain refused to quiet.

He eventually gave up, stretching his legs and pressing his feet into the floorboards. His joints popped loudly enough to be heard over the roar of road noise.

"How much longer?" he said quietly.

"Very nearly there."

"Hmm. Guess it's a big world."

It wasn't a foreign notion. In the service, he'd gone to places that felt like an entirely different planet. He'd seen stuff that made him wonder if he was still living the same life, if he was even the same person. The SEALs existed in a different reality, something sinister and harsh beneath the fabric of polite society. Clara, despite being enrolled in a military college, would never see that side of the world.

Connor was glad of it. Whenever it used to become too much—when he rang out of BUD/s the first time, when his hallucinating, sleep-deprived body was forced to tread water for hours during Hell Week, when one brother's skull exploded right next to him from a sniper's bullet on the shore of Somalia—he clung to gratitude. Gratitude that it was him there, and not her, or anyone else's child.

The first time he had held Clara, when he was a senior in high school and she was the size of a sourdough loaf, he had panicked. She was so fragile and petite; he didn't know whether to cling to her or to shove her back into Mam's arms. She'd come a long way since those early days, but he still had trouble letting go of that half-jealous awe.

He was supposed to be an only child, until he made the mistake of coming out to Dad at seventeen and then…well…nine months later, he'd been replaced with a baby sister. It took a trip to the Navy recruiter and two tries through BUD/S before Dad finally looked at him with respect again.

After the dishonorable discharge, looking after Clara was the call he needed to answer. Gran had lost her mind to dementia a few years later, so Mam and Dad moved to Ireland to oversee her final years. At sixteen, Clara needed a legal guardian in the States, and those responsibilities fell to Connor without fanfare.

For the first few years of her life, she had been competition—always topping his accomplishments with one of her own. The discharge had put everything into perspective. Once he came home again, he stopped seeing her as a perfect, spoiled doll and instead noticed the moments in between. His genius, athletic sister cried in the school bathroom because preppy brats said she had thunder thighs. She'd started walking around in high heels when she realized she wouldn't grow over five-foot-one. She skipped dinner whenever she fell off the balance beam.

And so, it became cruel to see her as anything other than his sister, a girl who needed an adult to support her instead of envy her. He cheered for her at gymnastics meets like she was an Olympian instead of an awkward teenager with an ill-fitted leotard. He was first to the mailbox on the day she got her Citadel acceptance letter, and he pinned it to the fridge as a surprise.

Now she snored in the back of the car—a car half-filled with gods. He'd failed to keep her out of this mess, so he had no gratitude to fall back on.

Their car slowed to a stop in front of a red circular sign with a single yellow bar. Connor didn't need a guidebook to interpret it. The road ended where the signpost hit the ground. His toes flexed in his canvas sneakers. Time to trek through the snow.

Raphael turned his head to look into the backseat. "Can you walk, Athena?"

"Of course," the goddess snapped through gritted teeth. Her shiver told the real story.

When they exited the car, the cold slapped Connor in the face. Not like that should have surprised him, halfway up a mountain in November. Slushy snow enveloped his feet, and ice-cold moisture sunk immediately through the thin material. He wrapped an arm around Clara for warmth as she exited the back of the car. They needed to move quickly, or both of them would lose some toes.

They followed Raphael down an unmarked path, with Athena bringing up the rear. Connor looked back at her periodically, scanning over her slumped frame and jerky movements. Despite the darkness, sweat shone clearly on her brow. Her chest heaved out cold steam, condensing in the nippy air.

The wind cut right through Connor's jacket, and whipped against his face enough to chap the skin. It stripped him of all body heat, frosting him from limbs to core. Inside his shoes, his toes tingled with numbness.

Instinct took him back to his old coping mechanisms. He got through Hell Week in subzero gales with nothing but a casualty "blanket." He could get through this.

Clara spoke, the words almost lost with the wind. "I wonder if he's actually leading us somewhere."

Connor's reply slurred with uneven shivering. "Y-you can't get more desolate than this. That's got to be a good thing, r-right?"

Raphael stopped and looked back. "Just a few steps more."

There was nothing but arid landscape and their feet crunching over snow. No house, no hut, and absolutely no one waiting for them. Just as Connor was about to bark something about how they were *clearly* in the wrong place, Raphael stepped face-to-face with the side of the mountain.

The angel's hand rested upon the mossy brown rock, and his lips whispered foreign words against the surface. Distant thunder followed the chant. Connor held Clara tighter, waiting for the ground to shudder beneath his feet, but it did not. The rumbling remained but a noise, before a white square of light carved itself into the mountainside.

Both hands supported Clara in his arms, so nothing blocked his eyes from the supernova brightness. Raphael remained still, haloed by the shine, a silhouette in a doorway of sun.

Finally, the rumbling stopped and the world stilled. The light had faded into two towering brass doors, etched with pictographs and undecipherable runes. A pair of golden suits of armor flanked each side of the doorway. They stood erect and menacing, each holding a spear fashioned in the same furnish as their bodies. The spears crossed in an X to block the door.

Connor shut his eyes, hoping the wonders would vanish when he opened them. They didn't.

Raphael eyed the statues. "Perhaps we should knock."

"Heed them not," Athena croaked, her words trailing off into a heavy cough. "They're merely Hephaestus's automatons. They will not attack without his command."

As Raphael stepped forward, the gilded suits of armor lifted their spears out of the snow and directed blank expressions toward the trespassers.

"Stand back!" Raphael demanded, waving toward Connor and Clara. Connor grabbed the first part of Clara he could reach and dragged her to stand behind him. Even Athena's eyes widened, and she haphazardly pulled a dagger out of her thigh holster.

The statues moved away from the bronze door and toward them

with surprising agility, aiming their golden spears. Small glass windows in the center of their breastplates showed a tangle of clock-work and gears.

"Raphael..." Connor said, slowly backing away. "Might want to start knocking."

# 6

As an engineering major, Clara couldn't help but *marvel* at the autonomous men. Metal and momentum substituting life. The careful details carved into their faces. Even their brows crinkled, sheet metal sliding against sheet metal. The cogs inside to make such expressions must have been tinier than dimes.

But as a young unarmed woman half-way up a mountain, where the temperature was surely near zero and her feet were already numb, she did *not* appreciate two robots pointing spears at her.

On her right side, Raphael's ivory hilt appeared in his hand. A metal blade materialized from a swirl of sparks, then a burst of blue fire coated it. The cool flame cast a cerulean glow across all their faces and the snowy expanse of Mount Etna.

As Raphael lifted the sword, a golden spearhead to his shoulder instantly disarmed him.

*Ouch,* Clara cringed, but Raphael barely reacted to the injury. The slender man lurched forward, spear still imbedded in his collar, to wrap both hands around his attacker's throat.

As the other suit leapt toward Connor, Clara dodged into the snow. She crawled in Athena's haphazard footsteps, staying low as spears and blades clashed over her head. Athena slumped against a boulder not far away, her body nearly keeled over. The goddess's face was so white, the snow nearly camouflaged her.

Clara's gaze flitted around for anything to use as a weapon. There was nothing on the side of Mount Etna except for snow and heavy stones too large to grab. She patted her jacket and pants, but only felt the outline of a wallet, a memo pad, and her Fisher Space pen.

But the backs of the suits were open, full of gears. Even something small could jam them if it had enough compressional strength to hold up to the force of the mechanics...

No time to run hypothetical numbers. She stumbled to her feet, ripping the silver pen out of her breast pocket. With the pen armed like a dagger, she leapt onto the back of Connor's attacker and jammed the pen between its central gears.

The machine jerked, nearly dismounting her. She wrapped her legs tighter around its waist, akin to the time she had ridden a mechanical bull at the fair and got tossed in front of a row of booing fifth graders.

Eventually, the guard stopped convulsing, but she clung to its rusty joints. *Can write upside down* and *jam a robot. They should add that to the label.*

The golden mountain doors opened, and rumbling snow sprinkled all four of them with chips of ice and rock dust. Clara instinctively ducked her head to protect herself from anything bigger, still clinging to the back of the automaton.

The silhouette of a short, muscular man stood starkly against the light. He called out in a foreign tongue, stern but not deep. The guards jerked erect, their spears still pressing into Connor and Raphael's throats. Clara slipped off the back of hers, untangling her legs from its waist. She hit the ground with an *oof,* the snow barely managing to soften her fall.

The man emerged from the doorway, and the moonlight revealed his features. Despite the chilly mountain winter, he stood shirtless and unshivering. Amber fractal markings crisscrossed his bare torso and arms, stretching all the way up to his skull. He appeared somewhat young, with curly brown hair closely cropped on the sides of his head, and twinkling, boyish brown eyes. He might have been halfway between Connor and Clara's ages, but supported every limping step with a brass cane.

"Hephaestus!" Athena said. "Call off your toys!"

As soon as the words left Athena's ragged throat, the man raised a hand toward his robots. They marched backward with creaking joints and clanging limbs, moving their spearheads away. Clara blinked rapidly, trying to make sense of the mysticism, but no sensible scene played out on the other side of her eyelids. It wasn't nearly the oddest thing she'd seen in the last twenty-four hours, but the oddness was starting to pile up.

Hephaestus lowered his hand, peering at Athena. "What are you doing here? Is something wrong?"

Raphael interjected before Athena could. "She's gravely injured. We were hoping Aphrodite could help. I don't expect you to do it for me, but as Athena's guard—"

"You want Aphrodite's help?" Hephaestus barked a laugh. "Well I can't promise you anything, Edenite, but you're welcome to try and sway her. This should be rather amusing to watch."

He waved a hand to his automatons. The metal men returned to their erect resting states—Clara's victim did so a little lopsided. She stared mournfully at her ruined pen, bent into an L-shape with its pressurized ink splattered across the guard's golden back. Dad had given her that pen for high school graduation. She'd always assumed she would have it forever.

Hephaestus held open one of the massive doors. Immediate warmth soaked into Clara's skin as they walked into the cave, the mountain's embrace protecting her from the frigid November air. She blinked away spots, crossing into the dimly lit tunnel from the bright threshold.

As Hephaestus moved past them to lead the way, he threw a glance back at Clara and her brother. He stopped in place, leaning into his cane.

"You two...you're human."

"Guilty, I guess?" Connor said. Clara's fingers itched to pinch him in his side.

"What brings you here with Athena and an Edenite? Are you their wards?"

Connor raised his branded hand and started to open his mouth, but Clara forced her way between them.

"It's a long story," she said. "Happy to tell you later."

Hephaestus shrugged and continued moving. "Doesn't make a difference to me. I probably like humans better than gods, if I'm honest."

They continued through the winding tunnel. Clara's damp shoes knocked against spare pieces of armor and other scraps along the way. Then, the rumble of metal upon metal and the crackle of fireplaces enveloped her with smells of ash and iron, like backyard barbeques and soldering guns.

The cave ended abruptly with a glorious cutout of the mountain's core. Ceilings stretched upwards over thirty feet, venting the smoky air from a dozen churning fireplaces. Forges burned and embers sparkled through the air, spreading warmth and light. Connor let out a low whistle, his shoulder bumping into hers.

Hephaestus brushed past them to lead the way, the sound of his cane echoing with every step. On the opposite side of the fire-lit cavern, a curved staircase led upward to a heavy oaken door. A woman descended the steps, striking and tall. She wore a simple white frock that complemented her olive skin. The slits of the dress ran all the way up her thighs. A wild mane of sandy hair flowed in waves to the golden chain belt cinching her waist. Her graceful hand slid upon the banister as she approached; her face stared calm and frozen.

Aphrodite.

Although lean and tall, as Athena had suggested, her composure was far softer than Clara expected. "Hello. We haven't had visitors in a long time. What brings you here?"

Raphael moved aside, revealing Athena behind him. "She was attacked last night with a sacrificial dagger. We were able to heal the physical, but she said you could help mend the soul damage. We were in Tunisia, so this was the closest place to go."

Aphrodite cast her hazel eyes upon the injured goddess. They narrowed, crinkling at the edges with penetrating curiosity. Both women stared each other down—Athena doing a rather impressive job of it considering she needed the help of a workbench just to stay on her feet. Aphrodite's expression remained stubbornly neutral, as if merely perceiving instead of judging.

Clara's jaw tightened. What if Aphrodite did turn them away? So far, she wasn't quite as cruel-looking as Athena had described, but Athena's judgement of character was probably a lot more tuned...

"Of course, I can help you. Come with me, Athena." The stunning woman glanced at her husband. "Help the rest of them settle in. I'm sure they're tired from the traveling. Especially the humans."

Raphael's head bowed. "Thank you, Aphrodite."

Clara, too, let out a breath.

Aphrodite placed a hand on Athena's shoulder, supporting her weak frame as she guided the goddess of war to the stairs. "This way," she said tonelessly. "You can relax. You're safe now."

## 7

The first thing Connor did when Hephaestus showed him to the guest suite was make a beeline for the damn bathtub.

Gods or not, Hephaestus and Aphrodite still had access to soap and hot running water. Connor had seen far worse in the field before—some weeks he'd bathed with thrice-used wet naps until the dried-out fabric was gray with his own grime.

When he lowered himself into the brass bathtub, he was half-convinced he'd never be able to climb out. Easy to forget that it'd been a straight day since he'd relaxed, or slept. Aside from the crumbs he'd forced down in the ferry diner, he hadn't eaten anything. Back in his SEAL era, a vigorous day without sleep or food would have been a breeze. But that was when he had been in his late-twenties and ripped, having conditioned himself for it for years. About all he was good for anymore was feeling sorry for himself, picking up the wrong people at bars, and fitting the perfect number of nachos on a ten-inch platter at his shitty kitchen job.

Damn. His job. He was on the schedule this week. But that probably wasn't going to happen at this point. He'd be fired, and sure, restaurant jobs were a dime a dozen. But with a less than honorable discharge on your record, things got a little...trickier.

A golden handmaiden made of steel and gears, looking very much like one of Hephaestus's automatons, moved slowly about the bath house. Her feet clinked across the mosaic floors, mechanical joints creaking with every step. With a smooth, expressionless façade of a face, she looked down at Connor in the bath, her arms extending a towel.

"Thanks..." He rose from the tub—his joints creaking a little less than expected—and relieved her of the towel. When her arms were empty, she gave him a jerky nod, then clink-clonked away slower than government paperwork.

Wrapped in the slightly itchy towel, Connor padded across the stone floor into the bedroom. Despite being a guest room, the wardrobe overflowed with fresh clothes of varying sizes—tunics, sundresses, trousers, jackets.

But no underwear in ancient Greece, apparently. Not exactly the type of commando he wanted to be, but whatever. He'd run out of fucks to give.

Once he'd adorned himself in the least Ren-faire-ish clothes he could find, Connor slipped out of his room and down the hallway. Aphrodite and Hephaestus's home was a winding mansion—multiple wings, an unfathomable amount of floors, stairs leading up to towers and others leading down to workshops. Outside of Hephaestus's main forge near the entrance, he seemed to have multiple rooms in the house dedicated to tinkering. Perhaps in a house of this size, it was a necessary comfort.

Raphael lingered outside Athena's room, leaning against a frescoed wall. Athena's door remained closed, and Raphael's shoulders hunched near his ears.

"Hey," Connor called, approaching him. He made a motion to slip his hands in his pockets, but there were no pockets in these stupid Greek trousers. Of course.

The angel straightened up, eyes flashing. "Connor. I thought you'd gone to bed."

"Just had to wash the grunge off me. Got a second wind. How's Athena?"

"To be determined..." Raphael glanced back to the closed bedroom door, worrying his bottom lip. "I hope we weren't too late."

"You did your best. We couldn't have gotten here faster."

"Yes." A frustrated huff. "But this never should have happened in the first place. I keep replaying that moment over and over in my head, wondering what I could have done differently to protect her."

"Hey. Mind if I tell you something I learned a long time ago? Back when saving the world was my day job?" Connor tilted his face forward, looking at him from under arched brows. Raphael gave him a barely perceptible nod. "Sometimes your best isn't good enough. It's a shitty truth man, but...it's life. And life happens, whether you want it to or not, like some kind of big chaotic monster. And just by standing up to it, just by *trying* to fight it, just by saving one person or two, you're winning. Because what's the alternative? Yeah, maybe you could have protected her better, but if you *hadn't* been there? She probably would have died in that hotel room."

Raphael stared at him, the corners of his eyes crinkling. Eyes that looked as old as his face looked young. Eyes that had likely witnessed eons of years, millions of souls. But he still peered at Connor as if...as if he was seeing something for the very first time.

Perhaps he'd never been told that it was okay to fail.

"Thank you, Connor," he murmured. "As much as I regret the circumstances that have brought us both here, I...I'm grateful you're the one I met last night."

Before Connor had to figure out a reply to *that,* Aphrodite slipped out of Athena's room, gently closing the door behind her. She regarded both of them with a tired smile.

"She should make a full recovery. She just needs to rest a few days. She's welcome to remain here, in the meantime. You all are."

"Thanks for letting us," Connor said. "She was half-convinced you wouldn't do anything for her."

Aphrodite's face betrayed nothing, except for the lightest twitch of her eyebrow. "Athena is a goddess of war. Her perception of the world is brutal. I am a goddess of love, which means I like to see the best in people, regardless of how they've treated me in the past."

She sported a small smirk, but shared it only with Connor.

Aphrodite reached for his wrist, and raised his branded palm to her face. "So...I see you've been marked as a ward."

Raphael took a step forward. "Mine. I mean to say...he's my...responsibility."

Connor's neck grew hot. *Mine.* Maybe to an angel of Eden, that word held no weight. To a human man on a ten-year dry spell, it *did things.* Hopefully Aphrodite wouldn't notice him shudder in her grip.

The goddess dropped his hand. "I wouldn't think an Edenite would need one. Aren't you powerful enough?"

"It wasn't on purpose. My Icon got away from me."

Connor frowned. "What's power got to do with it, exactly?"

"He might have told you that wards are messengers of the gods. But do you want to know the real reason we take them?" Aphrodite glanced up through long lashes. "Because it makes us stronger."

"That doesn't change anything, Connor." Raphael squeezed his shoulder, bare skin to bare skin, a hell of a lot warmer than he looked. "Believe me, I already have more power than I'd ever want or need. I'd never force someone to be my ward simply for that."

Connor swallowed, leaning every-so-slightly into the touch. "Yeah...I believe you."

Oh right, Aphrodite was still with them. When Connor looked back to her, she was smirking, something...*knowing* behind her expression. "It's almost a shame you're already claimed by him. I wouldn't have minded taking you as my ward, Connor."

Connor squinted, seriously questioning if she was coming on to him. Maybe the stories about her promiscuous pursuits were accurate. "Why's that?"

"Most men love me from the moment they see me. I can't control it. It's just the way I am. But you're completely immune, aren't you? It's rather refreshing."

The weight floated off of Connor's shoulders. She was beautiful, indeed—probably the most beautiful woman he'd ever seen in person. But between the two people he was standing with, she certainly was not the one that warmed his insides.

"Heh. Well, never really thought of it as a super power. But I'm sure Hephaestus appreciates it."

Aphrodite's dangling earrings chimed as she glanced back to Raphael. "There was something I became curious about, when I was healing Athena. Do you happen to have the weapon that stabbed her?"

Raphael hesitated, his hand resting above his shoulder-slung messenger bag. The moment passed, and he reached inside. "Of course..."

He fished out the black dagger, which he'd wrapped in a white cloth sometime between the attack and now. Possibly on the ferry—it looked like the same napkins used in the mess hall. Aphrodite gently took the dagger, balancing it with one palm as her other hand peeled back the dressing.

She hummed, "These are Aaru markings, on the hilt. See?"

Connor leaned closer, hovering near her shoulder. When he'd seen this weapon, it had been buried in Athena's gut, so he hadn't exactly gotten a close-up. The hilt of the dagger was gilded, leading into a smooth obsidian blade. But as Aphrodite said, a group of symbols wrapped around the hilt—pictograms engraved in red and green ink.

"Looks like...Egyptian hieroglyphs," he muttered.

Raphael paced before them, his arms crossed over his chest. "That's what she meant. Aaru is the kingdom of Egyptian gods."

"Oh." Connor rubbed a hand on the back of his neck, offering Aphrodite an apologetic smile. "Eh...sorry. Didn't meant to mansplain mythology at you."

She returned the smile, breezily. "I'm glad you're keeping up. You'll need to, if you're going to be a ward."

"I noticed the symbols myself," Raphael said. "But I haven't been able to make sense of it. Either a spectre stole an Aaru weapon, or..."

Aphrodite's slender hand ran across the hieroglyphs. "Athena has no quarrel with them, I'm sure. Why would Aaru send a spectre to attack her?"

Connor squinted, the world around him going fuzzy. It was easier to think when he let his eyes lose focus, let his mind drift a bit. The political dynamics of gods was far over his head. But targeted attacks on foreign nationals? That was like coming home.

And if there was one thing his time in the service had taught him, it was that people were not their nations. The will of a country rarely reflected the desires of its people. And the actions of a person, or even an insurgent group, did not justify the perdition of a nation.

"What if it's not *Aaru* who sent it, but someone *from* Aaru?"

Raphael and Aphrodite both leveled him with curious stares.

"You mean, someone acting as an individual?" Aphrodite said.

Connor shrugged. "I mean, why the hell not? You've got free will, don't you?"

Raphael steepled his fingers. "That's not entirely accurate. It's one of the primary ways we differ from humans. Certainly, we do have some degree of free will, but...we are generally held to the laws, customs, and missions of our kingdoms. An Aaru Sanctine would not act against the will of Aaru."

Well, there went Connor's brilliant idea. Perhaps the gods weren't so easily compared to humans, after all. "Guess the spectre stole the knife from someone, then," he said.

Raphael nudged him gently with an elbow. "It was a reasonable concept, Connor. I appreciate your insight."

Aphrodite handed him back the dagger, and he slid it back into its home. "What will you do now?" she asked.

"Once Athena is healed, I'll report this finding to Michael. Perhaps we can tell where the dagger came from—whether it was stolen or not. He's the chair of the war guild, so he'll have the jurisdiction to investigate Aaru, or anywhere else."

"Did Michael ever tell you why Athena was a target? Why would a spectre with an Aaru dagger want to kill her?"

"It was not a necessary part of my assignment to know what Athena may have done to warrant being attacked. My mission is to protect her and to serve my brother's wishes."

Aphrodite's full-bodied lips pursed into a thin line. It was the closest she'd looked to the vindictive vixen that media loved to paint her as.

"Interesting," she said quietly. "Either way, she should be safe here. Hephaestus has built our home into a fortress. If the spectre comes for her again, we'll be ready."

8

*This is heaven.*

     Or, at least that's what Clara thought when she opened her eyes the next morning.

But memories of emotionless automatons, of a scarred smith, and Athena's abdomen gushing gold eclipsed that thought. This was not heaven—it was purgatory. An oasis of safety in a sea of menace, a beautiful prison.

Clara crawled to the end of her bed and grabbed a muslin robe draped across the footboard. When she slipped it on, fabric pooled around her feet, like she was a girl wearing her mother's clothing.

A vanity and mirror sat near the French doors, where seashell combs and hair clamps lived. Clara cringed at the sight of herself, ruffling the thick, frizzy waves she earned from going to bed with wet hair. She picked a comb and gingerly ran it through her dark locks. Rather than catching on knots, the teeth glided with ease, smoothing every flyaway.

Apparently, the goddess of beauty had help with her perpetually splendid looks.

Clara smiled at her reflection for the first time in a while, and returned the comb to Aphrodite's vanity.

She exited the bedroom, strolling beneath hand-carved arches and walls imbedded with pearls. The building must have been thousands of years old, and Hephaestus's extensive restoration was obvious. Paintings over paintings, mismatched clay patching up walls, cracks spiraling across each column. Silver beams sat in the seams between walls, serving as extra support. Or perhaps protection against natural disasters, like the metal earthquake rods shoved through historic houses in Charleston.

Despite the gravity of their situation, the Thermo test on Monday kept creeping into daydreams and tangential thoughts, along with all the other tests and finals which would go untouched for the rest of the semester. If she didn't get home soon, it would be five failing grades—a devastating blow to her otherwise respectable GPA. Five classes to retake.

Few of her classmates had true engineering minds. They enrolled in the program for the job prospects, or to feel superior about their brainpower. But engineering wasn't about intellect. It was about instinct. About trusting yourself to work with the simplest answers. Clara rarely discovered like-minded people, even within her own major, so Hephaestus's presence was a welcome peculiarity.

Perhaps she could call this an independent study.

She reached what must have been the living space, divided by columns into three sections: a sitting area, a dining room, and a terrace. Once on the balcony, her robe was too thin to protect her from the winter breeze, but the sun prickled her skin with warmth.

The Sicilian horizon burned ruddy. The chateau was practically carved into the side of the mountain, with nothing but a ninety-degree slab of ice and rock beneath it. To fall off the balcony would result in nothing less than broken bones.

"Striking view, isn't it?"

Clara jerked, nearly tripping on her bottom hem. In the divide between the dining area and the veranda, Hephaestus leaned against a column with a bronze cane tucked under his arm. In the morning light, the amber markings across his bare arms and hands shone even more visibly than the night before.

Hephaestus limped closer, eventually resting his weight upon the balcony railing beside her. In one hand, he held a handmade ceramic mug. "Here. This ought to warm you up."

She stared, wide-eyed at both the steaming drink. "You have coffee?"

"Apollo brings me human artifacts to tinker with, occasionally."

"Thank you." Clara laced her fingers around the mug and bought it to her lips.

He nodded. Although a tuff of brown curls rested on top of his head, one side of his skull was shaven down to show how far the scars actually went up. They looked like tattoos at first glance, but they lived too deeply in his skin to be artificial.

They seemed...familiar. She'd seen the pattern before, during an electrical engineering lab about broken transformers—Lichtenberg figures. The scars of lightning.

He watched her with eyes of warm brown, quite different than her own. Bishara eyes were nearly black, constantly narrowed in some kind of skepticism. Hephaestus's eyes held some kind of heat, and an open, approachable curiosity.

Hephaestus rolled his shoulders. "You promised me a long story, yesterday. About how a human girl came to be caught up with an angel and a goddess?"

She snorted, taking a sip of the coffee. Rich, smooth, *so* much better than Starbucks. She'd never been able to drink coffee black like this.

"Believe me, it's probably nothing exciting by your standards."

"You underestimate how little I've left home in the past two thousand years."

Clara shrugged, leaning into the railing. "Maybe it's not much of a long story at all. Connor got marked up by Raphael's magic thingie, now he's gotta be his ward, and I'm...I'm here to make sure I can tell our parents about whatever the hell happens to him next. I guess that's about it, really."

"You seem to take the mystical well. Most humans would be bleeding from their eyes after processing such a thing."

"Well. Guess that's what you get when your mother is Catholic and your dad is Muslim. Hard to end up all singularly dogmatic."

Hephaestus hummed. "Raphael made the right choice to bring Athena here. I can't promise the company is positive, but I'm quite proud of it being one of the safest places on Earth."

"Did you build it yourself? It's quite beautiful."

He rubbed the back of his neck. Something about the way he moved, the way he talked, was far less *crisp*, than Raphael. Both Hephaestus and Athena could have easily passed as human, if she'd encountered them on the street. Aphrodite, a little less so, with such unnatural beauty. But she should have known from the moment she saw Raphael that he was no mortal man. His presence always betrayed something more.

"Yes, but, ah, the interior could use an upgrade. Recently I've focused more on keeping things out than on keeping the decor fresh."

"The forge didn't look so bad."

Hephaestus leaned farther into the railing. He arched his face closer to hers, as if letting her in on a secret. "Would you like to see it again?"

Clara's lips stretched into a smile. "Of course."

Hephaestus limped away from the balcony and into the kitchen, where a door—arch topped and walnut wood—waited for them. Clara stayed close, slowing her pace to meet his.

They entered through the walnut door and descended the staircase into Hephaestus's forge. The air tasted of molten iron; the metallic odors sank osmotically into Clara's taste buds. The warmth was a welcome reprieve from the nippy balcony, and Clara smiled at how this entire cavern—up to its thirty-foot ceilings—was lit effectively with the fire of three kilns. Smoke vented upwards and out through a gap in the rock.

"I selected this location to build upon millennia ago," Hephaestus announced, comfortably making the last step. "Knowing what I do about this mountain, it was the perfect site."

"Desolate?"

He pointed toward one of the open ovens. "The dragon Typhon

was banished here. The fires of his breath allow me to make weapons with extraordinary properties."

Clara meandered through workbenches, where a different work in progress occupied every tabletop. On her left sat a broadsword as long as she was tall, with script scrawling across the blade. Beige leather braided the hilt, and eyeball-sized emeralds embroidered the metal.

"This is gorgeous. Where do you get the materials?"

"Sometimes we get visitors. Artemis is usually good for wood. Hermes brings jewels every few centuries, when I can nab them off the bastard."

"I'm impressed," Clara confessed, moving around the bench. "I'm studying to become a mechanical engineer, which is sort of like this. But I design boring stuff. HVAC systems, industrial tanks…"

Hephaestus's back turned to her as he faced one of the fireplaces. "You know, you have a lot in common with Athena. She's crafty. Very bright."

"I like Athena, but she's…a little intense. I guess she's more a soldier, like Connor."

"Your brother's a warrior?"

"He was one of the best. I wouldn't have minded doing it too, but I couldn't. Not when it was taken from him." She bit her bottom lip. "I don't expect you know much about America, but a dishonorable discharge is unforgivable there. At least, his used to be. By the time the laws changed, he was too old to re-enlist."

"So, if war isn't your calling, what is?"

"I don't know…building things, I guess. But that'll never equal what Connor did. He was out there saving the world."

Hephaestus set his cane to rest against the table, crossing his arms. "I made Achilles' armor. I made Hercules' sword. You could pick up any discarded piece of weaponry in this room and I could tell you the legend it was crafted for."

His tone was wistful, nostalgic. Before she could jump to conclusions, Hephaestus finished. "Sometimes it's more important to be happy with what you do than it is to be renowned. I spent a long time worrying about my name being in the history I helped make. But when you live as long as we do, you realize no one's name lasts forever."

Clara slipped away, considering his advice. At least Hephaestus influenced the world. Connor had helped society more in three years with the SEALs than she probably would in a lifetime. Her parents were proud to have an "intellectual" in the family, but engineers rarely made history.

Her feet knocked against helmets and shields littering her path. Hephaestus said that building was all that mattered, but he must have longed for these pieces to fulfill their purpose. At least the gilded human shells in the back of the forge, similar to the golden guardians outside, might have been put to use. She approached one, peering up at its blank expression.

The open panel in the suit's chest suggested more than armor. Inside, it was full of gears and pulleys, making it impossible for a person to fit inside. Beside it, a half dozen others lined up shoulder to shoulder. The wall behind them jutted out twenty feet wide and twenty feet tall where a boulder had been rolled into place.

"These were outside. What are they?"

"Automatons. They help with lifting, mostly. But on my command, they can defend us."

"From what?" Clara moved away from the gilded soldier. "What have you been armoring your home against all these years?"

Hephaestus's face was only visible in profile. His chest swelled with a deep breath. "A man who wants me dead. There's a portal behind the boulder—it's a path to Paradisa. That rock and the automatons keep him from coming through."

"Paradisa? Is that your home?"

"Earth was always my real home. My mother conceived me alone, out of spite for Zeus's affairs." Hephaestus's face twisted halfway between a smirk and a grimace. "He didn't take kindly to that, so he fried me upon sight. Hera refused to raise a deformed child, so she threw me through an Olympian portal to an island on Earth called Lemnos. I broke my leg in the fall. Luckily, some human women took pity on me, and raised me until I was old enough to return to Olympus and face my bitch mother myself."

"Damn. So, is that who you're keeping out? Zeus?"

The door at the top of the staircase creaked before he could answer. Aphrodite glided into the forge, her white sundress immune to the soot spiraling throughout.

"Looks like you've found a friend," she called down to her husband. The hair on Clara's neck stood up upon hearing the goddess's voice.

Hephaestus kept his eyes downcast. "What do you want, Aphrodite?"

"I'm serving breakfast. The others are already at the table."

As she sashayed away, Hephaestus pressed his fists into his workbench. Beneath the sounds of fire raging, he growled, "Of course, milady."

I dling was never good for Connor's mind.

As important as it may have been for Athena to recover from her injury, and as important as it may have been for him to process what it would mean to be a ward, he couldn't help but want to...*move*. Forward, sideways, hell, even back. Less than a day had elapsed, and he was already cooped up, pacing his guest suite like a madman.

Without something to do, something to occupy him, his mind raced to burn the energy. His post-Navy shrink would call it a symptom of the PTSD, but this wasn't that. Combat and stress weren't the parts of his service that had gotten him slapped with a diagnosis.

No, this was the Bishara blood—that gung-ho mindset that made Bisharas rush headfirst into action while others turned tail and ran. Even Clara had had it in spades when she was a child, before society convinced her it wasn't ladylike.

A gentle rap on the door stopped him in his tracks. Raphael poked his head in, just opening the door enough to allow himself room.

"Connor? Do you mind some company?"

"Nah, come in." He was out of breath for some reason. Maybe the pacing? Sure, he could blame it on that.

He plopped down on a chaise lounge near the window. Damn. He was *really* out of breath. New air had a hard time reaching his lungs. He was some kind of worked up—more than he'd realized.

Raphael joined him on the other side of the couch, beyond arm's reach.

"Are you alright? You seem winded."

"I'm fine." It came out as a rasp, but by God, he was sticking to that story. "I'm fine, really. Just pacing around."

"What is it that you want, Connor?" Raphael tilted his head. "I know there are certain duties that circumstance demands of you right now, but I figure I should know the answer to that question. I should know what it is that you want, just in case…in case I'm taking it away from you."

Connor looked out the window, to the rocky edges of Mount Etna. To the snow-colored ridges, so bright he needed to squint. The answer wasn't out there, he knew. But it helped to sit in the light, and the silence.

"I want Clara to be safe. And my Mam and Dad too, of course."

Raphael smiled. "Of course. That's an easy thing to ensure. What else?"

"I want…"

*…to turn back the clock, and go back to the way things were. The way I was.*

*…to stop wondering if every person I meet is going to ruin my life the way Roger did.*

*…for you to touch me, and to know what we could be.*

*…to be fucking useful again.*

Connor sighed, shaking his head. "I just want to matter. To a person. To a group. To the world. I don't know."

Raphael watched him, both hands folded on his lap. "I can assure you, then, that I won't be taking that from you at all."

"Hmph." He leaned back a little, letting his head rest on the warm glass. "Yeah, guess being a ward is like being a fuckin' celebrity, huh? You told me they turn into saints."

"*Some* of them turn into saints. And that distinction is up to human churches, not to us. You would have to take any requests for sanctification up with the current Pope." Raphael let out a small laugh—probably the first time ever in Connor's presence. Connor certainly would have remembered the sound, because he would have filed it away in his brain the way he was doing right now.

"Yeah, yeah. Whatever. I guess I can't complain. I did tell you to come get me if you needed help beating up bad guys. Guess you couldn't resist me."

Raphael's smile turned sympathetic. "I would have liked to keep you out of all this. Perhaps it was you who couldn't resist me."

Connor's shoulders curved a little more inward, and he brought his knees to his chest. The banter was fun, until it wasn't. Until they played it too close to the heart. He could throw out harmless commentary and innuendo all day, but thrown back at him, calling him out like that…

He tried not to sour their easy rapport with his wariness. "They didn't call me Brash Bishara for nothing."

"I'd prefer if you didn't behave brashly. It'll keep you alive longer in Paradisa. I know we'll be bound together for life, but I do hope you get to live out the remainder of yours."

In the light of the setting sun, Raphael's onyx hair actually shone. The dusk filled his pale eyes with an amber film, and his porcelain skin glowed with a golden aura. Almost like he was haloed by illumination.

And as Connor stared at the other man—this *angel,* this being that was *more* than man—he was almost at peace with the idea of becoming Raphael's ward. Raphael had suggested, more than once, that he lacked the ability to lie. Which meant their meeting at the bar, though enigmatic, had not been a ruse. Raphael had never tried to deceive him.

Still, what did that really mean? They were of different worlds— Connor, a mortal human, and Raphael, magnificent and ageless. In the holy books Connor had grown up with, angels hardly even looked human, let alone thought of fraternizing on Earth. Sure, there was some questionable stuff about nephilim, but since the moral of that story was literally "don't fuck angels," it hardly reassured him.

Maybe he was projecting too much. If angels looked like men, if they had no wings, and if they comfortably cohabitated with pagan gods, what all did he really know about them?

Connor let himself enjoy the observations and mystery; let the small joy consume him for the time being. Better than focusing on the irrevocable punishment of touching Raphael's Icon. Or the irrevocable punishment for any number of small things he'd done, or had been, in his life.

Maybe *punishment* wasn't the right word for this. Maybe *opportunity*. Truth be told, it wasn't the commitment or the promise of violence that worried him. That part was like going off to war. It was a sacrifice, but the type he knew how to make.

No, it was the other thing Raphael had mentioned before—the sharing of souls. The sharing of emotions. Why couldn't they stay like this, forever? Hanging out in the same place, but still their own people? Sure, he'd be anchoring Raphael to Earth, which was the opposite of what Raphael needed to be doing. And sure, Raphael already told him that he lacked some degree of free will—that the will of Eden, and perhaps even of Michael, overruled any of his own desires.

But maybe that would have been nice. Life partners, at arm's length. Not bound by the chest. Not with Raphael able to *see* inside of him.

Not when he had so much to hide.

Before he could mull on it further, the window beneath his cheek seemed to vibrate.

Connor sat up, dizzy with the feel of it. But it wasn't just the window that was rattling. Everything in the room shook, from the hanging lamps to the bronze statuettes on every table, to the lounge they both sat upon.

They shot to their feet in unison, Raphael's hands extending to steady Connor's balance. Connor gripped his arms in return until the trembling room stilled.

Connor swallowed, glancing down. "Earthquake?"

*Bang.* No rumble this time. An absolute shockwave sent them both to the ground. Connor face-planted into the lion skin rug, getting a mouthful of mane in the process.

He lifted his head as the distant screams of combat began. He met Raphael's eyes, which were blown wide.

"Athena," the angel gasped. "It's here for her."

## 9

C lara had no cell service up on Mount Etna, but her fingers still itched to whip out her phone and refresh Facebook. Connor had ribbed her at breakfast the third time she'd reached into her pocket. *"You are in the company of literal fucking gods but your phone is more interesting? You millennials are something else."*

He was just mad 'cause he was an extroverted eighties kid. As much as Connor refused to let people too close, he still thrived off their company. Meanwhile, if Clara never had to talk to another person again, she'd get along fine. Social media was a way to feel social and connected without actually having to be in front of people.

And sure, it was a…habit. Maybe that part was harder to admit. It wasn't like she was proud of her millennial dependency on instant gratification, but maybe she did worship Samsung more than she worshipped any Greek heroes or archangels.

Additionally, typical boredom busters were not available at Hephaestus and Aphrodite's house. Not one of their books was written in a language she understood. They certainly didn't have crossword puzzles or television. All that was left for her to do was to lay across a lounge in the common room and let her thoughts chase their own tails.

She simply couldn't find a way to start a conversation with three gods who seemed intimately familiar with one another—their relationships and rapport going back eons—especially when she had so little to share with them. Making conversation with Athena on the ferry had already been a struggle, and Aphrodite reminded her way too much of the girls in gymnastics: thin, blonde, perfect nose. Intimidating.

Hephaestus had been kind to her before—had a lot in common with her, actually—but he seemed too preoccupied for small talk. He tinkered with something near the fireplace, some kind of geared contraption, and was lost in muttered conversation with Athena. Even if Clara could hear them properly from fifteen feet away, their conversation was entirely in Greek.

Clara stared at the gold-leafed ceiling. Maybe figuring out a conversation in another language could be a puzzle to calm her restless brain. Like a crossword cryptogram.

Their body language spoke loudly enough. Athena talked with her hands, rapid and intense, almost as if giving him some kind of frustrated lecture. Hephaestus just made a noise in the back of his throat and continued to stare down at the contraption in his lap. After a couple minutes, one word of Athena's spiel became clear through the foreign tongue—*Aphrodite*.

At his wife's name, Hephaestus's face jerked up from his work. He rubbed his forehead, muttering *Aphrodite...Aphrodite...*back to her. The name emerged multiple times again through the gibberish. Always said tiredly. Always said with reluctance and weight.

Every now and then, Athena would let out a short laugh or nudge him with a foot or a hand. It was almost like she was roasting him, the way one does with someone they're comfortable around. He'd protest weakly, rolling his eyes, snarking back something in a disbelieving tone.

Their conversation died when Aphrodite entered the room, a large clay urn held in her arms. She didn't regard them much at all, aside from a curious wrinkle of her nose. Instead, she moved from potted plant to potted plant, pouring water gently into the soil.

"Hephaestus looks guilty about something," she commented mildly, in English. She glanced at Clara. "What were they up to?"

There was something playful in her voice, something that could be mistaken for flirtation in a different context. Clara moistened her lips, because how the hell was she supposed to reply to a question like that?

Hephaestus butted in with a scoff. "Leave her be, Aphrodite. And have I told you that I hate that power of yours? My feelings are my own."

Aphrodite sighed, setting down the empty water pitcher. "You know I can't control what I see."

"I have no shame in what I said," Athena said. "I told him that it's been five thousand years, and if he doesn't start appreciating what he's got staring him in the face, I'm going to start appreciating it for him."

Clara's eyes widened. Certainly, it was a joke, but a day ago she wouldn't have expected Athena to go to bat for Aphrodite.

Hephaestus shot his friend a sour look. "An empty threat coming from a virgin."

Aphrodite smiled. "Oh, I'm sure Athena and I could do plenty of things that wouldn't tarnish her virginity."

Hephaestus buried his face in his hands, and Clara's own cheeks grew warm from the secondhand embarrassment. "I'm beginning to miss when you two hated each other."

"There's no strength in hating each other," Athena said, a little sobered. "We're all we have left anymore."

They sat in companionable silence for a moment, the four of them. Clara wasn't really part of their conversation, but they'd gone out of their way to make it understandable for her—so at least they'd tried to include her somehow. Hephaestus remained the most unchanged by the banter, still looking preoccupied and frustrated as he tightened a latch on his mechanical work-in-progress.

In the silence, it was easy to hear the remarkable *groan* that echoed throughout the room, almost seeming to arise from inside the mountain itself.

Clara sat up so fast she saw stars. "Uh. This is an active volcano, isn't it?"

"Only if Typhon is in the mood for it to be," Hephaestus said. "And that was definitely not him."

Another noise, this time closer. Acute. Like a stampede.

Hephaestus stumbled to his feet and reached for his cane. "That's coming from the forge."

Pale-faced, he ran clumsily past the columns, through the dining area, and toward the door of his forge. Aphrodite and Athena followed on his heels, with Clara rushing to bring up the rear.

She met them at the base of the staircase, looking around the forge. "Is anything here?"

*Thud.* Aphrodite fell against Hephaestus, and Clara stumbled back into a rocky wall. Hephaestus enveloped his wife with both arms, and Clara wondered, briefly, if it was the most intimate they'd been in centuries.

Clara rubbed her shoulder, ducking away from the gravel falling from the ceiling. The rock cracked beneath one of her hands resting on the wall.

"What if it's spectres?" Athena asked. "I knew they would come for me, even here."

"I don't know much about them," Hephaestus said. "But my defenses could keep out a skyfather."

The next sound was not a thud, and did not shake the mountain. It was the groan of bending metal.

Hephaestus slowly limped to the center of the forge. The dark exit tunnel framed his short stature in silhouette. Athena joined Clara at the wall, pushing herself between the girl and whatever horrors could emerge from the tunnel.

And horror did. From the darkness of the exit, a group of spectres —in numbers vast enough to overflow the tunnel—shambled into the light with razor-toothed smiles.

Athena's voice cut through the foggy molasses of Clara's brain. "You need to hide!"

Clara's body felt like a heavy puppet, pulled and pushed to the ground, shoved under the nearest workbench by Athena's impeccable strength. Immediately, she scooted back to conceal her balled-up frame. So weird, the way hiding spots provided an illusion of safety. She had been an anxious child, afraid of monsters in the closet, but concealing her face with the sheets always made her feel safe. *If I can't see them, they can't see me.*

The blurred images of Hephaestus and Aphrodite reflected in a nearby silver shield. In the mirrored metal, the spectres moved as blurs of limbs. Their growls echoed through the cavern, both humanoid and distinctly monstrous. Clara's vision darted across them in a futile attempt to count. *Five...eight...no, wait, nine? More? They move so quickly. God.*

Aphrodite grabbed a curved knife from the nearest workbench and emerged from behind her husband. Hephaestus gripped his cane with both fists and twisted the center. A blade popped out of the bottom, effectively converting his cane into a spear. Elsewhere, Athena had apparently grabbed some kind of weapon off a work-bench and was challenging her own spectres to a fight, but she was out of Clara's line of sight. All Clara heard were her fierce yells and the clang of sword against sword.

The more immediate spectres leapt at Hephaestus and Aphrodite in a cacophony. They each landed with a clatter, toppling Hephaestus's wares off workbenches and shelves. Clara cringed at the clang of metal against metal, covering her ears.

Hephaestus yelled in his native Greek, and the half dozen automatons lined against the far wall jerked to life. Their golden legs rushed past Clara's hiding spot, lurching to protect their master.

She poked her head out from under the table. Aphrodite tangled with three spectres in graceful slaughter, turning them into a shroud of smoke with the dagger. Not far away, Hephaestus whipped his cane around to clobber one spectre in its milky face, then jerked the cane back to spear another in the chest. With every fatal injury, the spectres exploded into smoke. They were either dead or merely dissipated, but Clara couldn't be sure.

Back to back, husband and wife defended each other as Clara remained under the bench. Her nails scraped against the floor as her fists balled up. A countless number of enemies outnumbered them, and Hephaestus's posture grew ragged. He'd planted his cane on the ground, supporting his weight, and he now batted off the spectres with nothing more than a fist and his good leg. Aphrodite's moves remained deft, but her face screwed up as she struggled to protect both herself and her husband.

As Hephaestus elbowed one spectre in the throat, another kicked the back of his knees, sweeping away his balance. His cane flew out of his hand and rolled under a workbench.

Clara barely cut off her scream before the shrill sound escaped. A whimper came out instead, a pathetic juvenile noise. She couldn't even think. She was about to learn the repulsive, unimaginable pain of having an arm ripped off, maybe see her insides on the outside.

All because she sat cowardly, waiting for someone to defend her. Waiting for Connor to hear the noise and save her, or for Athena to remember to protect her.

But, no. She could *do* something.

Clara's ears roared with blood as the spectres crowded around Hephaestus and Aphrodite, who kicked weakly at their assailants. One of Hephaestus's hands sprawled across Aphrodite's waist, but the other reached toward his distant cane.

Aphrodite tried to push herself off the ground, but a spectre landed a hearty kick into the small of her back. As she groaned, it grabbed her by the ankle and dragged her across the sooty floor toward one of the kilns. Another spectre joined and grabbed the goddess's arms, lifting her helplessly off the floor.

"No!" Hephaestus's limbs struggled to push him up, and the foot of a spectre stomped him back onto the ground. Most peculiarly, thorned, leafy vines emerged from the spectre's foot, latticing across Hephaestus like a net.

"Aphrodite! I'm coming!" Athena called, struggling to move past her two opponents. But there was something odd about the spectres she fought, as well. One was like the spectre back at the hotel--he seemed to teleport, almost, turning to smoke at will and dancing around Athena in a blur. The other held the goddess of war back by her upper arms, considerably stronger than he appeared and too strong for Athena to untangle from.

Each of these spectres was different. Different abilities, different strengths, perhaps even different powers.

Clara swallowed, gritted her teeth, and crept out from her hiding spot. She reached up, groping for a sword on her sanctuary bench. The spectre tying down Hephaestus met her eyes, tilted its head. Staring into its eyes was like staring into fog.

Clara jumped to her feet and crossed the distance between them. She thrust the end of her sword toward its face, slashing it from temple to jaw. The spectre stumbled backward with an angry screech, and dissolved into smoke.

Hephaestus ripped the vines off his chest, his arms slicked with tiny golden cuts from the thorns. "My Icon," he gasped. "The cane..."

"Over here!" Clara gripped Hephaestus's arms, her back straining as she hauled up his dense weight. Once on his feet, he slung an arm over her shoulders and they staggered, together, to the workbench where his cane had rolled. He fell to his knees and reached under the table for his lost totem. As soon as Hephaestus reunited with the cane, a red glow bathed his skin, reinvigorating his entire body. His thorn-ravaged arms healed, and the golden sheen of blood vanished.

He stretched a hand toward his wife's attackers, who had reached the edge of the kiln with Aphrodite in tow. His eyes flickered orange, a flame blooming in his hand, albeit slowly.

Clara watched back and forth between them, at Aphrodite screaming and twisting in her captivity, to Hephaestus with his gritted teeth and sweating brow. Maybe she could have run to Aphrodite, helped untangle the goddess from her entrapment...but that would put her in the path of Hephaestus's fire.

Hephaestus's defense never got the chance to bloom. A single remaining automaton speared one of Aphrodite's attackers through the ribcage. The spectre exploded into smoke with a force great enough to douse the kiln's flames and to knock the automaton on its back. Hephaestus's shoulders slumped, the miniature flame dying in his hand.

"Clara! Clara are you okay?!"

She spun, heart hammering. Connor and Raphael rushed down the staircase together, splitting up when they reached the base. Raphael made a beeline for Athena while Connor navigated a labyrinth of upturned tables and weaponry to get to Clara. The remaining spectres threw anything within reach, from heroically heavy shields to rusted broadswords. Connor dodged the chaos on his approach, grabbing one of Hephaestus's abandoned battle axes and swinging it in defensive arcs.

"Are you okay?" he shouted to Clara.

As her lips parted, a spectre tackled Connor from behind and tossed him into a pile of twisted metal. He rolled across the heap, feet over head, and Clara's mouth turned sour.

"No!" She lurched toward him, but two arms encircled her waist and lifted her off her feet. She kicked against the air, grunting in protest as the arms pulled her under the same bench she'd hid before.

"Clara, they're too strong! They'll kill you!"

"Goddammit." She forced her head out from under the bench anyway. Although the spectre numbers had dwindled to half-dozen, natural selection had done its work. Only the strongest remained. And the largest of them all stood on a workbench in the middle of the room, rigorous flames engulfing both of his arms.

She turned in Hephaestus's grip, her voice cracking. "That spectre can control fire, like you. Can't you fight him?"

"I can't. I'm no better than damp flint. I don't have that kind of power anymore, you saw that yourself!"

The room seemed to grow small, honing in on the narrowest of paths. Aphrodite was alone and weaponless now, cornered by the overly strong spectre Athena had fought. On the other side of the forge, the teleporting spectre hit Athena across the face with the broad side of a sword, knocking her cold to the ground. Raphael wasn't there to catch her, but his flaming sword shot forward into the spectre's chest, at least managing to avenge his charge.

All of this occurred around the spectre in the middle of the room, who kept their opposing sides separated with intense walls of heat.

Connor had managed to untangle from his earlier spectre foe, but the wall of flames emitting from the pyrokinetic spectre kept him locked behind a pile of Spartan shields. Clara barely avoided singeing her own face and ducked back under the bench as a rush of flames whizzed past their table.

No one could save them from this. No one other than Hephaestus.

She took a deep breath and blurted the words before she could regret them. "If you need more power, then make me your ward."

Hephaestus choked a noise halfway between a whimper and a scoff. "You don't know what that means."

"Connor's told me enough. I know it's permanent, but you know what else is permanent? Death! Which we're about to get a taste of if you don't stop that guy from frying us."

"Clara…absolutely not. I am in pain every moment I wake. I will not burden you with that."

*Damn the gods,* she thought. Damn the gods and their immortality. Damn them for thinking their petty self-conscious bullshit was more important than peoples' lives.

"You're not a burden." She could have shaken him. "None of that matters right now, because you can save us."

"You barely know me at all. If you really knew me, you'd want nothing to do with me—Aphrodite could tell you that."

Hephaestus looked past her, where his wife had nearly gone still, slumped against one of the brick forges. Her wild blonde hair frizzed, and her lips leaked golden blood as the spectre continued to beat her with its bare hands.

The cogs twirled inside Clara's head as she looked back and forth between husband and wife. She hated to use the manipulative idea, but she could apologize for it later.

"She cares about you, Hephaestus. And if you care about her, you'll save her."

Hephaestus struggled for a moment, too long a moment, squeezing his eyes shut, before letting out what sounded like a curse.

"You can't say I didn't warn you."

"It's not about what I want."

He cleared his throat, clasping one of Clara's hands. His other hand settled upon her chest, above her heart.

"Do you vow upon the River Styx to share your soul for the remainder of your mortal life?"

*I'm not really ready to share my soul, but go off, I guess.*

"Fine, fine," she breathed, her chest pressing into Hephaestus's hand. "Yes, I do."

"To strengthen and assist us both, unite two races, and make two halves a whole…"

"Ahh!" She nearly buckled. Light glowed where Hephaestus's hand touched her, dancing in tendrils around his wrist. Something yanked a tether in her navel to unravel her insides.

"I vow to protect you as my ward, to prevent harm from coming to your body or soul, to remain by your side in the same realm…"

Clara covered the hand upon her chest with her own, digging into his skin. She gritted her teeth, refusing to scream. As the yellow light reached Hephaestus, she barely had enough breath in her lungs to scream anyway. Her chest constricted; a limb somewhere was being pulled too harshly, a tendon was about to pop, a blood vessel was about to burst.

Hephaestus continued talking in a beautiful, lyrical language far from English. When Clara could no longer hold back a sob, it was done. The yellow light wrapped around Hephaestus's chest and burrowed into his skin. He gasped, his eyes flashing a brief, brilliant gold before returning to their usual mahogany.

Clara groaned, falling against her newly minted companion. Luckily, Hephaestus was not quite as overwhelmed, for he managed to haul her to her feet. Although the ritual had ended, she was still…extended. The overdrawn tether was simply taut, when it had not existed at all before.

But what truly engulfed her, what truly made her want to sit down, was the instant rush of hot tension to her chest, and sharp pain down her right leg.

"Don't let go," he instructed, his arm tightening around her waist. "Don't let go, or you'll burn."

She cradled his side, dizzy, as his cane dug awkwardly into her back. As she clung tighter, Hephaestus's eyes glowed bright gold, and fire licked up his arms. He outstretched a palm toward the spectre in the middle of the room a spark already blooming.

What started as nothing more than a simple flame grew outward and upward, weaving through the forge as a compressed stream. It hit the spectres one by one, charring them into oblivion while narrowly avoiding their friends. The heat and power blew back Clara's hair, but the fire did not burn her either. She reached into the orange light, stunned as the flames twirled around her fingers and caused no harm. Just heat, lovely and radiant. This fire had been caged in his blood for centuries, finally experiencing release, and it greeted him like a familiar lover.

With a final roar, Hephaestus pushed the fire forward, creating an obliterating wall of smoke and flame that engulfed the pyrokinetic spectre. Clara closed her eyes against the bright light, every one of her cells igniting against the warmth. The fire consumed itself in the shape of a dragon, then all fell silent.

Hephaestus collapsed to his knees, dragging Clara with him. His forehead pressed against the warm ground as one hand remained upon her back. Footsteps clambered over and a soft hand caressed her back. Clara gasped, sucking in dry, electrified air.

She lifted her head. Raphael looked down at her, and his blue healing light blanketed her skin. But what about Connor? Fatigue kept her down, but she forced her eyes to not blink.

Connor surfaced from under a pile of smoking metal, and a cry escaped Clara's throat. Soot caked his cheeks and thin scratch marks crisscrossed his arms, but he was alive.

Drunkenly, her thoughts and feelings overlapped each other and contradicted. None of it was tangible—the moment she experienced godlike thought, the sensation slipped away and something else replaced it. Clara danced between her heart and Hephaestus's, all of it a blur, with no discernible barriers between hers and his.

This was how it felt to be a ward.

# 1 0

Connor pressed his face against the floor-length parlor window. The lounge reeked of perfume, and of old mottled liquors evaporating into thick syrup from the decanters. A layer of dust coated every piece of furniture.

Beside him, Clara hugged herself, looking down at the golden threaded rug. She hadn't said a word since they'd emerged from the forge. As for Connor, he was okay—barely a scratch. A little out of breath but too high on adrenaline to give a shit.

Clara, though, moved like some kind of zombie. Even her gait looked lopsided.

He reached for her, gripping her shoulder.

"You're okay, right?"

"I'm not hurt."

"That's not what I asked."

"I'll be okay."

She was still so young and out of her element. His conditioned mind found battle familiar, but he could no longer imagine how it looked to a layman.

"It's important to check in with your headspace." He walked closer, still a little uncomfortable in those damn Greek pants, and still in want of pockets. "I had nightmares every day after the discharge. Still do, sometimes. That memory was worse than the combat or the killing or the guilt. That very last day, I...I used to replay it in my head. Over and over."

"Why'd you torture yourself like that?"

"It's not like I could help it."

"So...how'd you get rid of it?"

"Time. Distractions. You. When Mam and Dad told me to take care of you...it was the best thing that could have happened to me."

"Really?"

"Yep."

She looked down at her hands, covered in white ash. "You never told me that."

"Yeah, well," he tried to smile at her, to bring back the levity, "you never would have let me live it down."

She had danced among death with the smoke of spectres twirling around her. It was terrifying to know she could have been killed, but there she stood: whole and near him.

Connor touched the back of her neck. "You were pretty great out there, you know. Dad would have been proud. Between the two of us, you weren't the one who needed Hephaestus to save your ass."

Clara leaned into him, slipping both arms around his waist. Her hair reeked of soot, but he pulled her close anyway. At least it was something. Walls coming down, and Clara—his Clara—emerging from behind them.

"He had some help," she said softly.

He frowned. That sounded way more meaningful than it should have. "Help?"

Clara pulled away, lacing her hands over her stomach.

"I'm his ward now. I had to do it, to give him the power to stop that fire spectre. We were all trapped, Athena was out...I just...he was the only one who could stop it, and he couldn't do it without me."

Connor huffed, shaking his head. When the wall of flame engulfed the forge, he assumed Hephaestus found hidden power within himself, not because he needed the help of Clara's *soul.*

"I didn't get a choice to do this to myself, Clara. Why the hell would you do it on purpose? You could have gone home, you could have..." He raked a hand through his hair. The adrenaline inside of him spiked again, perhaps fueling itself. "Just, *why?*"

"Because I had to do *something!*" Her face screwed up. "I wasn't going to let any of us get killed when I could have stopped it."

His shoulders slumped. She really was their father's daughter. Brash Bishara 2.0.

"Guess I can't blame you for that."

Clara tilted her head. "I don't regret it. I just need time to figure out what this means. Until then, I'll deal with it."

Deep in the inner folds of his conscience, he was grateful to be in this with Clara. It was a selfish, poisonous thought he should have buried and never admitted to, but the prospective isolation of becoming a ward had been the most terrifying part.

His memory stretched back twenty years, to the dock of the U.S.S. George Washington. Mam clasped him by the arms to wish him farewell, never completely sure if he'd come home. But never once did Connor see his mother quiver. Perhaps she cried once they were asleep, perhaps she bemoaned her worries in letters she never sent to anyone. Perhaps Dad wasn't the only one good at keeping secrets.

He called upon her strength and her resilience, knowing it was buried dormant in his genes. If his mother had seen him off to war, then he could do the same with Clara. Except he wouldn't force her to go off alone.

He crossed his arms over his chest. "What does it feel like? Raphael said we'd see each other's feelings or...whatever."

Clara peered at him. Or, more accurately, *through* him, off into the space above his head. "It's weird. I can sense where he is and what he's feeling. He's terrified right now. He feels like he's right here next to me. And it makes me feel...stronger in a way. Like I feel his powers, but I can't access them."

"Can you read his thoughts?"

"No. Only his emotions."

Well. At least that was a relief he could look forward to.

"But do you think he can read yours?"

She didn't answer, instead offering him a frank expression. "I think you can trust Raphael."

"What does that have to do with anything?" Connor grumbled, turning his back on her. The phrase was familiar. It came as her warranty label on every friend-of-a-friend she'd tried to hook him up with, every *"isn't he cute?"* at a bar. *You can trust him, you know.*

But this wasn't that. This wasn't sharing a warm bed with a hook up, or having drinks with some heavily pierced coworker he'd never commit to, or playing on some swiping dating app on Clara's phone. This was handcuffing himself to a man he barely knew, for the rest of his life, and giving up every iota of internal privacy.

Clara lifted a shoulder. "But you like him, don't you? What's got you so bent of shape about it?"

"That almost makes it worse."

If anyone was capable of withholding judgment, and not sneering at Connor's insides, it had to be Raphael. But to expose his soul to someone he was drawn to...

It would have been a helluva lot easier if there was nothing between them to hide.

The door creaked behind them, and Raphael poked his head into the room. Connor glanced away, his face burning up as if Raphael could already read him.

"Connor? I need to speak with you."

Clara squeezed Connor's elbow, granting him a small smile. She looked tiny on the other side of him, as she always had. But he was plenty aware of the fire beneath her skin, and of the invisible bond she shared with a god. Connor shuddered, for the same fate soon came for him.

Clara exited, leaving him in solitude with Raphael. Connor turned back to the window, squaring his shoulders. Time dilated around him. Tunisia seemed weeks away, not days. He almost couldn't picture his father's face.

He finally glanced back at Raphael. "It's time isn't it?"

"I'm afraid so."

"Well. Let's get this over with, then."

Connor studied Raphael, eyes slipping down his lithe frame. Raphael's voice was gentle, his touch a beacon of hope. But there was no mistaking the stress weighing upon his frame. The fine lines etched into Raphael's face told a perfect story of pressure and of bearing the responsibility of every human life. Raphael, the man who loved his duty, but undoubtedly resented the lack of freedom. He was given an inch of free will, forbidden to take a mile.

And just like in the hotel bar, during their first real conversation, Connor didn't see him as an angel. Raphael's shoulders hung with an invisible weight, his face stiff beneath the serene smile. He knew next to nothing about Raphael, from his unfathomable age to his history of human interactions, but he knew what loneliness looked like. It showed itself in his mirror every morning.

Connor rubbed his neck. "If I've gotta be a ward, I guess I'm lucky I'm yours."

Raphael let out a nervous noise. "You give me too much credit, Connor."

Connor dared to draw closer, shrugging. "Even when I've found it hard to trust you, and cut me some slack 'cause most of this is ludicrous, I've never found it hard to be honest with you. Believe me, that means a lot. It's been a shitload of time since I could be myself with someone new."

Connor blew out both lungs, heart racing. "If I have to do this, I need it to be as painless as I can make it. And I could have a total stranger messing around with my guts, or I could have you." As if Raphael wasn't a stranger too...but he didn't feel like one. He never had.

Raphael leaned forward, placing both hands on Connor's collar bone. Connor tensed beneath the touch, but Raphael didn't seem to notice. "Right now, I'm in the middle of a war that could cost you your life. I could leave you here, have you wait until I come back. The distance apart would make you sick, but perhaps you'd survive it. You're more likely to survive that than traveling with me."

Connor forced a smile. "No. I've been in a few wars before. It's where I'm meant to be."

Connor envisioned Clara and the range of possibilities he had imagined for them fell apart. He used to think he'd watch her grow into a leader, an inventor, a champion of change in the world. Not anymore. Their future had become masked in fog.

But at least they still had a chance to make an impact on the world —together.

"Are you ready?"

Connor nodded. "Let's do it."

His film of certainty was thin, but present. He sucked in a breath, focusing on the relief it brought. Raphael grabbed his wrist in a firm handshake, then placed his other hand over Connor's heart. Connor's skin tingled beneath the touch.

Raphael began the ritual, asking him a few questions about what he was getting himself into. It sounded a bit like wedding vows, not that such a comparison soothed his nerves.

Pain started on the last *I do*, a fiery tourniquet around his ribcage. Yellow light emerged from his chest in a vine, stinging like poison sucked out of a wound. He was unabashed to yell out, the guttural noise filling his own ears.

Raphael did not appear to take joy in causing him pain, but he continued with his elegant language. The flowing lyrics spiraled into Connor's ears and nested into his soul.

He forced himself to open his eyes and watch what was happening, but there was only Raphael's calming gaze engulfed by golden light. That's all Raphael had to soothe him. His touch, which was normally a balm, caused the bizarre agony.

Connor's lungs grew too tight to breathe, and heat flared across the back of his skull. As a gasp rose in his throat, the curtain of pain finally pulled away. The light dimmed in the center of Raphael's chest, and Connor physically felt its descent. Like an extra limb.

Connor fell to his knees and pressed his forehead against the carpet.

*What have I done?*

C lara felt everything.

Plenty of religions or money-happy life coaches claimed they could connect people to the universe. To build them a way outside of themselves. To make them feel things like they never had before.

None of that was ever true, no matter how authentic the promise. Until now.

Her hands trembled in her lap. It was all so damn *loud*. Her and Hephaestus's souls, tangling and fighting over the same space, struggling to find some sort of agreement on territory. He was too strong to push out, so overwhelmingly full of emotion and pain that her body threatened to buckle. This is what he had warned her about.

At least Connor was going through the exact same thing.

Near the staircase, a vacant look filled her brother's eyes. He hovered wordlessly near Raphael, arms crossed over his chest. But the longer Clara watched him, the longer it was obvious that he was *hugging himself*.

Becoming a ward had not settled kindly with either of them.

Clara sucked in a breath, refocusing on her own companion. The more she honed in on Hephaestus, the more sense her brain made of all this. Whenever she was tempted to occupy her thoughts with someone else, or anything else, he existed like a raving distraction in the back of her brain.

Near one of the hearths, he puttered around Aphrodite like a moth. His anxiety flowed off him in a tendril, snaking over to connect in Clara's gut. The bond was a tether between them, giving them a sense of each other at all times. If his tension glowed any hotter, she might have been able to see the bond.

It was the closest Aphrodite and Hephaestus had been in Clara's presence, aside from during the battle. He muttered things to her occasionally, reached for her, even. Cupped her jaw in his calloused hands and tilted her head, checking her for the third or fourth time, until Aphrodite waved him away. It didn't take knowledge of Greek to know she was telling him to buzz off. But through the goddess's frustration, her voice retained some level of fondness. Clara's gut lurched when she heard it, before realizing she'd just felt Hephaestus's response to his wife. The more Clara stood in silence, watching them move around each other, the more the longing infected her from Hephaestus's side.

He loved Aphrodite. He *adored* her. But despite their many years of marriage, his heart felt caged, like…like he still feared rejection? Or that there was something he could not trust. There was so much reluctance, so much fear, so much heart-in-her-throat-and-sweat-on-her-palms emotion that Clara had to inhale her own air deeply and exhale out his pain.

She looked elsewhere in the room. Athena sat upon the lip of a table, nursing a silver goblet of mountain water. She'd woken up shortly after the battle, a bit dazed, but mostly pissy that a spectre had managed to disarm her so profoundly. Golden blood still stained her hairline, but her lacerations had healed minutes ago. It seemed that she, and Aphrodite, didn't actually *need* Raphael to heal them—they were capable of healing from their own injuries, albeit slower, and perhaps only from conventional wounds.

Athena held the goblet in both hands, staring down at it. "This was my fault. They wouldn't have come here if it wasn't for me."

"You're a victim, Athena. You don't deserve to be hunted." Raphael ran a hand over his hair, shaking his head. "But...the spectres have clearly become more aggressive in chasing you. I think it's about time we stopped acting defensively, and instead try figuring out who is sending them after you in the first place."

Hephaestus, having finally left his wife alone, joined the circle of their conversation. *Curiosity.* That felt...blue, for some reason. The feeling was fleeting, slipping across Clara's neck like a silk scarf, before meandering beyond her reach. What a synesthetic trip this bond was. How would she ever get used to sharing Hephaestus's soul? He seemed somewhat unaffected by sharing hers, at least so far.

"Why do you think there's someone behind this?" Hephaestus said. "I've never seen creatures like these spectres before, but how could you possibly know their motivation?"

The angel shrugged. "Because they don't seem sapient enough to have one. If they were founded or...pray tell, *created*, then they must have been instilled with a mission by someone with an agenda. Why this agenda includes hunting down Athena, I'm not aware. But it does not seem like something they could have chosen for themselves, especially with how single mindedly they behave."

Raphael paced, stroking the side of his chin. He froze a few feet away, stopping short of something tiny on the floor. A small brass token on a leather cord glinted on the tile, so simple Clara had hardly noticed it.

He knelt, twirling a finger around the necklace and holding it up. "Does this belong to any of you?"

Athena circled closer, hands on her hips. "What is it?"

"A ward medallion for those living at the Embassy of Wards. It allows them limited passage to Earth."

"I've never been to that place," Hephaestus said. He jerked his head in Aphrodite's direction. "I can't speak for her, but I would have noticed that here in my forge before."

Connor finally cleared his throat to speak. His voice was small, croaky, so unlike the typical strength Clara knew of her brother. But they were discussing tactics, and maybe that would help ground him back to Earth. "Do you think one of the spectres dropped it?"

Raphael rubbed a thumb over the relief. "If they did, it means the spectres must have been at the Embassy. Perhaps it's where they came from in the first place."

Clara found her own voice. Had to dig it up from the bottom of her lungs, but she found it. "What's the Embassy of Wards? *Where* is it?"

Raphael stepped closer to her, extending the medallion with his hand. The token swayed, the size of a quarter, etched with a relief of a mountain city.

"Normally, humans go to an astral heaven when they die. They lose their physical form and can no longer travel through realms. We treat wards with greater dignity upon death—we invite them to the Embassy, which allows them to stay in Paradisa with us."

"Then we leave for the Embassy. Now." Hephaestus stormed closer, but he stumbled on his poor leg and was caught by Raphael's swift hands. He shoved the angel off him, grumbling to himself. Clara nearly buckled as his shame flooded her chest, constricting around her lungs.

"We?" Athena snorted. "Hephaestus, isn't your role inside the forge, making weapons for the rest of us? You are not fit for a battlefield."

Rage flared next, burning across Clara's cheeks. Hephaestus cut his eyes at his friend, despite her light tone.

"I saved all of you tonight. And now that I have a ward...I suppose I should use this extra power for something. It's not like I'm safe sitting here in a house I thought was good enough."

Raphael placed a hand on his shoulder. "You can come with us, if you'd like. But the Embassy will still be there tomorrow. Athena is still recovering from her wounds, and the humans need to rest. We can leave in the morning."

"Yes, we humans appreciate sleep." Clara smiled, tongue shoved firmly into her gums. Like she could sleep at such a time, with

Hephaestus roaring inside her and adrenaline still thrumming through her veins.

"My health is irrelevant, as I'll be leaving here immediately." Athena said, looking to the floor. "The longer I stay here, the more endangered you are. And I need to inform Michael that things have escalated. The safest place for me right now is with the war guild."

Raphael frowned. "I understand, but Connor and I will need to accompany you. You're still my charge."

"You're far more useful trying to hunt these spectres down, Raphael. And that's possibly safer than trying to watch my back. You have your ward to protect now. I can take care of myself. And if I can't..." She sighed with the weight of millennia. "So be it."

Something sank inside of Clara. It was the first sensation since binding to Hephaestus that she recognized as her own, not his. No, this was her own sense of despair. Her own premature mourning for Athena's will.

"Don't give up," she said, barely loud enough to hear herself.

But Athena heard her. The goddess's brow softened, almost hiding the severity of her facial scarring for a moment.

"I'm not giving up," Athena said, scanning the room to look at all of them, one by one. "I hope to see you all in Paradisa later. Try not to get yourselves killed."

---

Humans appreciated sleep, as Clara had said. Clearly, gods did not, as Clara laid awake with Hephaestus practically *pacing* inside her head.

At least, it started with the pacing. As the hours grew darker, the bond poured worse and worse things into Clara's half. A throb in her skull, a dizziness when she moved her head too quickly, a bubbling sense of nausea in her throat.

Almost like...being drunk?

That wasn't an incredibly familiar feeling. The Citadel could throw some parties, but she spent most of them at home with Connor, studying in her bedroom. The only time she ever passed out was under a thermodynamics textbook at four in the morning.

Still, her twenty-first birthday gave her enough familiarity with the buzz of alcohol, since *Connor* had taken her to Applebee's for midnight Fireball shots. Sure, they'd both agreed the place was a dumpster, especially the one on Rivers, but it was "tradition." He'd had his own first drink there with his Navy buddies, nearly two decades before. So, either squids had shitty taste, or Applebee's had been way better in the 90s.

Eventually, the ill-feeling became too much. Maybe if she could tell Hephaestus to go the hell to sleep, it'd quiet down the torrent within her.

She climbed out of bed, her gut lurching just from the upright position. Clara grabbed the bedpost, steadying herself. Anxiety had given her enough of this feeling before, the ball-in-her-throat feeling that would keep her awake at night. There were plenty of ways to cope with that, mostly going back to deep breaths and distraction. Strangely, those same coping mechanisms seemed to work on her now. *Inhale. Tongue against the roof of the mouth. Focus on the feel of the carpet beneath my toes...*

The coping mechanisms got her all the way to the living room and down to the forge without puking or falling over, and that's where she finally found Hephaestus.

He was hammering something with one hand, and held a goatskin flask in the other. Hammering, of course, was a loose description, because every other swing missed the bench entirely.

"Hephaestus," Clara said, watching him take a long gulp from the flask.

He regarded her with hazy eyes, wiping the back of his hand across his mouth. "Clara? Whadaya doing down 'ere?"

"I can't sleep."

"Ah. 'Ave a drink, it'll help."

He thrust the flask to her chest, and she had no choice but to take it from him. As soon as the cap approached her nose, the harsh sting of alcohol flooded her sinuses. Clara sputtered, covering her cough with the back of her hand, thrusting the goatskin back to Hephaestus.

"Jesus, what is this, moonshine?"

He frowned at her, eyes glazed. *Confusion.* More confusion, that is. If she thought he couldn't feel more confused, he somehow managed it.

"This's unmixed wine."

"Damn." Not that wine could be as strong as liquor, but it sure as hell explained the headache. "So, you are drunk, huh…"

He raised the goatskin to his lips again, wobbly, purple liquid spilling down the scruff on his chin. Clara reached for it, gently prying the container from his flimsy grip.

"I think that's enough for tonight."

She felt it before he acted upon it—his frustration, the entitlement, the tantrum. His reflexes were so sluggish compared to her own, he barely opened his mouth before she was shutting him down.

"I mean it," she said. "We have to leave here tomorrow. I can't be dealing with your…hangover, or whatever!"

He slumped against the bench, using that to hold himself upright instead of his cane. Another spike of pain shot through Clara's temple, almost migraine intense. She winced, gritting her teeth, going through the motions of intent anyway. She fought through the ache of uncut wine coursing through her system secondhand, fought through the haze of confusion, and tossed his goatskin flask right into one of his forges.

The alcohol caught fire in a flash, blowing a small puff of flames upward until, in a heartbeat of a second, it was gone.

Hephaestus groaned weakly, watching her from his slumped position on the workbench. He laid half-sprawled across it, resting his chin on the side of a broadsword without a care.

"It's for your own good," Clara said, approaching him again. "And mine too."

"M'sorry, Clara. Wassn't thinkin' about you. Never 'ad a ward before."

His slurred speech was half-spoken into the side of his arm, still sprawled limply across the bench. Clara stopped, closing her eyes for a few seconds to keep the world from spinning around her. She dutifully pushed back, visualizing the world as *she* saw it, not as he did. She had her own sense of self. She did not need his overcoming her.

When she opened her eyes, the world was right again.

"Why haven't you ever taken a ward?"

"Noonewannetme."

The pang of sympathy? That was definitely her own. *No one wanted me.* She'd said the same words herself before—to Mam and Dad, to Connor, to her childhood best friend Brandi. *No one wants me.* There was no lonelier feeling in the world.

"Hey. I wanted you, okay?" Maybe the circumstances hadn't been ideal. Maybe she wouldn't have chosen this at all, if they'd been in a better timeline. But she would have died before swearing an oath to someone reprehensible. If the devil himself had said, "I can save us," she would have proudly given him the finger.

"Dun even know whatta do with you. Whatta do with a ward…"

"Neither do I. So, who cares? Who says we've gotta do anything, right?"

For a moment, his brown eyes seemed to sober up some. They stared at her, wide and wet, his body still lopsided.

"You're here forever," he said quietly. "You'll wantta leave, soon. And you can't, cause of me."

She reached around him and slipped his arm over her shoulder. "Don't worry about that right now. Let's get you to bed. Try to work with me, okay? You're heavier than you look."

He was also much warmer than he looked, hot like a cast iron pan as he leaned into her support.

Hephaestus, to his credit, seemed to make some effort to walk on his own. The cane took a good bit of his weight, at least, and she took the rest. He moved away from the workbench, each step tiny and unstable, when something golden caught Clara's eye.

He'd been laying atop it, before. A pair of golden pistols, glinting in the firelight.

Clara forced herself not to pause, because that would probably send them both stumbling to the floor. But as they took baby steps toward the staircase, maybe conversation would sober him up some.

"What are those guns? I wouldn't think you'd know how to make guns."

"Guns been 'round for centrieeees." A hiccup, a cringe, a wobble in his step. Clara stopped walking long enough for him to rebalance himself against her side. "Apollo brings 'em. I tinker with 'em. Those're for Connor."

"You made guns for Connor?" How was that possible? It'd barely been four hours since their fight with the spectres. How had he managed to throw together two weapons from scratch in that time?

"Dun'be jealous." He looked down at her, offering a sleepy smile. "Axes are for you. Have to be useful to you some'ow."

She half-wished she could go back and look, see what axes he was talking about. But she said to herself, as much as to him, "We'll look at those in the morning."

The stairs were a trial, but by taking them one at a time, Clara maneuvered Hephaestus into the common area without anyone busting their face open. By the time they'd hobbled to the bedroom wing, her shoulders seared with pain, and her hips popped with every other step. Hephaestus had grown heavier against her, less and less aware of his weight distribution. If it weren't for his cane sharing *some* of the burden, she probably would have dropped him back at the living room.

So, she approached the first room she saw, fingers crossed that it would have a bed in it.

When they pushed their way through the heavy wooden door, they did score a bed, but they were not alone.

Aphrodite turned in her vanity chair, a seashell comb in hand. Her eyebrows raised, puzzled, but not offended.

"No," Hephaestus groaned, jerking Clara to a halt. "This's *her* room. I dun sleep 'ere."

Aphrodite rose from her chair, her night robe flowing behind her. "What's going on? I don't remember the last time I saw you drunk."

"I drink'n special 'ccasions." Hephaestus patted Clara's shoulder awkwardly, his grip slipping halfway down. "Clara's my ward now. I mourn her life! All the life she could've had, 'fore getting roped to me."

It was the longest uninterrupted thing he'd said since Clara they'd left the forge, and damn, it *showed.* He barely caught his breath at the end, whole body swaying, head hanging.

"You'll sleep here tonight," Aphrodite said. She rounded Hephaestus's other side, taking his weight off Clara's shoulders. Hephaestus grumbled something incomprehensible, perhaps even half Greek, but leaned into his wife anyway. By the time his knees hit the side of Aphrodite's bed, he easily slumped face-down into the bedcovers.

Aphrodite smoothed out her robe, turning back to Clara. "I'll watch over him tonight. Thank you for bringing him to me, Clara."

"Yeah…" Not the intention, but not a poor outcome. "Goodnight."

"Goodnight. Try to get some sleep. It should be easier once he does."

A heavy wool feeling blanketed Clara's skull. She nodded, moving back into the hallway as quickly as she could. Her own room was only a few doors down, and when she was finally reunited with her own bed, she slumped onto it with the same gracelessness as Hephaestus.

One final taunt echoed inside her head before sleep came – *All the life she could have had, before getting roped to me.*

## 12

C onnor groaned into his pillow when morning broke. *Fucking finally.*

Sleep never came, not once in that long night. As much as his mind and body willed him to rest, one blue-eyed, black-haired difficulty kept his thoughts active. Since their binding, Raphael's soul had bled into him like a bullet wound. Connor already dealt with the voices of doubt and paranoia brawling in his mind, and now he had to deal with everything inside Raphael too? All that emotion and personality? All those curiosities?

It was too much, and yet…there was nothing he could do but lay there and deal with it. With his phone long dead and no clocks on the walls, he'd waited *hours* for sunrise. No idea what time it was, or how long he had left. Just curled in itchy cotton sheets with another man's heart in his chest.

Sunrise was salvation, because at least he didn't have to fake it anymore. He could get up, wash off, and prepare himself for whatever Paradisa had to offer.

At some point, those golden handmaidens in his bathroom must have washed his clothes, because they sat folded on the bathroom counter. Jeans, t-shirt, jacket, underwear. Even his black socks, too. He gave the idle automatons in the corner a little salute.

"Thanks, ladies."

Connor brought the Flaming Lips shirt to his nose, inhaling deeply. *Lavender.* He was gonna smell like an old lady's spice garden, but it beat reeking of B.O.

Jeans hadn't felt this good in almost a decade. Nor had boxer briefs. It sure felt more like home, more like he was in his own skin, than wearing odd handmade Greek clothes. And it was important to feel like himself, then. Because every footstep, every turn of his head, every *breath,* reminded him of the foreign body within.

There had to be a way to deal with this. He couldn't *not* sleep for the rest of his life. Maybe it was just going to take some getting used to. Or maybe it was going to take some effort.

He closed his eyes, imagining a soaring wall partitioning himself from Raphael. His mind's eye looked up, watched the wall rise past the break of the sky, tall and wide, without beginning or end.

The roar within him dulled. There. Better.

When he walked into the common room, Raphael was already there – not too surprising. It didn't seem like the angel ever slept. Clara, however, also lounged across one of the chairs nearby, not sitting in it with any sense of propriety.

"You're up early," Connor said.

"Yeah." She yawned, stretching her short arms. "Couldn't sleep more than a few hours."

"I feel you there…"

Raphael stepped closer, tilting his head. As he moved, Connor sensed the angel's presence in addition to seeing him. Like reading text overlapped on itself. It was faint, with the wall between them, but it was there.

"I'm sorry you slept poorly, Connor."

"It's fine." Connor squirmed, wrapping an arm over his abdomen.

"Have you adjusted to the bond?"

"It just feels weird. Like you're on top of me all the time."

Inside of him, really. Stripping him open from within.

"You'll grow used to it. I haven't had a ward in some time. I forgot it was so jarring at first." He placed a hand where Connor's shoulder met his neck, and offered a small smile. "Don't worry. You have nothing you need to keep from me. I don't cast judgement."

So, he knew. He knew Connor was trying to blockade them, hide something from him. *No. Get out. Let me breathe.*

Slowly, Raphael released his shoulder, leaving Connor floating in a lonely but private abyss. Raphael's emotions lingered, but now felt immensely far away.

Raphael's brow creased. "Is there something wrong?"

"It's fine." Connor repeated. "Just gotta get used to knowing someone is under my skin."

"I'm still getting used to it too," Clara said. She seemed like Mam for a moment, with a soft face and her touch brushing through his hair. Of course, Mam would have followed it with a smack on the back of his head and some quip about being a grown man. Clara, mercifully, refrained.

The storm inside him was far from stable, but there was no time to focus on that. He wasn't allowed to feel sick with the consequences, not when this was his choice. And not when the alternative was death.

He cleared his throat. "Guess we're heading out soon?"

Raphael nodded. "I believe so. Aphrodite and Hephaestus are already downstairs in the forge. That's where we'll be departing from."

"And Hephaestus has a surprise for you." Clara winked.

"Oh?" Connor perked up, and of course Clara noticed. She snickered, probably thinking he looked like a dog that had just heard the food dish rattle.

"Just follow me, big guy."

He focused on Clara's swinging ponytail as she walked toward the forge. And for a moment, it was helpful to pretend he was tethered to her instead of Raphael. He followed her in a sleep-deprived daze, his balance teetering a few degrees to the left.

But Raphael was there with a steadying hand on his upper back, and all Connor's coping mechanisms blew straight to hell. He was back in that pit, building a fortress out of his own heart. Trying so hard not to focus on the warmth of Raphael's fingers, on his soft voice whispering *"There, I've got you."* Fuck, how was he supposed to live the rest of his life like this? How was he supposed to live the rest of one *day* like this?

He pulled back his shoulders, fixing his balance so Raphael would deem him steady. The angel pulled back, allowing Connor to enter the forge on his own. Clara was already at the base of the staircase talking to Hephaestus, a small handheld axe in each fist.

When Connor approached the landing, he waved a vague hand in her direction. "What the hell are those?"

Clara tilted her head innocently. "Tools."

*Not buying it, kid.* "Yeah, an Allen wrench is a tool. Those are weapons." He crossed his arms over his chest, staring her down.

"Becalm yourselves." Hephaestus shuffled to the bench nearest Connor. "I had them in mind for an inexperienced fighter like Clara. Let's test their distance ability, shall we?"

He plucked one of the axes from Clara's grip and reared back his arm. The axe somersaulted with a deceptive amount of strength toward the rocky eastern wall of his forge.

It sunk in almost to the hilt, cracking the wall up and down from the blade. But judging from Hephaestus's expression, they hadn't seen the real trick yet.

"Raise your hand, Clara. And brace yourself. Don't be afraid of it. It won't hurt you."

She lifted a shaky hand. The axe wiggled with her summoning, releasing itself from the volcanic rock. It flew backward, flipping in the air until it smacked her outstretched hand.

"Now for Connor." Hephaestus smirked. "I have something for you as well."

Hephaestus reached under his bench and withdrew a compact metal box, intricate with runes. Clara stood on her tiptoes, peering over Hephaestus's shoulder to see it more closely.

Connor accepted the gift with both hands and set it on the closest table. The box had some weight to it, and not just from the contents.

The metal must have been something dense, like iron, if its black sheen was anything to go by.

He couldn't possibly imagine what was inside. If Clara had gotten weapons, maybe that was the theme of the day. But about the primary weapon Connor was comfortable with was a Sig Sauer 226. If there were throwing knives in this box, he was doomed.

His thumb ran along the box's front latch and he lifted it, pouring light over its contents. With a slowly growing smile, Connor removed two striking golden handguns.

"Sick."

Each gun looked similar enough to the Beretta M9—slender and lightweight, perfect for one-armed shooting. Whenever he went to the range, Connor always preferred something with more kick, like a Desert Eagle, but that kind of recoil was tough to handle in actual combat. And at least with Hephaestus's own design, the safety didn't look to be a godawful hassle like on the actual M9. Connor turned one of the pistols over in his hand, admiring the engraved scripture and elegant design.

"Meet Castor and Pollux. An old experiment of mine once Apollo started delivering firearms to tinker with. I figured you would be able to give them a good home."

"Damn." Connor already felt like he wanted to shoot something. He glanced down at the box, then froze. "Wait. Where's the bullets?"

"There are no bullets." Hephaestus looked undeniably self-satisfied. "They're enchanted to never run out."

A strained noise escaped Connor's throat. *Holy shit. Bottomless fucking bullets.*

"Wow. Thanks, dude."

Still awed by the gun in his hand, he barely managed to catch the bundle of leather hurtled toward his face. Hephaestus threw a similar strappy mess in Clara's direction, and that's when it became clear: harnesses.

Connor slipped the straps over his shoulders and went to work disassembling the guns. Call it habit, but he couldn't help it—a new gun in his hand demanded to be checked out from top to bottom.

He flipped one magazine over in his fingers, squinting. If he wanted an answer to what magical nonsense filled it instead of bullets, there wasn't one.

Clara's hip bumped against his. "Feels good to be back, doesn't it?"

He looked down at her, fondness swelling in his heart. "You have no idea."

"I saw them down here last night. Knew you'd get a kick out of them."

"Your axes are pretty sweet too. And hey, that means you can't shoot your eye out."

He should have anticipated the shove that followed.

Hephaestus had moved on to his next gift recipient. Aphrodite's leg was propped on a footstool, long skirt slid thigh high, as she tied on a thigh holster. Hephaestus passed her a dagger far different than the Aaru sacrificial blade—this one rose gold and embedded with sapphires. He muttered something about *making it stylish for her.* The barest hint of a smile crossed Aphrodite's face as she hooked the dagger into her holster, and lowered her skirt.

Hephaestus touched his wife's elbow. "We have to be careful. We're not made for this and I...I can't exactly protect you."

Aphrodite nodded, quiet. "It's fine. It's better than nothing."

Hephaestus returned to Connor and Clara, clearing his throat. "I have one more thing. But just for Clara."

"Oh?" she said.

Connor winked at her. "Don't act so surprised. You are *his* ward."

*And I'm Raphael's.* The thought spiked his brain, intrusive, and drew his eye to the angel. Raphael was pacing the other side of the forge, near the big boulder blocking Hephaestus's portal. Aphrodite chatted quietly with him, nothing too important-looking from the outside eye.

Connor looked away from them, refocusing on his guns. He clicked both magazines into place with the heels of his hands, letting out a satisfied grunt. Each gun fit nicely into the holsters under his arms.

Nearby, Clara held some kind of amber, suede waistcoat in front of her face. It was shaped like a corset, with six brass buttons running from the base to the collar. On both sides of the collar, Hephaestus included patches of short amber fur, perhaps to pad her shoulders from the harness's weight.

"Cute. Uh…is this so I blend in?"

"No," Hephaestus said. "It's so you don't get hurt. Connor is a soldier, and Raphael's a good bodyguard. You and I are neither. This is a sort of armor, made from the impenetrable hide of the Nemean lion. The spectres, and anyone else for that matter, shouldn't get through."

Clara slipped on the Nemean vest, then moved to apply the shoulder harness over it. She groaned when the straps caught against her shoulder blade.

"Need help?" Connor snorted.

"Here," Hephaestus offered, with a laugh. "I'll help before Raphael has to fix a sprain."

Raphael. Raphael drew closer now, moving through the aisles of workbenches. Connor felt him before he saw him as the tether between them burned hotter.

The angel cleared his throat and gestured toward the boulder. "Do you have a way of moving the stone, so we can use this portal?"

Hephaestus whistled around two fingers, summoning his two intact automatons from different corners of the forge. One of them wobbled, its left leg dented from the fight with the spectres, but it still found its way to the rock. With their joints groaning, the automatons rolled the boulder enough to reveal a swirling blue glow behind it.

When the automatons stopped pushing, the liberated portal cast a blue glow across Hephaestus's forge. Connor stared, mesmerized by the watery vision of Paradisa on the other side. All he could discern was the edge of a cliff leading down to a clear blue lake, along with a crystalline city in the distance. Everything was too far, too massive to make out the details.

But the details were soon to come.

Raphael's hand slipped into the crook of his elbow, and Connor shuddered, right the hell there, in front of everyone.

"Connor? We can go first, I think."

"Fine…fine. I'm coming."

Raphael nodded, then led him closer to the ethereal light. His hand fell lower to interlace with Connor's fingers, and it took everything Connor had not to shiver at that too.

He looked over at the angel, who watched him with soft confidence. Raphael lifted their joined hands, squeezing. "Ready?"

"Guess so."

Connor squeezed his fingers back, and braced himself to be tugged across dimensions.

# 1 3

I t was like diving into a lake—wet, cold, and airless. White noise filled Connor's ears and meandered into his sinuses. Although the portal smothered his senses, his pulse remained steady. There was something peaceful about being desolate between worlds.

After a couple steps, he emerged on the other side, fingers still wrapped around Raphael's. The sooty, humid warmth of Hephaestus's forge was replaced with perfect, breezy weather and a spicy, crisp scent.

A stone arch enshrined the portal he'd just walked through, which looked like a reverse mirror with a watery reflection of the other side. Raphael gently pulled him back, making room for Aphrodite, Clara, and Hephaestus to join them in the ethereal world.

Connor looked down at Raphael's hand, still interlaced with his own. He glanced over to see Raphael staring at the contact and clenching his fingers. Connor grunted and pulled away. He crossed his arms, tucking his hands near his guns.

The tether between his soul and Raphael's still smarted, fresh and noticeable, like he couldn't walk too far away from Raphael without it being yanked. Although Connor strongly sensed that Raphael was always with him in spirit, he fretted to think of the angel more than a few feet away. The bond felt tighter when they were apart, like something strained within him.

To the left of the portal, a limber black man stood with a silver, winged staff in one hand. He wore a plain white frock with a rope cinching his waist. A thin circlet rested atop his shaved head, and a small horn hung loosely from his belt.

"Aphrodite? Hephaestus?" he greeted the Olympians in a surprisingly lighthearted tenor. The next thing he said was foreign, but it sounded of pleasant bemusement.

Hephaestus placed a hand upon Clara's back. "English for my ward, please. This is Clara. Clara, this is Hermes. Herald of Olympus. He guards our portal and ferries our dead to Hades...when he's not chasing naiads."

Hermes extended a palm toward Clara. She tentatively placed her hand over his, and he kissed her suavely across the knuckles. Under less pressing circumstances, Connor would have laughed aloud at his sister's blush and frozen stature. Now, he just bowed his head with a smirk.

"Lovely to meet you, Miss Clara. A bit unorthodox to see Hephaestus out of his forge. I'd almost forgotten what he looked like."

Hephaestus smiled tightly. "Do you remember what spectres look like, and if you've let them through your portal lately?"

"'Course not. Who do you think I am?"

Aphrodite cleared her throat. "They attacked Athena at the forge. We're hoping to find where they came from."

"Ah, everyday it's something else." He acknowledged Raphael for the first time, nodding with tense disdain. "Ever since his kind took over, the whole place has gone to Abyssus."

Even through their blockade bond, Connor could feel the spike of offense rise in Raphael's throat.

"Taken over? I believe Eden was the first kingdom to propose the unity."

"Lighten up, angel." He lowered his voice as if Raphael wasn't standing in earshot. "Just like an Edenite. None of 'em have a sense of humor."

Raphael's nose wrinkled, the only physical sign of his frustration bouncing down their invisible bond. Connor shuddered to shake off Raphael's feelings, but the mental wall barely muffled them. It took half of his concentration to maintain the barrier, and sometimes he was too damn curious. He could see into Raphael, which was tempting, but that also meant Raphael could see into him.

Hephaestus waved a hand in front of Hermes' face. "Are there still carriages at the base of the mountain?"

"Of course. I've kept yours in working order all these years."

Aphrodite moved in front of them all and wrapped Hermes into an embrace "Thank you, Hermes. We'll see you soon."

"I hope so. Good luck, Dite."

Raphael walked away first, and Connor trailed close by. Mount Etna had seemed breathtaking, but the view from Hermes's portal made Connor's eyes wet. He blinked away the mysterious tears with no sense of when they'd come.

He approached the cliff's edge, ignoring his companions. Jagged steps carved into the rock wound down the side of the mountain and led to a crystal blue lake. Even with the dreary sky, an expansive city glimmered in the center of the water. A granite bridge stretched miles and miles across the lake, from the Olympian shoreside town to the tall city. Similar bridges emerged from territories on the horizon, but all converged at the crystal metropolis like spokes on a wheel.

Raphael appeared at his side. Connor slid his hands into his pockets, swaying on the balls of his feet. "Hey, Ninja Turtle."

"Ninja...turtle?"

"Yeah, you know, one of them was named...shit, never mind." Connor shook his head, gesturing to the city in the lake. "What's that place, out there?"

"The capital, Concordia. Built after the unity to give us an equidistant meeting place. Technically, everything on this lake is part of Concordia. Our old kingdoms were much larger and spread out. These are almost like satellite cities."

"What do you mean by 'the unity'?" Even though the Greeks and Raphael got along well enough, and even though their politics seemed intermingled, they hardly represented the same religion. And as many times as Connor heard someone sneer the word "Edenite" in the last three days, bad blood clearly remained.

"The kingdoms of Paradisa maintain cohabitation and alliance. Our guild system allows us to share information and spread the balance of power. But it's only been this way for the last thousand years or so. We used to use Earth as a battleground, constantly waging wars to gain human followers."

"Huh. I imagine a thousand years still feels pretty recent for you guys."

"Incredibly." Although Raphael's voice hardly betrayed dryness, their bond did.

Connor turned away, fidgeting. His skin itched and his heart seemed to throb with an extra murmur. Raphael's was a twin pulse echoing his own.

Raphael leaned slightly closer, his breath ghosting Connor's collar. "Connor, I can feel that you aren't—"

Before he could finish that hushed sentence, Hephaestus inserted himself between them, excitedly grabbing Connor's shoulder. "You look up yet? That's where the real magic is."

Swallowing thickly, Connor followed where Hephaestus pointed, up and behind them both. Twin marble staircases from the sides of Hermes's portal meandered upward. Embedded in the side of the mountain was a columned façade painted in vibrant indigos, reds, and yellows, adorned with gleaming shells and seaside gems, and stretching high into the clouds. The most similar human achievement Connor had seen was Petra, in Turkey, but that was a faded relic. Olympus looked as if it had been carved yesterday.

Connor craned to look beyond the grand entrance to get a glimpse of the city within the mountain. An arched, frescoed ceiling seemed to emit its own illumination, as if the white paint was light itself. Columns continued back infinitely, supporting the structure of their metropolis.

"How could you have stayed away from this place, Hephaestus?"

"It never felt like home." The smith let out a low whistle. "But it is a beauty, isn't it?"

Hephaestus limped away, following Raphael and Aphrodite down the stairs. Clara was the last to join Connor at the cliffside, looking up at him with an unrestrained grin.

"They don't get it, do they?"

"No, they don't, kid."

They descended the innumerable steps in silence. Connor's knees strained, and his neck dripped with sweat. Hephaestus and Clara lagged behind a few feet, slower than the rest. Clara never parted from her partner's side, a hand grasped on his arm to steady him. Much as he hated the fact that Clara had been roped into this, at least Hephaestus seemed like a good fit for her. They had a lot in common. Including a lot of stuff Hephaestus probably didn't know yet. But Connor bit his tongue. It wasn't his place to tell Clara's secrets, just like it wouldn't be Clara's place to tell Raphael about…about where everything in his life had gone wrong.

It was a two-mile hike to the carriage station at the base of the mountain. The covered station occupied several hundred square feet of the shore, with chariots and carriages lined up in four lanes. The vehicles varied in size and material, in ornamentation and symbology. But the most curious difference among each was the set of animals pulling it. A chariot pulled by goats drew Connor's eye, and he couldn't help but snort. Of all the animals, in all the world, why would some god pick goats?

Hephaestus broke off from the group, limping his way to the rear of the station. In the back of the first lane, red fabric covered an out-of-service vehicle. Hephaestus ripped back the cloth, revealing an expansive brass carriage hooked up to six mechanical horses.

"Thank you, Hermes," Hephaestus muttered. "Let's see if she still runs."

He opened the side gate and jumped up on the driver's mount. With a golden whip from the carriage's front railing, he cracked the air above his clockwork horses. All six roared to life with a mechanical groan. Their eyes glowed red, and their front legs arched off the ground. Smoke billowed from their nostrils as they whinnied, metallic and tinny. Behind them, their creator beamed with boyish joy, and Clara's expression mirrored his. She couldn't have been more different than Connor—an open pool for her companion to pour himself into, an eager mirror.

"Hop in!" Hephaestus waved a hand. "Should be an hour ride to the Embassy from here. These horses can outrun the wind."

Connor stepped into the carriage body and pulled Clara to sit beside him on a bench. It was a tight squeeze, even for both of them being relatively small. Raphael and Aphrodite took their seats on the other side. The goddess and the angel looked even more cramped— Raphael flushed completely against Aphrodite's right side. He moved his knees away from her, in some futile attempt at politeness, but the carriage wall stopped his pivot at thirty degrees.

Connor's eyes trailed over Aphrodite's smooth jawline and down to the swell of her breasts. All at once, the strange desire struck him to bury his face in her neck, drink in her sweet scent, and *holy shit, what?* His back straightened against his seat, and he scanned his comrades as if they somehow overheard those bizarre thoughts. Clara and Aphrodite idled, preoccupied by their own thoughts, but a red bloom slowly shaded Raphael's ivory face.

*So even you're not immune to her, huh?* At first, Connor hid his laugh in an awkward cough. But like cheap whiskey, a sour aftertaste from the thought overstayed its welcome. His jaw clenched, and he rein-forced the mental wall. *It doesn't mean anything. It's just her powers. He doesn't actually want her.*

A small window behind Connor's head slid open. Hephaestus poked his nose in. "Ready to go?"

Connor nodded automatically, but his thoughts lurched to a stop —was he ready? He had no idea what was about to happen. The mili-tary had acclimated him to complacent agreement; the "follow orders, ask questions later" mindset drove his acceptance of this strange new world. But perhaps complacency wasn't the best route when myste-rious travesties ran amok and even the gods couldn't make sense of them.

As the carriage kicked into motion, Clara divested herself of her axe harness and relaxed into the cushioned bench. Seeing her as she usually was, an unarmed girl with a ponytail and bangs, brought Connor down to ground level again.

She asked, "What's this Embassy like?"

"I've only been there once," Aphrodite said. "Long ago, to visit an old ward of mine, Paris of Troy. He practically raised Hades to see me after his death. He wanted to know why I didn't protect him enough, and why I didn't protect the woman he loved. I told him I couldn't fix foolishness."

Connor's lips pursed. "I thought you guys had good relationships with your wards."

Raphael tapped his thumb against his bottom lip. "Not always. Many of mine were martyred by other humans. Immortal souls can hold a grudge, and I'd just as soon not harm them further with my presence."

"Immortal souls?" Clara sounded soft beneath the thunder of mechanical hooves and carriage wheels. "What, are there...mortal souls too?"

Raphael sobered. "Us. No one can be fully immortal, Clara. But we are aged by lack of belief rather than time."

Aphrodite nodded. "When none of you worship us anymore, our Icons no longer function. It is traditional to go to The Graveyard of Gods in Abyssus and let ourselves be consumed by stone."

Connor trained his gaze on his angelic companion. "Even you, one day?"

"Everyone dies sometime, Connor."

Connor lifted a knee to his chest, turning away from the Sanctines. It was perplexing to consider a scenario where he could be in Paradisa, a dead soul still kicking, but Raphael would be a statue. What would that even be like? Maybe his soul would eat grapes in a palace while Raphael stood on a threshold, a lonely old man forgotten by Earth who succumbed to his rocky fate.

It only proved that all stories—all lives—became tragedies if allowed to run long enough. Even in heaven.

C onnor watched the horizon meet Hephaestus's mechanical carriage as they approached a villa cradled in rock. The Embassy stretched for miles and was carved into the cliff sides of two mountains. Dozens of buildings called it home, with each section painted in a different pastel. The foremost buildings – the most official and regal behind an iron gate – arched into the sky with golden spires and robin's egg domes.

Raphael pointed to Clara's axes. "Hide your weapons. We don't want to look conspicuous."

As Clara slipped the harness over her shoulders and concealed both compact axes beneath her gray canvas jacket, Connor nudged his foot against Raphael's. "How *should* we look?"

"Casual. Nonthreatening. That spectre with an Embassy medallion would not have stolen it. It wouldn't have been valuable enough, which means it may have been given the medallion by someone here."

Their carriage pulled into a covered station within walking distance of the front gate. A ten-foot wall with brass spikes and pale bricks created the Embassy's façade, but the wall continued until it hit the mountain. If Connor didn't know better, he'd assume it was a fortress.

He was last out of the carriage's golden doorway. They crossed the station and approached the entrance gate—a pair of iron doors stretching twenty feet across. Clara stayed behind to help Hephaestus down from the driver's mount, but her presence hung acutely in the back of Connor's mind.

The iron gate dissolved into shimmering air, opening the Embassy to visitors. Connor lingered close to Raphael and kept both hands tucked under his arms. Despite their attempt to remain casual, they were walking into unknown territory. Spectres could have been lurking behind every taffeta curtained window or have been eclipsed by every shadow.

A dozen marble steps led them beneath an embossed archway. Some runic phrase was etched over their heads, but one perk Connor hadn't inherited from the bond was Raphael's gift of tongues. He tried not to inherit much at all. Having to cope with being around Raphael was hard enough, with Connor's gaze always catching the handsome line of the angel's jaw, or Raphael's hand constantly brushing his skin.

At the top of the steps, Connor finally absorbed his surroundings in full. It was the cleanest air he'd ever smelled, rippling down up his nose and across his tongue like cool spring water. The main courtyard could have fit hundreds, though no one occupied it during that sunny afternoon. Odd. No one was around to enjoy it on a nice day like this. The place was like a ghost town.

Well. It technically was a town for ghosts, he supposed. But where was the haunting?

They continued walking down a narrow path lined with trees that had seen better days. The ground retained jagged rocks from where a mountain had been demolished in favor of architecture. A few hundred yards beyond the entrance, another courtyard appeared in the distance. Over a dozen archways of different colors lined the circular pavilion, capped together by a jade dome.

"What do we have here?" Hephaestus said, walking into the circle first.

Aphrodite paced the pavilion. "Each gateway leads to the dormitories and pavilions for wards of every kingdoms. Avalon, Olympus, Amaravati...they're all represented here."

Hephaestus groaned. "How massive is this place? It could take days to interrogate everyone here."

"You saw it coming in, didn't you?" Aphrodite arched a thin brow. "The Embassy is almost as large as the capital. This place has acquired wards for thousands of years, and still has room to grow."

"I believe we already know where to go." Raphael said, standing beneath one of the gates. He tilted his head to look up, golden light sparkling in his eyes. "Markings on the sacrificial dagger were from Aaru. I thought it may have meant it was stolen from there, but maybe...maybe it came from the Aaru pavilion here?"

Connor shrugged. "As good a place as any to start. Lead the way, boss."

Without another word, he followed Raphael along the Aaru path. The gold-slicked pathway meandered up to a temple at the top of the hill. In style, it resembled some of the towering stone shrines in Cairo or Karnak with its sphinx monuments guarding the front and round pillars embossed with hieroglyphics. A thirty-foot obelisk carved out of pure onyx stood as a welcome pillar before it, which emphasized the major difference between Aaru's style and the ruins of Egypt—these materials were absurdly lavish. Rubies and emeralds buried in the outer walls glinted in spite of the overcast sky. The entire temple shone gold, and every engraved pictograph was as vibrant and multicolored as the day it had been painted. Whatever the Egyptians had built three thousand years ago must have been a mundane approximation of divine architecture.

They approached the front of the temple, close enough to bump elbows. An open archway past the obelisk led into a massive atrium.

Raphael raised a hand. "Stop. I hear something."

Aphrodite rushed to stand behind the outer wall. Connor crouched on the opposite side of the doorway with one gun already in hand. After a heart-hammering moment, he peeked around the door's corner to see an organized meeting of people gathered in the middle of the temple.

Before the altar, a towering figure in a headdress made of orange fur walked among two groups of kneeling subjects. Golden trinkets and a pale waistcloth adorned his muscular, dark-skinned body.

A dozen men and women stood by the altar, each armed and ornamented in distinct garments. Black leather armors, sashes bright with primary colors, helmets made of bronze. Everyone looked plucked out of a different time period and country, but they shared the same stern expression.

The subjects were divided distinctly by appearance. On the left, one group dressed with black smocks and head-caps, blending them into a uniform abyss. The group on the right wore varied garb like the altar people. The commonality among them was old age.

The man with the staff stopped in front of his devotees. With every foreign word, he thrust around a gilded staff with a fox head adornment.

"That's Set, the pariah of Aaru." Raphael said. He leaned closer to hear from the other side of Connor, close enough for his breath to brush Connor's cheek. Connor turned his face away, resisting the urge to lean into him.

"Pariah for what?"

"For killing their king, Osiris. He fled Aaru not long after. Hasn't been seen for centuries, by all accounts."

Hephaestus let out a low groan. "I've heard of him. Piece of work, inn't he? Killing his own brother?"

Connor squinted. "Why would he do that? Jealousy?"

"It's presumed so," Raphael said, "But he left so quickly after the murder. Made no attempt to overthrow Aaru and replace Osiris. Either he didn't want to fight Prince Horus for the throne, or…maybe it was more personal."

Set's foreign words stopped, and one by one, spectres crawled up from an unseen pocket in the floor. Glossy eyes bulged, jerky joints creaked, and they wore the same rotting appearance as all the others. But the crowd of followers did not cower or shriek. Rather, they shifted from kneeling positions to bowing, their foreheads pressed onto the polished tile.

Set spread his arms with a flourish. Kneeling by the edge of the doorway, Raphael translated the words under his breath.

"He's speaking Sancti, the common tongue. I hear…*The day is coming. We will seek justice from those who have wronged us.*"

The followers responded with a fierce yell, their fists pumped into the air.

"This is not good," Connor croaked.

Aphrodite gingerly elbowed her way in front of Clara and Hephaestus, then turned her nose around the corner. "Those on the right are Sanctines. Old ones, it looks. They must be powerless by now. Why haven't they gone to the Graveyard?"

Connor jutted his chin toward the other group. "What about the people on the left?"

"Wards who live here at the Embassy." Raphael answered first. "They all dress like that. Black frocks and caps."

With a wave of Set's hand, the spectres swept back to the far corners of the temple. Each group of followers, both wards and old Sanctines, rose at the command.

From the ward group, a skinny blond man no older than twenty stepped forward. He met with a woman from the Sanctine group whose body was so weathered that she could barely walk. The young man stretched out a hand to the crone, looking upon her leathery face and corkscrew hair without judgment, and she gratefully folded her fingers through his. With her other hand, she presented a gnarled wooden object to Set, who tossed it into a fire bowl roaring behind him.

With a burst of volume, Set recited the Sancti language with a hand extended toward the pair. The ward screamed as yellow light poured from his skin, slipping into the body of the old goddess. She looked no better off as she threw back her head and her throat caught as she struggled to breathe. Her hands embraced the young man's, but both of their skeletons twisted beneath their skin, crackling and snaking to swallow them into one body. It looked disturbingly like a bonding ceremony, like they were becoming wards, but so much worse.

Connor rose to his feet, a gun in hand. "He's killing them. We've got to do something!"

Raphael yanked him back down, his voice shaky. "Connor, stay back. Set is extremely dangerous."

Set circled the writhing pair, unsheathing a glowing golden sword from his waist. His words grew harsher, loud enough to overwhelm their screams.

"We can stop it," Connor hissed. "We can save those people, I can't just sit here and—"

The wet squelch of metal through flesh cut the words out of his mouth. Set's sword plunged through the hearts of both his volunteers, binding them together in sick impalement. Beams of yellow light exploded from the tangled bodies, and Set held onto the hilt of his sword with both hands. The temple rumbled, threatening to knock Set askew, but his strong legs stayed grounded.

He ripped the sword out of the couple, and they crumpled together, obscured by dozens of members of the crowd.

All stayed silent. Connor craned to look into the atrium, squinting through the smoke filling the temple. The haze and crowd cleared, revealing a ball of white flesh whimpering at Set's feet.

"That's a spectre," Clara whispered. "He *made that.*"

With an almost gentle hand, Set dragged the newborn to its feet.

Connor grabbed Raphael's arm, forcing the angel to look at him. "Raphael, he is going to force every person in the room to become one of those monsters. He's alone except for a few spectres. We can *take him.*"

"He's right," Hephaestus said from the other side of the doorway. "When the wards realize they don't have to obey him, they'll help us."

Raphael glanced back into the atrium, where two more people rose from the kneeling crowd.

"Stay behind me, Connor."

"Got it, boss."

Their stampede into the Aaru temple was a blur. Connor's senses lit up in ways long forgotten, his sharp eyes scanning the room for targets like a digital scope. The dozen or so spectres at the front of the room, with their dull skin and ill-fitting bodies, stood out profoundly from the kneeling crowd.

When the crowd shot to their feet and scattered, and the spectres leapt into action.

Connor followed Raphael closely, staying behind him because, hell, he wasn't enthusiastic about going one-on-one with a crowd of shadow monsters. The fight in Hephaestus's forge stayed fresh in his mind, from the stench of spectre breath in his face as the creature held him down, to the spray of warm spittle soaking into his clothes.

He targeted Raphael's six, shooting into the chest of the spectre dodging closer. As the creature exploded in a wave of black fog, he realized with a strange sense of wistfulness that it was the first time he'd fired one of these guns.

A cold hand encircled Connor's arm. Without looking, he threw all of his force into spinning and colliding his fist with his attacker's jaw. With a slight tilt of that same hand, his fingers found the trigger of Castor. The spectre vanished with a screech, although he couldn't be sure where that shot made its mark.

They were about halfway into the room when Set finally gave them some kind of reaction. But instead of terror or rage, he was cool as gunmetal. He remained near the altar, watching the fight with patient satisfaction, his arms crossed over his chest.

*"Stop your spectres, Set!"*

Aphrodite's voice reverberated throughout the room with a supernatural rumble. Even though the command wasn't directed at him, Connor's ribcage rattled with the force of it. *Damn. Note to self: never piss her off.*

Instantly, Set lifted a hand. He called out a short word to his shadowy army, and the spectres slunk back like wounded puppies.

"The power of persuasion," Set hummed, clapping his hands. "Incredible. But luckily for me, I don't need the spectres to help me."

At a wave of his hand, one of the wards in a black cap threw his hand over Aphrodite's mouth, while another ward forced her to the ground. She twisted and screeched, but her persuasive words were too muffled to be obeyed. With a curious expression, the ward pinning her down untangled the chain belt from her waist, and twirled it around his wrist.

As Hephaestus reared back a handful of fire aimed straight for Set, he received a similar treatment. Wards came from everywhere around them, ruthless in their disarmament. Clara shrieked as they pinned her down against the floor. An orange-haired female ward wrenched the axes out of Clara's hands and stepped away, twirling them in her hands.

Connor's shoes skidded on marble and he aimed Pollux at Set's forehead. He wouldn't shoot, not unless this guy gave him a true reason to, but it wouldn't take much to find one.

"Call them off," he rumbled.

Set stilled, and dared to *smile* back at him. He replied in English, which sounded even stranger from his throat than Sancti. "You humans have a fascinating level of confidence. I almost admire it. I'm afraid, my human friend, you are not as persuasive as the goddess."

Before Connor could reply, one of Set's wards jammed a kick to his lower back. He hit the ground with an *oof* and Pollux skittered across the tile. Set casually approached the pistol and plucked it off the ground, peering at it curiously.

"I cannot promise this will be easy," Set murmured, running a dark finger over the engraved script. "I cannot promise you won't come to harm. But I hope we can come to some sort of agreement."

As Connor twisted to find Castor under his left armpit, he found the man who kicked him had already wrenched the gun away. *Dammit!*

"Take them upstairs, and disarm them of Icons and weapons. I don't want them using their abilities anymore here." Set waved an order to his cult as simply as he would order a glass of pinot noir. His varied ward henchmen tore away Raphael's sword and Hephaestus's cane, in addition to the weapons already confiscated.

"Get off of them!" Connor yelled. He looked from ward to ward, begging to find some spark of humanity left in any of them. "Come on, I'm *one of you*. Don't let him do this. What are you *doing?!*"

They stared back with glazed indifference.

A flurry of hands ripped him away from the ground. In the corner of his vision, equally dirty hands roughed up Raphael and Clara. They were pushed toward the staircase where an unpleasant fate surely waited.

## 14

Clara was not raised to accept injustice. Dad, the fierce Marine, never mustered more than aggressive glares. But Mam had climbed over more than one store counter after hearing slurs about her husband.

Clara twisted in the grasp of strong fists, one on each of her arms, and she screeched to be released. Behind her in the distance, Connor's voice reproached her, but goddammit, there was nothing just about this. Set had created a monster before their eyes, using the bodies of the weak and desperate.

"You don't want this!" she cried, looking back and forth to the wards restraining her. "I'm a ward too! I'm one of you. Let us help you!"

One of them finally granted her a dead-eyed stare. "You are not one of us."

They shoved her through a doorway and out onto the glass roof. Clara's throat tightened as she looked down. The temple and altar were visible below, probably thirty or forty feet, but the crowd of Set's followers had long dispersed. It looked as if she was walking on air with nothing but this thin pane to protect her from the fall.

The men tugging her arms let her go near the roof's edge and pushed her to her knees. The glass groaned as she slumped onto it, further spiking her slight fear of heights. Really, it wasn't the heights she was afraid of. It was the falling part. Force equals mass times acceleration. And while she didn't have the stability to calculate her kilos times the acceleration of gravity, the answer was not a friendly number.

At least she wasn't alone. Connor fell to his knees beside her, his expression forcefully neutral. Hephaestus limped in behind him with some muttered curses to his captors and was followed by Aphrodite, her mouth still covered with a burly ward's palm. Then finally, Raphael brought up the rear.

Set paced before them, sizing them up as his followers arranged them on their knees in a semi-circle. His hands clasped behind his back, almost patiently.

"You okay?" Connor's voice, near her cheek.

"Fine." The orange-haired ward snickered as she scraped Clara's axe blades against each other. Clara lowered her voice in Connor's ear. "How're we getting out of here?"

His brown eyes didn't bullshit her. "I don't know, kid."

Strangely, his uncertainty hardly fazed her. She considered the possibility of dying and found she wasn't afraid anymore. Not like in the hotel or in Hephaestus's forge. No, she was *pissed* at the thought of dying, of abandoning a life that had been ultimately unremarkable, especially when she was so close to making it mean something.

Raphael hung close to Connor, never tearing his gaze away from his ward. Clara glanced leftward, where Aphrodite and Hephaestus curled against the roof's ledge. As their captors abandoned them there, Aphrodite whispered to her husband, "Don't do anything stupid."

Hephaestus scoffed under his breath. "Your confidence is inspiring."

Set stopped pacing and tilted his head. "Who told you we were here?"

"No one did," Raphael answered as he knelt squarely in the middle of the glass roof. "One of your spectres had an Embassy medal. We never would have found that clue had you not sent them after Athena."

Set struck the back of his hand against Raphael's cheek, knocking the angel askew. Connor barked a curse, lunging at Set best he could, but that only earned him his own slash across the face. The sound was sharp, like a *whoosh* of metal through the air followed by Connor's pained hiss. Clara's heart lost all rhythm when she finally had the nerve to look at him. Blood seeped from beneath Connor's eye, and his skin ruptured in four deep lines.

Set stood upright, rubbing his hands together. "I know your brother sent you to protect her, Raphael. You're such an obedient child, aren't you? Always doing what Michael says." He snorted. "I suppose I can't blame you. He's quite persuasive. Can promise the world, only to ride away with all the glory for himself."

"My brother has nothing to do with this," Raphael said, his mouth dripping red. "This is between you and Athena. You're targeting her—why? Is this some feud between Aaru and Olympus?"

Set shrugged a shoulder, pacing before them. He approached Aphrodite, bending his face to hers. His jackal headdress framed his soft features with menace. The closer he drew to Aphrodite, the more Hephaestus strained against his captor's grip. Clara's blood warmed in turn, echoing his scorched emotions.

"I have nothing against Olympians," Set said. "At least when they're not standing in my way. But *Olympian* is not the only label Athena goes by. You should ask her, sometime, what it means to be called *Inquisitor.*"

"Athena is a good person," Clara blurted at the opposite end of their lineup. She wasn't sure if that was true, really. Athena could be prickly, after all. But she'd also defended her friends and had been willing to change her opinion about Aphrodite in gratitude.

Regardless of whether Clara believed the words, it had a more desired effect. Set moved away from Aphrodite and Hephaestus's emotions calmed within her. He slowed to a stop in front of Clara, kneeling to meet her at eye level.

"You're a rather confident young human. Do you want to be like Athena? Is that it? I can find you plenty of better role models."

Clara looked between Set, towering above them with dripping malice, and the woman carrying her stolen axes. She swallowed, subtly pulling her legs beneath her to bend in a crouch.

Set continued, sighing. "None of you realize that Athena is not the only one I'd love to see dead. But Michael wouldn't have told you that, would he? He would decide what information he wanted you to know, and you would blindly follow."

He looked at Raphael with a cruel smile. And with his eyes on the angel, Clara threw her head back and then forward, headbutting the Egyptian god right in the face.

As much as her forehead throbbed from the unceremonious attack, Set was worse off between them. He fell over with a graceless flop, windmilling his arms to catch his fall while letting out a guttural roar.

Clara moved before he could catch her, catapulting herself at the orange-haired woman. The ward felt far denser than her waifish appearance suggested, but Clara's surprise attack hit with enough force to topple her. They rolled together across the glass, tearing at each other until Clara's hand wrapped around one of her axes. She untangled from the woman enough to position herself over an intersection of the glass floor.

Summoning every ounce of energy within her, she slammed the axe into the glass floor. The glass cracked in spidery veins around the axe head, but did not break.

A few feet away, Connor went for the man who'd taken his guns. His foot collided squarely with the ward's skull, crushing it between his boot and a brick wall. The man crumpled into a heap, letting Connor's guns clatter to the clear floor.

The orange-haired ward wrapped hands around Clara's throat from behind, pulling her backward into a chokehold. Clara strained, the heels of her feet sliding against the steadily cracking glass. Her gaze darted over each of her friends, but they were too occupied to notice her struggle. Set himself stood in the middle of it all, yelling to his comrades, pointing a finger to the horizon. The wards who held their confiscated weapons followed the gesture, leaping off the roof without question.

One of Set's men—the burly, Viking-looking ward from earlier— pinned Aphrodite to the ground with two meaty fists. Hephaestus dove at him, latching onto the Viking from behind, and his arm wrapped around the man's neck as he tried to peel the brute off his wife.

A *whoosh* in Clara's peripheral tore her away from them. Raphael flew through the air in a heap and hit the temple wall. When Clara's blurry eyes darted back to the source, all she saw was Set, his arm outstretched. As Set gained on Raphael, a bullet struck his face and knocked him to the ground. Connor!

Her brother fell to his knees beside the angel, his hands already tending to the potential wounds. *Cuuuuute,* Clara thought blearily, as time slowed to a beautiful, technicolored halt.

Raphael waved him away with urgent words that slurred and stretched in Clara's hearing, but through her hazy vision, she saw his finger pointed at her.

Clara wheezed, writhing against the woman choking her, stretching a hand desperately toward her axe. The blade wiggled, trying to detach itself from the glass, followed by the prickling sound of increasing cracks. Her throat vibrated either a low hum or a pathetic cry, she wasn't sure. All she knew was the vignette of black closing in on her vision and the exploding shockwave of a bullet whizzing past her ear.

"Clara?"

Connor swooped down on her, big damn hero, muttering apologies and placing his gentle hands on her bruised throat. Clara unfolded herself from the limp woman, gasping. The burst of new oxygen to her brain woke her up better than a slap in the face.

"Bluh...huh?"

"It's okay, you're safe now. I got her."

Behind her, the orange-haired woman was no more; her face was a bloody wreck. One thick bullet hole stood out between her eyes. She pried one of her axes out of the woman's stiff fist.

"Thanks," she muttered, promising herself she'd never again make fun of Connor's accuracy.

"You good?"

"Yeah…? Yeah, sure?"

"Set's getting back up." Connor's arms wrapped around her back and hoisted her to her feet. "We gotta go."

Raphael, Hephaestus, and Aphrodite, all ruffled in their own ways, joined them in a semi-circle on the roof. The world sharpened, the noises lost their haze, and Clara looked at the warming corpse of Set a few feet away. The golden bullet had already wormed itself out of Set's temple.

Connor followed her gaze to Set, and nodded. "Get to the ledge, all of you! I've got an idea."

The three Sanctines listened, and Clara limply allowed Connor to escort her. Together, they hobbled across the groaning glass and reached the roof's stone edge. As they passed Clara's second axe buried in the glass, she reached down and yanked it out of the pane.

When all of them were safely off the glass, Connor fired one shot to the center of the roof. The glass shattered, and gravity swallowed it along with Set and his crew's slowly reanimating bodies.

Connor jerked a thumb over the other side of the ledge. "Now we've got to jump."

Clara's stomach flipped when she glanced over the edge of the roof, at the thirty-foot leap onto hard stone that was their only way out. She didn't want to imagine how a compound fracture of the femur felt, but she consoled herself with the knowledge that Raphael was a healer.

So she jumped, following her brother in the leap of faith. And only when she approached the abrupt kiss of gravity, did she remember Raphael's lack of Icon—and powers.

*Shit.*

Connor braced for impact. The air beneath his feet vanished, replaced by hard ground. The force rattled him from toe to shoulder. He curled his body into itself to roll and was grateful to glimpse Clara performing the same motion nearby. When he finally stopped moving, spread-eagle beneath a marble canopy, his left shin throbbed with the echoes of a fracture.

When he flexed his leg, the pain did not intensify. Frowning, he crawled to his feet and scanned their new surroundings for Raphael.

A few feet away, his companion crouched with a hand on his leg and an obvious wince. Connor rushed over and slipped his arms around Raphael to pull the angel up.

Raphael met his eyes. "I think I broke my leg."

Shit. Of course. No Icon, no healing, no immortality. Raphael was just as human as he was, like this.

He tried not to find any of that appealing, particularly when it caused such pain.

"I can feel it. Can you walk?"

"Perha-ah!" Raphael attempted to press weight upon his damaged leg. He retracted the leg, letting it dangle above the ground, and leaned the rest of his weight into Connor. "No, I don't think so."

"We need to get out of view," Aphrodite declared, blowing past all of them. Hephaestus stumbled after her slowly, still hindered by his normal limp, while Clara stayed tight on his side.

Connor hauled the angel into a support carry and bolted. At least he still had enough strength to pull off such a move. Raphael's grip sunk into his skin, tense and pained, and he muttered groans into Connor's shirt.

Connor didn't look back. His legs had to move faster, he had to activate muscles long dormant, and his focus had to remain on the back of Aphrodite's rippling skirt. As he lagged behind the others, he instinctively scanned their surroundings for Clara. She ran safe amidst all of them, protected in all directions by their alliance.

When they turned a corner, Aphrodite pulled open a door nestled in a stone nook. Hephaestus and Clara stumbled together into the room, but Aphrodite remained outside, her stare locked onto Connor's.

Adjusting Raphael's weight, Connor let out a yell. He sailed through the doorway, barely careful enough to avoid hitting Raphael's limbs on the frame, and skidded to a stop to avoid hitting a wall. The door slammed as Aphrodite slipped inside.

Clara and Hephaestus rushed to Connor's side and helped him lay Raphael on the ground. The angel winced, grasping at his broken shin. Connor reeled in his own exhaustion and forced himself to think of something else. Raphael had enough pain without Connor adding to it.

This was a closet, saturated with the smell of freshly washed linen. Hundreds of bed sheets, towels, and robes on the twenty-feet-tall shelves. A small ladder leaned in the corner of the room.

Clara touched Raphael's shoulder, looking sympathetically at his leg. "We need to find your Icons."

Through a twisted cringe, Raphael managed to gasp, "Perhaps one of the Embassy wards knows where they stockpile stolen Icons."

Connor knelt too, his stomach unsettled by phantom pain. "Why would they tell us anything? Every ward we've seen here wants to kill us."

"No." Raphael sucked in a breath. "No, there's someone. Someone I know would never join Set. You and I can go to her while the others look elsewhere in the pavilion. I won't be useful in a fight right now."

Clara stepped around Raphael and past Aphrodite, who braced the door.

"I can lead the way. Out of the three of us, I'm armed."

"Clara..." Connor groaned her name before he could stop it.

Clara's ponytail whipped through the air as she cast him her scrutiny. "You know I have to do this."

Connor walked over to her, feeling small despite his height advantage. He stood over her petite frame, but her steely eyes kept their fire. Deep down, he was glad of it. She would make Dad proud, but that didn't make it any easier to let her go.

She stared him down, only softening when he wrapped her into an embrace.

"Don't get killed," he said, their mother's catchphrase. He looked at Hephaestus and Aphrodite. "And you keep her safe." Both of them nodded. Maybe he didn't need to tell them anything.

"I'll keep my eyes open," Clara assured, offering a small smile. "You be safe too."

Connor nodded and settled back on the ground at Raphael's side. As the others slipped out of the room, Raphael's hand squeezed his shoulder. Despite Raphael's lack of powers, it still brought Connor comfort.

---

Clara sped down a passage in the Aaru temple with an axe in each hand. Jumping off the roof landed them in the back of the temple, which extended into a labyrinth of other halls, buildings, and nooks.

Hephaestus walked beside her shoulder to shoulder. She didn't know how well Raphael and Connor fared with their connection, especially considering the way Connor's nostrils flared every time Raphael got too close. But being a ward to Hephaestus was easy, except for the occasional bursts of panic creeping on her every hour or so. They always arrived with sudden intensity and brevity.

Aphrodite caught up to them. "Clara, where are you leading us?"

"I saw the spectres with the weapons go north somewhere. Maybe we can find them if Raphael and Connor's plan doesn't work out."

Aphrodite glanced over her shoulder. "We should be less conspicuous. If the spectres haven't gone far, neither have Set and the rest."

Clara heard the footsteps: too distant to be dangerous, but close enough to make the hair on her arms prickle. "Yeah. Let's just be quiet and keep moving."

The deeper they traveled, the darker the corridors became. They no longer walked through porticos and beneath awnings. These were the cool, tomblike hallways of a temple interior. And every time Clara led them around a dark corner, she thought she heard a growl from a spectre. But the attacks never came to fruition. The only movement was from firelight dancing across the walls.

Deep into the labyrinth of the Aaru pavilion, they came across another atrium, probably fifty feet by fifty feet. Pale, dispersed light shone in from the glass ceiling while the halls beyond the columned perimeter remained in shadow. In the middle of the sun chamber splashed a magnificent fountain where stone carvings of four sphinxes served as the base for a twenty-foot tall, black obelisk. Water spurted from the mouths of each statue, trickling into three layers of increasingly larger pools.

And there was, moving around the fountain with erratic movements, a spectre. The *new* spectre, freshly born, merged from an elderly crone and a blonde young man.

Clara extended both arms. "Shh! There's one."

Aphrodite teetered, looking over Clara's head at the spectre pacing around the Aaru fountain. "Why isn't it with the others?"

Clara tiptoed behind one of the columns, and her comrades did the same. The spectre leaned over one of the fountain pools to watch its clear waters. It screeched at the sight, writhing and scratching at its pale body.

Hephaestus's nose wrinkled. "What's wrong with it?"

Clara squinted to get a closer look at the oddly behaving monstrosity. "It's just been created. Maybe it doesn't have any idea what it is or what's going on."

"Can you hit it from here?"

"Maybe."

Clara sucked in a deep breath and emerged a thumb's width from behind the column. The axe weighed down her arm as she readied to throw it at the spectre's skull.

She reared back her arm and threw. The axe somersaulted through the air and buried itself into the creature's shoulder with a sick *thunk.*

*Dammit.*

The spectre bayed, its screams loud enough to nauseate Clara. As it bent over and back, it jerked erect and clawed at the embedded axe. *At least it didn't turn to smoke. I guess it hasn't learned how to reformulate itself yet.*

Hephaestus pushed Clara's arm. "Hurry! The screams will draw attention."

Clara dodged the spectre's field of view while eyeing a vulnerable spot in the back of its neck. But amidst its thrashing, the spectre jerked to a stop. And as if all pain was forgotten, it spun, locking its gaze completely on her.

No malevolence shone from its milky eyes. Its mouth didn't drip with the desire for blood. It lunged at her, hissing, but it seemed more afraid of Clara than Clara was of it.

Clara lifted her other axe, hesitant. *I can't just kill it. Not when it can barely defend itself.*

She almost scoffed. She was sympathetic toward a spectre—the same type of creature that had tried to kill her and Connor multiple times, a creature with no other purpose than to perform the bidding of evil.

That was before she had known where they came from. *But...this isn't a person anymore. You're putting it out of its misery. Just do it.*

Clara hacked at the back of the spectre's neck, severing the top of its spinal column. It lived long enough to cry one final wail before exploding.

Smoke blasted Clara in the chest like a bullet, lifting her off her feet. She hit the stone floor with a rough slide as her lungs flattened into airless pancakes. She wheezed, clutching her chest, willing herself to catch her breath.

Hephaestus's face appeared over her. His hand stretched toward Clara, and she offered her right arm. He pulled her up with his natural strength, nothing godly about it, just decades of hammering away at swords.

Aphrodite appeared on her other side, her hand outstretched with Clara's axe.

"Let's keep moving," the goddess said. "They're not all going to be as hesitant as that one."

W ith Connor's support carry, Raphael hobbled along toward the Embassy rotunda on his uninjured leg. Most of his weight pressed against Connor's armpit and ribcage, which strained Connor's back, but Connor pushed out the nuisance. No man left behind—even if he had to be carried, and even if his physical closeness, constantly brushing against Connor's body, made Connor lightheaded.

Unfortunately, their destination seemed miles away. They passed monuments and black-smocked wards who barely spared them a passing glance. The wards kept their heads bowed like nuns, eyes fixed upon the ground, refusing to acknowledge the world around. Connor ignored them in return and heaved out a sigh when they reached the familiar rotunda gateways.

"Eden pavilion. That must be the path." Raphael pointed to an arch with a star, a crescent, and a cross engraved into the stone.

"I'll buy it, but how are we gonna find your friend? Even you don't know where she is."

They staggered beneath the Eden gate, and Connor tried not to be frustrated at the steep descending staircase that awaited them. Raphael moved away from him, pushing his weight into the stone railing instead, so perhaps it was for the best. The angel winced with every step, and Connor felt it in his own calf, but managed to move a bit ahead. Strange; now that Raphael was no longer against his side, he felt miles away instead of too close. Goddamn bond.

"I suppose there must be living quarters somewhere." The skin creased around Raphael's eyes. Connor didn't need to ask if he was okay—he wasn't.

Connor shrugged, joking, "Maybe her name is on the door."

They reached the bottom of the staircase, Raphael tucked back against Connor's side. The angel gestured toward an arched brick corridor that contained copper-painted doors every four feet.

As they approached one of the doors, Raphael let out a relieved noise. He jerked his chin toward the dark gold runes engraved upon the metal.

"Brilliant, Connor. You were right. The names are on the doors, alphabetical by Sancti runes."

"Hey, humans run this place, right? I'm not brilliant just because I think like one."

Raphael smiled through his pain. "There's a reason why we were made for each other. Gods and humans, that is. We all have blind spots."

Raphael abandoned Connor's side and hobbled, supporting his weight with a hand on the wall. Connor could only follow, unable to read Raphael's language and having no clue who they were looking for anyway.

They reached the end of the corridor, and Raphael took them left down another curved tunnel of brown-washed bricks. The tunnels allowed light in at the front and the back, and wall-mounted torches provided the remaining illumination.

"We're in the right letter now." Raphael scrutinized each door, mouthing the words he read upon them. In the third corridor, he stopped before a door.

"This. This is it." Raphael's knuckles rapped against the door. Seconds passed, then a girl younger than Clara peeked through the door's crack. Her delicate features, porcelain skin, and pixie haircut did not suggest much strength. But her catlike eyes shone with intelligence.

"*Bonjour mademoiselle,*" Raphael greeted her. "*Parlez-vous anglais?*"

"Saxon?" Her eyelid twitched. "Who are you?"

Connor could sense Raphael swallow every influence of leg pain to deliver his message with appropriate dignity. "Raphael. I'm a brother of Saint Michael. We need your help."

The girl had squeezed between the door and its frame, preventing either of them from seeing inside her quarters. After a moment of consideration, she stepped back, allowing them to join her inside.

Her candlelit abode was no bigger than a hotel room. The basic décor in all the ward condos was likely identical, but the girl had made it her own with wall-mounted swords and leather-bound books with French titles. Once she closed the door and secured a chain lock, she eyed Raphael's limp with suspicion.

"You're hurt?" Despite years in Paradisa, her French accent remained thick. "Angels do not get hurt."

Raphael lowered himself into an armchair, wincing. "We do when our Icons have been stolen."

Connor chewed the inside of his cheek, an old habit from before the service. Nothing he could do would make Raphael more comfortable. The pain was so real, and Raphael's reaction to it so natural, that Connor had nearly forgotten he was an angel.

"I suppose I should introduce you both," Raphael said. "Jeanne, this is my ward, Connor. Connor, this is Jeanne. She was one of Michael's wards from fifteenth-century France."

It took a moment for Connor to connect the dots. When he did, a cold sense of majesty settled on his shoulders. *Saint Joan of Arc was a ward?*

Jeanne stared blankly, oblivious to his recognition. "A pleasure, Monsieur Connor."

Raphael sat straighter. "We know Set has taken over the Embassy and has swayed the wards here to his favor. What all do you know about this? Have you been threatened?"

Jeanne lowered herself into a chair across from them. "It started with people disappearing. Friends, neighbors. We thought they had made a trip to the capital and never returned. Then Ji Gong found the monsters made of shadow."

"We call them spectres. Go on."

"He managed to tell us his findings before he vanished. A few of us tried to flee, but that night, Set and his spectres arrived, and locked down the entire Embassy. We're forbidden to leave or to allow visitors. We cannot speak a word of his occupation. He cannot kill us if we defy, but he could lock us in the darkest dungeon and throw away the key."

Connor tilted his head. "They *can* kill you. That's how they're making the spectres. They're combining the wards who live here with ancient gods."

"They cannot do it unless we willfully give ourselves to the binding." She shuddered, gaze locked on the floor. "Unfortunately, many are more than willing. Some of the wards have been...disillusioned with their lives here."

Raphael hunched, setting his elbows on his knees. "Do you know where they'd keep stolen Icons?"

"I know Saint Cosmas saw a cache of them in the Avalon pavilion, but I don't know where. They may have moved it by now."

Raphael bowed his head and rubbed a hand over his brow. That look, and the flash of pain pounding against their mental wall, was more than empathy. It was pity.

Connor jumped in before Raphael could propose something crazy. "We can't free the whole Embassy today. This place is huge. You're injured. What we need to do is get your Icon back and get the hell out."

Raphael sucked in a breath. "I know. I wish we could do more. But if we can get out, we can return with Michael's army. We can't fight Set and his spectres on our own."

As Raphael forced himself to his feet, Jeanne rose with him. Tentatively, she grasped his arms, looking into his porcelain face. "Saint Raphael, how is Michael?" Her voice broke, slightly, with feigned nonchalance.

Raphael's pained expression eased. "He's well. He's general of the war guild now, so as soon as he hears you're in trouble..."

"Can you tell him that..." She glanced at Connor, then lowered her voice. *"Il me manqué."*

Raphael squeezed her thin shoulder. "Of course. If all goes well, you will see him soon yourself."

Molecules vibrated between Raphael and the French girl. The air throbbed with divinity, warming Connor's flesh and chilling his bones at the same time. A knot welled in his throat—probably from Raphael's nerves and the sense of responsibility reflected upon him— as mutual pain made it hard to maintain their bond's dividing wall.

"I'll ensure we return," Raphael vowed. "Be safe, Jeanne. Avoid leaving your room if you can."

Jeanne nodded and ushered them out of her tiny home. When the door closed behind them, Raphael groaned, groping at his crooked knee and leaning upon the wall for support.

"Hey…" Connor tucked both arms under Raphael's and slipped a knee between the angel's legs, supporting his whole frame. By the time Connor's ballast position locked in, he'd crowded Raphael against the brick wall with barely room for a slip of paper between them.

Raphael's face was inches away, and his pained breaths brushed Connor's throat. The small illumination bleeding into the corridor reflected in Raphael's blue eyes, lighting them up to be more ethereal than usual. Connor shivered as divinity molecules lit up around him again. At the same time, Raphael's pale skin showed a faint dusting of freckles across his cheekbones and nose, humanoid flaws which Connor had never before noticed.

"Thank you…" Raphael's hands dug into Connor's arms. "I'm almost fine. Just…just a moment."

"I'm sorry. I wish I could help you, I really do…"

"No, no." He laughed under his breath, weak and strained. "Just needing this is bad enough, isn't it? I'm the one who is supposed to take care of you."

"You still are. But we're not gonna pretend you aren't hurt." Not only was Raphael's rapidly declining state worrisome; it was disturbing to see that he expected himself to be indestructible. Sure, the guy was used to being a god, but when their enemy's entire plan hinged on stealing powers and immortality, Connor wished Raphael wasn't so hard on himself.

Connor moved as far away as he could while still holding Raphael up. The angel shifted his weight, using the wall to support himself instead. When Connor grew confident that Raphael wouldn't teeter, he released the other man's arms. Moving farther apart squashed the tingling in his gut, but the ongoing separation anxiety made him miss Raphael's touch.

"Can you walk again?"

"Yes, I think so."

"Where to now?"

"The Avalon Pavilion is a good a lead as any."

They returned to the rotunda with the same tiresome system as before: hobble, rest, hobble, rest. The phantom pain covered Connor with a sickly sweat all over, but Raphael looked far worse. Connor set him against an archway with a Celtic knot on it, letting them both rest for a moment.

An explosive boom sounded from up on a hill, beyond the arch, with enough power to rumble the ground. And within the noise, so obscure that it took Connor a moment to identify, was a shrill female scream. Clara.

## 15

C onnor closed his eyes, torn between Clara's voice and the needs of Raphael's injured body. After counting five breaths, he turned his head toward the Celtic knot arch and the hill Clara's screams seemed to come from.

He looked down at Raphael slumped against the arch and found it difficult to breathe. He couldn't leave the mortal angel alone, but Raphael was too injured to haul up the hill. Likewise, the screeches of spectres and a rumbling stampede grew louder beyond the Celtic arch, and he surely couldn't leave Clara to suffer either.

Before he had to make a choice, three familiar figures emerged in the distance, running full speed in their direction. Aphrodite led the pack, her long legs carrying her farther than limping Hephaestus or Clara, who always had had the body of an endurance runner instead of a sprinter.

Connor spied what they were escaping from: spectres in the dozens, roaring and spitting as they chased his friends out of the Avalon village. Quickly, he hauled Raphael into another support carry. There was nowhere to really hide, but a few of the other arches were cast in shade. Connor and Raphael hobbled together behind the Eden arch, its structure barely obscuring them as Clara, Aphrodite, Hephaestus, and the spectres ran through the rotunda.

As Clara passed by, she looked leftward and met Connor's eyes. Her arm lifted, fingers opening as she sent a black velvet bag soaring into his hiding spot. Connor caught the ripcord without fumbling it, gasping at his own reflex.

Crouching, he reached inside. Subtle grooves carved into ivory rubbed against his palm.

"Think this belongs to you." He returned the Icon to its rightful owner with a toss. As soon as Raphael's hand wrapped around the ivory, a blue glow washed beneath his skin. Connor's throat tightened at the crack and twist of Raphael's healing shin, only to relax as pain ebbed from both of their bodies.

"Are you okay?" Connor asked.

"Let's go," the angel said, now on steady legs.

The spectre stampede finished, leaving Connor and Raphael to follow from behind. Connor lifted both golden guns level with the spectre swarm. He and Raphael ran side by side, Raphael a little slower as he readjusted to his healed leg, but the angel still carried his flaming sword in one fist.

Connor's feet smacked against the cobblestones hard enough to echo. The Embassy sounded disturbingly peaceful despite the violence waging within its walls. The streets were now clear, no wards in sight, no screams or reactions. Now that Connor knew the evil within, it bothered him that every bystander had retreated in silent fear from the spectres in their citadel. The Embassy was a ghost town, and he tried not to think about what was happening to its residents.

Raphael and Connor passed through the cascading entrance gate as Connor's lungs burned. He lost his breath even more upon noticing a distinct lack of Clara under the station canopy. Hephaestus's carriage waited beneath the awning, its doors spread with the invitation to board, but the carriage remained empty.

Connor hunched, hands on his knees, his breath coming in bursts. "Where are they? How did we get here first?"

Raphael pointed, and Connor followed the gesture to the Embassy's gates. Running down the entry stairs, among a tsunami of shadow and fire, were their detoured friends.

Connor's first instinct was to run toward them, but Raphael grabbed his arm before he moved. *God damnit. He knows what I want.* Frustrated, he half focused on rebuilding the wall between them. Just because he liked Raphael well enough, and just because they were in a life or death situation, didn't mean he wanted someone dumpster diving through his heart. Even with his eyes on his rapidly approaching sister, half his worries lingered on protecting his deepest truths.

"Connor, we need to get on the carriage."

"We can't leave without them!"

"We won't." The serene voice vanished, replaced with stern unease. "I promise you, we are not leaving your sister. But when those spectres come, we need to be under cover."

As Raphael hopped up into the driver's mount, their friends passed the gate. Hephaestus lagged behind with his limp, but a trail of fire remained in his wake.

Clara reached the station first but stopped to look back. Connor groaned, was about to yell out to her, when both Aphrodite and Hephaestus stopped too. Hephaestus faced the spectres head on, his hands blooming a fire that shielded his wife and ward for a few seconds.

"Keep going!" Hephaestus shouted. "I'll hold them off!"

"What are you doing?" Aphrodite faltered. Even from the other side of the platform, Connor heard her reel in a note of persuasion at the last moment.

"Just go!" Hephaestus waved one hand at her while his other held the cane, lifting it like a beacon. Fire smoldered in his outstretched left palm, as well.

Aphrodite slung an arm around Clara's shoulders and guided them both to the carriage. As the spectres rolled toward them with frightening speed, the fire in Hephaestus's hands grew outward. With his roar, the simple flicker exploded outward and upward, consuming the spectres with a twenty-foot wall of fire.

The heat and power of the wall blew back Hephaestus's hair and coat. As the spectres burned with a wave of wails, Connor reached for Clara's hand and pulled her into the carriage with him. Aphrodite stumbled in afterward, her gaze still locked on Hephaestus's show of might. When the spectre howls stopped, the flames devoured themselves, leaving silence. Hephaestus teetered with exhaustion in the gateway of smoke and ash.

The spectres were no more, along with most of the Embassy's front barricade. The entry cobblestones were charred black, and the iron gates faded from molten orange, their gooey forms slipping into new designs.

Connor would have applauded if he wasn't so spent. He slumped onto the bench, arms around Clara's waist, lactic acid burning his muscles. Clara's head lolled on his chest, every pound of her weight dead against his side. Her forehead shone with sweat, but she was sickly white, as if all her life force had drained.

Hephaestus joined them in the cabin as Raphael lurched the carriage to life. Aphrodite swooped down on her husband almost instantly, with a level of concern that pulled a surprised noise out of Hephaestus himself.

Connor looked at Clara to share a weak laugh, but all she returned was a shell-shocked stare.

---

Their carriage rode for nearly an hour until the bright sky darkened into smoky, technicolor night. None of them spoke the whole ride, but Connor made sure Clara always remained in the corner of his vision. Otherwise, he was like a detached string, floating lost in the wind. His only other connection was to Raphael, but the post-battle calm allowed him to keep the wall between them thoroughly reinforced. It wasn't hard, with how calm and reserved

Raphael remained on the trip. Sometimes, it seemed like Raphael was keeping up walls of his own.

The vehicle finally stopped, and Connor climbed out first. His legs and back popped with the movement after being cooped up. Fog filled his head, but the overwhelming aroma of a thousand flowers cut through the daze. He took a deep breath, filling his lungs with the scent of nature, and exhaled out every toxic atom in his body.

When he rounded the carriage, he saw the source of the smell. Raphael had pulled up to a modest white cottage—the only building for at least half a mile. The rest of the scenery was full of lush, vibrant gardens with a single brick road winding through. Beyond the gardens and the cottage, miles away but still within sight, was the lake that seemed to bring all of Paradisa together. A light breeze from the water still managed to reach the cottage.

Connor moved to get a closer look, admiring a batch of lilies hanging over the road's edge. Almost all the flower bushes were in a similar state of bloom.

He returned to the carriage as Raphael hopped off the driver's perch.

"Welcome to Eden." Raphael gestured to the cottage. "Make yourselves at home."

Clara, Aphrodite, and Hephaestus walked silently to the cottage's front door, their shoulders slouched like zombies. Connor turned to follow them, but Raphael brushed his arm.

"Connor, wait."

Connor looked back. "What is it?"

"I've wanted to do this for hours." Raphael touched both sides of his face, and Connor's throat tightened. His heartbeat throbbed in his neck, hyperaware of what those words meant, and the warm hands on his jaw, and—

Blue tendrils of light radiated from Raphael's fingertips. The sparks cascaded across his left cheek, sewing up the crusted-over scratches Set left on his face. *Oh. Healing me. Of course.*

Connor shivered, but not from the tickling magic. "I'm fine," he insisted half-heartedly.

"Now you're more than fine." With nothing else to heal, Raphael's hands fell away.

"Guess you don't like looking at me all scarred up, huh?"

"I don't like seeing you hurt." He met Connor's gaze and the corner of his lips twitched upward with a hint of smile.

Connor couldn't help but return it. "Well. I like getting myself into trouble, so you might have to get used to that."

"Speaking of trouble, we have some more to deal with today. I reached out to Gabriel on the way here, to alert Michael we were coming. There's much we need to tell him about the Embassy. Follow me—Michael's house is less than a mile away."

"Contacted Gabriel? How does that work?"

"Gabriel is a herald, which means he can be invoked with a thought. We conduct all long-distance communication in Paradisa through them. Their messages can even cross realms or fill multiple minds at a time."

Connor followed him, and surprisingly, his body did not complain. His joints didn't enjoy being confined in a carriage, but he still felt better than he had any right to, considering the day's events. He wasn't even tired or hungry, though it had been...he couldn't remember how long it'd been since he tended to those necessities. In recent years, he could barely get through a regular work out. Maybe activating some old tactical moves warmed him back up.

He was so lost in his thoughts, he almost missed Raphael's bright gaze upon him. "I apologize, by the way. For doubting your theory about the Aaru dagger."

"Huh?" Connor rewound his memories to the day before. "Oh. That it was from an individual, and not from all of Aaru?"

"Exactly. And it was. You were completely right."

Connor shrugged, slipping his hands into his pockets. "Made enough sense to me at the time. No war I ever fought was with a country. It was always with a handful of assholes trying to ruin it for everyone else." He bumped Raphael's arm with his own, and it warmed his body in a slow wave. "You don't need to apologize, though. My theory didn't make any sense at the time."

"But it does now. Set is a pariah. He's no longer bound to the covenant of his kingdom. He has free will, truly. And he acted on it."

"There's not really any way you could have known that. But hey, maybe that's why having different perspectives is useful, right?"

Raphael bowed his head, but Connor still caught the corner of his smile. "I agree."

They fell into silence and continued down the garden-lined road for minutes until they approached stone steps to a skinny, ornate house. Michael's home soared with whitewashed marble, and its deep blue stained-glass windows swallowed the night. Even though Michael was no king, this house looked like the quarters of royalty. Far less modest than the small bungalow they just came from.

Connor crossed his arms over his chest. "Will he be awake?"

"Angels don't need to sleep, and Michael certainly wouldn't," Raphael reminded him. "You probably won't need to either when you're in Paradisa."

*Eh. Guess that explains why I'm not falling over.*

The door opened without a sound, and a sturdy man filled its frame. He voiced a single droll question to Raphael in a foreign tongue.

"My ward, Connor," Raphael responded in English. "He was a military man. He'll be of great help, Michael."

"Hi," Connor answered lamely. *Honored to meet you,* he should have said to the patron saint of soldiers, whose statues adorned every shelf in his mother's house, but the words didn't come.

Michael shared the shining icy eyes and black hair that seemed to be angelic commonalities. He may have been fetching once, but millennia of battles had weathered away his good looks. He was the only Sanctine Connor had met so far, with traces of gray in his cropped hair.

Connor knew how it felt to be sized up. Michael's cool gaze roamed across him with narrowed eyes. The angel of war made a noncommittal noise in the back of his throat.

"You've never taken a soldier before, Raphael."

Raphael's lips thinned. "This one is special."

Connor's blood flashed hot from his toes to his ears. *Special.* He didn't particularly care if that was true, so long as Raphael meant it.

Michael stepped back, allowing them inside. The fireplace warmth immediately wrapped around Connor, and he let out a relieved breath. Mam had given him a lot of things, but not her Irish tolerance for the cold. He was warm-blooded Tunisian, through and through.

He wasn't sure what to expect out of Michael's home, but it wasn't too different from a human structure. The materials and design were obscure, but the cathedral ceilings and crown molding looked oddly mundane. Additionally, the area behind the staircase, which would normally be a kitchen, was wall-to-wall with swords and armor.

Connor followed both angels into a room with a long table that a dozen other warriors already surrounded. Women and men were among them, their armors and skin reflecting different territories. From her spot at the end of the table, Athena regarded him with a nod.

Michael circled the table to stand at its head. An intricate map of Paradisa was sprawled across the mahogany, its structure reminiscent of an eye. The capital was the pupil; ten bridges across the lake, from Concordia to the kingdoms, were lines in the iris. The rest of the world, including the Embassy, filled in the white.

"Gabriel said you needed to speak with me urgently, Raphael." Michael pressed his fists into the map, eyes downcast. "I took the liberty of summoning my chief advisors to hear you out. Make this important."

Raphael straightened his posture. "As some of you might not know, I have been assigned by Michael to protect certain individuals from attacks. To date, all of these attacks have been orchestrated by the mysterious creatures we call spectres. I intercepted one in Tunis while protecting Athena, which is where I met Connor. But days later, a large group attacked Mount Etna, the home of Hephaestus and Aphrodite. One left behind a travel medallion from the Embassy of Wards."

He continued. "When we arrived at the Embassy to investigate, we found it completely under the control of Set, the Pariah of Aaru. We have reason to believe that some wards are being held by force under his control and that he is the one orchestrating these attacks."

"Set? He hasn't been seen in centuries," said a curvaceous woman near Connor who laced her English with a significant Irish lilt. Her long mane of curly red hair was rather distracting, but her bold features drew focus back to her face. Dark eyebrows twitched above fierce green eyes. "Where did he find spectres? How is he controlling them?"

Raphael's lips tightened. "He's creating them, Badb."

The table erupted in murmurs, all the comments swelling up and overwhelming each other. With one lift of Michael's hand, the war guild shushed instantly.

Michael made a skeptical noise. "No one can create life. Are you sure of this?"

"We saw it ourselves," Raphael said. "His sword showed unique properties that allowed him to bind dead wards to elderly Sanctines. If you want further witnesses, Aphrodite and Hephaestus of Olympus were with us as well."

"Hephaestus? That rat was with you?" A tall bear of a man sneered from the corner. "Where is he now? Tell me!"

"Silence, Ares," Michael said harshly enough to tighten Connor's stomach. "You may have earned back privilege as a witness, but you have not yet earned your voice."

The man slipped lower into the corner, fuming. Ares. Connor should have guessed. He was towering, broad-shouldered, and wearing a long braid of dark hair. A beard covered most of his face, although he looked handsome beneath it. He stood like a perfect warrior, right down to his scowl. The warrior was burly enough to snap Hephaestus in half, and the madness in his eyes ensured he would do it.

Michael stroked his face as he turned away from the table. He whispered into the ear of a stocky samurai with a sleek black ponytail, standing silently in the corner. The man muttered something back to Michael, who paused for a long while.

Finally, the war chief turned back to his guild. "This meeting is adjourned. All of you are dismissed, save for Raphael and his ward."

No one else defied the order. Athena brushed past Connor, offering him a small nod. The remainder of the war guild shuffled out of the house in silence, with the exception of clanking armor, until Raphael and Connor remained alone with Michael.

"What I'm about to tell you," Michael began, watching them with dark eyes, "does not leave this room."

Connor glanced to Raphael. He was okay with confidentiality; he damn near lived it for years. But this was so not his turf.

Raphael looked between him and Michael, before slowly nodding his head.

Michael sucked in a deep breath. "I believe the sword you saw Set wielding is an ancient weapon known as the Sword of Creation. It was forged by the skyfathers to create life and was hidden by them millennia ago."

Raphael's brow knitted. "Why have I not heard of this?"

"The information was only available to a handful of people. Even most kings do not know of it. If news of the Sword's existence became widespread, it would have created turmoil. Our unity would have collapsed as every pantheon in Paradisa would fight over each other to find it. To create life in their own image."

"Damn," Connor muttered, taking a seat at the end of the table. Raphael and Michael surprisingly took his lead, lowering themselves into nearby chairs as well.

Michael continued. "I know of its danger because I nearly succumbed to it myself. Years ago, long before the unity, and when Lucifer was still our beloved brother, I sought out the Sword. Lucifer and I worked together to find its location. When he said he knew where it was, that he had found its location, I was overjoyed. I knew we could use the Sword to make Eden more powerful than anything."

He shook his head, shielding his eyes with shame. "He refused to tell me. Said it was too much power for one man. I wrapped my hand around his throat and demanded he give up the location, and if it weren't for Gabriel walking in on the moment, I might have..." He scoffed, looking away. "I was ashamed of almost killing my twin, at the time. Now, I think of all the pain I would have saved our worlds if I'd gone through with it."

"So, Lucifer found the Sword, you think?" Connor asked.

"No, I don't think he ever did. It wasn't long after that he betrayed us, and I was forced to imprison him. But I believe he had the knowledge. And as far as I've ever known, he is the only person who could tell of the Sword's location. Set must have conspired with him to find it."

Raphael's eyes widened. "Lucifer is rotting in a cell at the bottom of the Claustrum. Hardly anyone can enter that prison and keep their life. Set never would have come out."

Michael tilted his chin upward, challenging his smaller brother. "Lucifer is the ultimate deceiver, and he hates us. He hates *me*. He would salivate at the chance to help Set undermine our peace."

"Your own hatred blinds you. Lucifer's knowledge of the Sword could have been wrong. And how would Set have known to go to him? There must be another explanation."

"Regardless." Michael waved a hand. "He has it now. And he's using it to build an army. If he's holed up in the Embassy, he won't be letting go of that territory. He'll wait as long as he has to, until he's gotten what he wants. Until he can take me down with the rest of them."

"Set spoke about you as if he knew you," Connor commented, crossing his arms over his chest. "What *do* you know about him? Do you know why he's sending spectres after Athena?"

"And after others, if he's to be believed?" Raphael added. "Michael, you cannot keep secrets from us anymore. Not when so much is at stake."

The general took a hulking breath. "There are others. Shiva of Amaravati. Lugh of Avalon. Perhaps five or six more. I've given them all protection, and it's gone about as poorly as it did with Athena."

Connor leaned into the table. They were getting close to the truth, he could almost smell it. "So, what do all of those people have in common?"

"I'm not revealing that information in a human's presence."

Raphael stood, abruptly. "Anything you need to say to me, you can say to my ward."

Michael's sigh dripped condescension. "Don't act like he's your equal. He may be a soldier, a step up from a prophet, but he's still a human. Our world is not their business."

"He *is* my equal. We share our souls one to one. Do you suggest to me that Jeanne was a lesser companion to you because she was human?"

Connor nearly buckled at the effort it took for Raphael to confront his brother; the heartbreak it caused. It was a breathtaking wound—a pain that would leave a scar—and the mark would merely add to the network of scars already crisscrossing Raphael's lonely heart.

Connor's throat constricted as Raphael's reaction invaded him. But he didn't push the angel out. Raphael needed to share the pain with someone. He would be far too caught up in his own problems to notice Connor's.

Michael slowly rose from his chair, eyes twitching in their sockets. "I don't want to talk about Jeanne, brother."

But Raphael persisted. "We saw her, just today. She misses you, Michael. And you can help us save her, and all the others trapped hostage there, if we go back to the Embassy."

"It's a death trap. He wants us to go. He's waiting for us, waiting for *me*." Michael's tone softened, offering a silent olive branch to his brother. "But you're right. He must be stopped. None of us have ever set foot in the Embassy, so we'll need your guidance if we go."

"We'll follow you," Raphael agreed. "Connor and I, and the rest of the war guild. Take as much of an army as you need. He is, at the end of the day, only one man."

The general steepled his fingers. "Alright. Leave me, for now. I'll prepare a plan the guild sees fit and will reconvene with you in the morning."

Connor turned to leave, but Raphael's feet seemed stuck to the floor. Connor leaned close, slipping a hand onto Raphael's elbow. He could tell Raphael ached with more to say, but Connor didn't need to be Michael's ward to see the general's mental walls come up. The conversation was over, whether they liked it or not.

His breath ghosted Raphael's hair. "C'mon."

He met Raphael's chilled gaze. His insides relaxed as Raphael nodded, letting go of the burden. They exited the house together and closed the door on Michael.

# 16

Clara sat in the center of Raphael's common room, legs crossed underneath her. She planned on sitting in silence, but a handmade lyre in the corner of the room proved too captivating. Against her intentions, the lyre had floated into the air as soon as she'd touched it, with its strings plucking themselves in a soft continuous lilt.

Her Nemean vest and axes were piled in the corner of the room. It felt good to give her shoulders a rest for a while. Maybe it would feel good to give her spirit a rest too. Her eyes drooped heavy as the lyre's song enabled her fatigue.

On the edges of her bond, Hephaestus drew nearer. He'd been down the hall moments ago, setting up one of Raphael's larger meditation rooms with Aphrodite. Something like reluctance pulsed in their bond when he heard about the sleeping arrangements.

He appeared in the doorway of the common room, gesturing at the self-playing lyre. "Huh. That's Apollo's."

Clara looked up from her lap, bangs obscuring her vision. "Oh? Are Raphael and Apollo friends?"

"I suppose they're both in the healing guild."

He limped toward a nearby armchair. With his movement, her internal sense of him matched her vision.

"It's weird," she said. "Knowing where you are all the time."

"It's new for me, too." He unsuccessfully masked a grimace as he bent his knees, the strain obvious in his bad leg. All his weight went into the cane until the chair's support was beneath him.

They spoke no more, but real silence was impossible with him. He still thrashed beneath his skin; there were parts he chose to show and parts she knew he kept from her. She was the same way, though. She hid everything she felt by avoiding his gaze.

Hephaestus set his cane against the accent table and leaned forward, elbows on his thighs.

"What are you doing out here?"

"Nothing. Just thinking, I guess. I wish I had something to…work on here, you know? I feel like I'm going nuts just sitting here. It's like I'm waiting for the world to end."

She dodged his eyes, but his watch continued. "I know. After Aphrodite's affair, I stayed in the forge for months."

"Affair?" It was baffling to think of the goddess of love, as she was today, hurting Hephaestus with such indifference. But she couldn't hate Aphrodite for an old mistake. Creeping into Hephaestus's heart, she saw that he didn't hate Aphrodite either—but the distrust was clear.

Hephaestus sighed, slumping back in the armchair. "I felt like metal could bend to my will when she couldn't. But that was wrong, wasn't it? Thinking I needed to control her at all. I thought jewelry and pretty things could get her to love an ugly smith. But now I know she didn't give a damn about that. All she wanted was for someone to look her in the eye and love her truly, without it being from her power. And he convinced her that he did."

His longing filled her chest with cotton. Clara shivered, pushing the weight away. "It was Ares, wasn't it?"

"Mm. When I caught them in bed together, I trapped them in a net to humiliate them, as they had humiliated me. I dragged them naked through Olympus. But my peers laughed at me just as much as they laughed at my wife. She may have been adulterous, but I was the fool who couldn't please his own wife."

He shook his head. "Ares and Aphrodite didn't go unpunished from the rest of Paradisa. They were debarred from guild leadership. And the last time I saw Ares, he vowed he would kill me if we were to meet again. He thinks I ruined his life. Maybe I did."

Clara's voice grew small. "It's weird to imagine anyone hating you."

"I'm starting to feel like you're the only one who doesn't."

"You've been kind to me this whole time."

He snorted. "It's easy to like an ideal version of me."

Clara chewed at her lip, running a hand over her sleeve. "We all show ideal versions of ourselves. There are plenty of things that are less than ideal about me, too."

"Everyone is imperfect," he acknowledged, "but I don't think you're any less than ideal, Clara. Why would you say that?"

*Ow.* A sting of teeth through skin and the tang of blood. Clara ran her tongue over her bitten lip, wiping away the evidence. It was a nervous habit, but at least it never left a permanent reminder.

She could have blurted out the truth to him. Could have opened her side of the bond like a levee, and flooded him with her pain.

But she probably couldn't make him understand. Couldn't put him into the shoes of a sixteen-year-old girl whose thighs were too big or whose nose had its own cruel nickname. Couldn't make him feel the shame of ranking third in her graduating class and everyone treating her like a scandalized failure for not being valedictorian. Couldn't make him see what it was like to be the only girl on the dance team who didn't have a boyfriend, or even see the point in them. The other girls just assumed she was a lesbian and refused to change in the same room with her. It was no use telling those cruel harpies that she found them even less attractive than boys.

"I've spent a lot of my life in pain," she said, summarizing it all in a few blunt words. "I hated myself. I'm better now, I...I don't feel like that anymore, but it's still part of me, I guess."

Her tongue felt so big in her mouth, and her throat so tight. It had been years since she'd dragged any of this to the surface. Normally she just avoided mirrors, buried herself in Thermo and CALC III, tried not to think about the past. It worked...for the most part.

Spilling this to a man who didn't have a choice in the state of his flesh or the fault in his gait made it all so juvenile, though. The petty trials of high school that forced her into self-loathing didn't compare to being abandoned by your mother and fried with lightning.

But Hephaestus, it seemed, didn't see it that way.

His hands grabbed each of her shoulders. "The pain of the past only means one thing." He lifted one of his forearms, letting a scar reflect the fire's orange glow. "That we survived."

"N-Never thought of it like that."

Hephaestus pulled her into his arms, his hands falling modestly to her shoulders and elbows. He wasn't tall, but he was taller than her, and her face ended up somewhere near his collar, where his shirt had absorbed that campfire smell from his forge.

Clara blinked away tears—when had those gotten there?—but they fell on his shirt anyway. She wrapped her arms around his back, like he was a pillar to hold her up.

"Hephaestus...?"

That quiet voice was not Clara's. It came from the threshold of the doorway and the common.

Normally, anxiety and shame felt hot. It made her heart race, made her cheeks flash with fire. Now, Clara's blood turned to absolute ice, and her feet were frozen in blocks of it.

She sucked in a shaky breath, glancing over her shoulder at Aphrodite. How unusual, to watch the goddess's normally confident face contort into awkward disbelief.

"I'm...I was going to retire..."

She slinked out of the doorway in a blonde flash. Even though the goddess was already gone, Clara untangled from Hephaestus.

"I'm sorry," she blurted. "It wasn't like that, but she's going to think—"

"No, I'll talk to her." Hephaestus's hand found its way back to her shoulder, squeezing. "Don't worry about us. You..." He sighed, ending his thought with a chaste kiss to her forehead. "You're brave, you know. Aphrodite sees that too, and for all her faults, she's got the patience of an Edenite."

Clara's throat remained full of tears and sandpaper, but she huffed out of laugh anyway. "I'm going to tell Raphael you said that."

He groaned. "Don't you dare."

⸻

The night deepened, blanketing Paradisa with a kaleidoscope bruise of flashing clouds. Connor tossed upon a cot in what Raphael called a *"meditation room."* What an awfully appropriate name for it, with the neutral colored walls and blackout curtains, with the no-nonsense candelabras made of animal bone and the array of pillows spread across the wooden floor.

But meditation didn't come. Nor did sleep.

Connor's body may not have required sleep in Paradisa, but his sanity did. During the most hellish weeks of SEAL life, it had become a limited resource, a precious escape. Years later, he still needed the cleansing relief of unconsciousness. Without it, his mind accumulated too much garbage, too much chaos.

Footsteps crossed the threshold from the hallway to his room. Connor snapped upright, fumbling toward the side of his cot, before remembering this wasn't his room. His guns were too far away, and the person standing before him was no enemy. Just an archangel in white cotton clothes.

He collapsed back into the pile of pillows. Rubbing a hand over his face only brought marginal comfort.

"I felt your stress," Raphael said, kneeling by his side.

"I just want to sleep." Connor groaned, palms pressed into his eyes.

Raphael responded with a sympathetic breath. "Oh...you can't sleep while I'm awake. I'm sorry, I forgot. I didn't think you'd need sleep here."

He grunted. "Is it always going to be like that?"

"No." Raphael patted the coverlet over Connor's leg. "For a few days. But for now, I can sleep, too. For you."

He settled onto the rug near Connor, not bothering with blankets or pillows, and laced his fingers over his stomach, the effigy of peace.

A strip of purple and blue lights from the window illuminated the space between them. Paradisa's night sky looked like a hurricane swallowed the Aurora Borealis, and it cast similar light throughout the meditation room.

Raphael turned upon his side, a lock of dark hair falling into his eyes. "Is there anything else you need?"

Connor let out a quiet laugh, rolling through the myriad of responses he could offer that question. At least it would be hard to see a blush on his dark skin.

"No, this is...fine. Maybe you weren't the only thing keeping me awake."

"You're worried about Clara."

Connor squinted. "Careful. I'm gonna start thinking you're a mind reader."

"I assure you I'm not. But...the bond does help."

He huffed out breath. Sure enough, thoughts of Clara storming out that linen closet with her axes in hand and of headbutting a fucking god kept replaying in his brain. Even though Raphael couldn't read his mind or see his memories, he surely got a sense of them. And they all radiated with the same energy.

"Fine, Dr. Phil. I guess, it's like...my baby sister doesn't need me anymore."

Raphael frowned. "She'll always need you in some way."

"I can feel her slipping away. Guess it's nothing new. Been that way for years now, but I keep getting the sense like she doesn't need me the way she used to. Or maybe she never needed me at all. Maybe I told myself she did so I'd have something to do." Connor covered his face with both hands, blocking the room out. "I get it. I was the same way at her age. But I didn't know how much I considered her my kid before. I mean, she's my sister, but she's still *my* kid."

"I am the youngest of my brothers, but many of them show the same concern for me as you do for Clara. It's not abnormal, even for us."

"Really? Michael wasn't exactly warm and fuzzy tonight." He sat up on an elbow, now farther from sleep, but engaged enough to not care.

He expected Raphael to nod with enthusiastic agreement, but the angel looked away. Perhaps Connor had broken an unspoken rule about siblings. *That was probably wrong of me. I'm allowed to make fun of Clara, but if anyone else does it, they're getting punched.*

"Michael was first. Our world needed protection, so he was given a sword." He pulled his knees to his chest. "As the eldest and a warrior, it's natural for him to be blunt."

"Yeah, I got that impression."

"Your actions toward Clara come from a place of compassion. I do sometimes wonder if Michael's come from a place of doubt. As if he sees the rest of us as incompetent."

They had said nothing to each other on the walk home from Michael's. Raphael's emotions collected in Connor's chest like iron drawn to a magnet. The wall between them had eroded some, mostly because Connor could not command the focus required to keep it perpetually raised. But now, more than ever, Raphael needed to feel their bond. And Connor accepted that it was okay to let some of his emotions slip under the fence and over to Raphael to help soothe the angel. His feelings returned to him in the quietest echo.

"Do you want to talk about what he said?"

Raphael's features glazed over. "Michael is stubborn. And always fixated on Lucifer. He was hurt by Lucifer's fall, and since then, he wants to find Lucifer behind every plot. It's unbelievable that Set would have trusted Lucifer enough to collude with him. No one would."

Raphael ran a hand over his brushed back locks. The ends of his dark hair were long enough to curl under his ears. Connor caught himself staring at that small detail, same as he'd stared at Raphael's freckles outside Jeanne's dorm. Miniscule features that should have separated the human from the divine. He had to be careful, noticing such things about an angel. They could trick him into believing Raphael was just another man, instead of something far greater and untouchable.

Connor shook his head. "Well, maybe he could be on the right track? Where I come from, Lucifer isn't known as a good dude."

"Some of what you've heard is probably true. The rest…perhaps not. Lucifer thought himself better than humans and couldn't understand why we wouldn't conquer you. Truthfully, he thought we should conquer most of Paradisa."

"You said he was in the Claustrum…?"

"Our most damnable prison. Michael seized his Icon and stabbed him in the stomach, banishing him from Paradisa. For thousands of years, he has remained locked in the Claustrum. No visitors. No promise of ever returning home."

Connor shifted on his cot and closed his eyes, imagining a window growing in their mental barrier. Through it, he extended a mental touch of comfort to Raphael's side before retreating to his own headspace.

Raphael continued. "Lucifer and I were close when I was young. He was like me—emotional, you'd say. Unfortunately, his emotions always included an appreciation for mischief and pride. But the day he turned on Paradisa, I could swear he was a different person. His 'gift' had always been troublesome, but it never manifested so ruthlessly before then. He loved Michael more than any of us. The past is buried, and he must pay for what he did but…I still want to know what changed in him."

Never had Connor heard a person speak of Lucifer with sympathy. "Who made him that way?"

It was a heavy question, and he didn't expect an answer to it. But Raphael looked to the ceiling with a mysterious smile.

"Ah, you want to know about the creation. If I knew the answer, it's probably not information that humans should know. But the truth is, we're not sure."

Connor could have laughed if it wasn't so monumentally disappointing. "Is that the big secret, then? That no one knows?"

"Every kingdom has its own story, particularly one that benefits them," Raphael offered, opening his palms. "We do know there was some kind of creator, or creators. After it, or they, seeded the realms with life, they sequestered themselves where no one could find them. All they left us were a handful of prophecies for how we should run the universe. And to prevent others from replicating their work, they locked the secret of genesis away with them. They feared that the power of creation would end up in the wrong hands, with life being created for ill gains."

"Seems like that's what happened anyway."

"No one knows the whereabouts of the creators, and a new race of life has never been created outside of their influence. Until now, I suppose." Raphael returned to lay on his back. "Curious, isn't it? How much the spectres are similar to us and our binding. Humans and Sanctines seemed destined to be intertwined as equals, in whatever way fate desires."

"Yeah. Just wish Michael saw it that way too."

"He's a brilliant battle strategist. I shouldn't take have taken his words personally, as he would not have expected me to." Despite the stoicism, his voice told the real story. He turned on his side, looking earnestly at Connor through the darkness. "Really, I mostly felt wronged on your behalf. I don't see you as disposable. You do know that, right?"

A lump swelled in Connor's throat. No, he didn't know that. Not for certain. Not until now.

"Yeah. Thanks for uh…heh…defending my honor, I guess."

His hand moved to his back pocket and hesitated over it, as he debated whether to expose what was on his mind.

*You're stuck with him for life. You're going to have to tell him sometime.*

Holding his breath, Connor pulled out a ratty wallet and flipped to the photographs. The picture of Eric was torn and faded within its small protective flap. Still, seeing Eric's face always steadied his pulse. As long as he had a picture, he could never forget what Eric looked like. Just like in the Tunisian bar, he glanced between Raphael and the photo, and was struck by the resemblance.

He passed the wallet so Raphael could view it. Raphael's face flickered with something mysterious upon seeing Eric, but it soon vanished.

"Who is this?"

"His name was Eric. We were together about six months when he went out to a bar to meet up with some friends and never made it back to his house. They found him in an alley beaten so bad they had to pull his dental records."

If Raphael judged him for the word *together,* it wasn't on his face. Nor was it in the bond.

Connor swallowed. "People like me, we know the risks—everyone had some friend of a friend whose body was found in a dumpster, or in the woods—but I never thought it would be him. He was a quiet guy. Really careful about who he opened up to. I guess some gang saw him coming out of the wrong type of club after a night with some friends."

Rationalizing the hate crime never got him anywhere, except angry. Justice was served on paper: Eric's murderers were eventually caught, put on trial, and jailed til they rotted, but getting there had been exhausting. Their lawyers talked for them for months, painting a thick layer of buzz words. *Broken homes. Bad educations. Wrong friend circles.* It must have been society's fault, or bad parenting, or undiagnosed mental illness that made them gleefully hold a stranger down and smash his face with a brick.

"About three years into the SEALS, I got that phone call about Eric. I kept in touch with his parents for months after, following the trial and stuff. I tried to keep it together, but my bunkmate, Roger...he was a good guy, but he was a stickler to the rules. He knew I was distracted, and the truth just came spilling out of me. I thought he was cool enough to keep it secret, but he ratted me out as soon as I hit the bed that night. Because it was *nothing personal.*"

He shook his head, realizing it had been almost a decade since he recounted the story aloud. "When the CO confronted me about it, I just...I couldn't lie to him, man. I wanted to say that Roger was full of shit, but it wouldn't have been true. I kept seeing Dad's face in my head and how disappointed he'd be if I pretended to be something I wasn't. It took him a long time to get to that point, but that's how he accepted me, in the end. So, they told me to pack my bags, and that was it."

Raphael watched him silently, serenely. While he offered no verbal reply, his comforting presence in their bond was nearly palpable.

Connor sighed, tucking his wallet back into his jeans. "I went from the Navy's best to a kitchen sink 'cause of that guy. He didn't give a shit. It was just *the rules.*"

The painful memory bloated his gut, but his lungs breathed easier. When he first connected his soul to Raphael's, all he could think about was how raw the past still burned him, like sandpaper rubbing across his ribs. If he couldn't trust the men who were supposed to watch his back against guns and insurgents, how could he trust a stranger with the rest of his life? A stranger whose entire institution apparently damned his state of being?

But Raphael was not an institution, and he had never felt like a stranger. He was a man of patience, and he had a saint-like capacity for empathy. And as Connor allowed the aperture between them to slowly slip open, confessing his ills made him far more weightless than shamed. Raphael did not slap him in the face with the parade of well-meaning statements he'd grown tired of a decade ago: *people aren't all bad, you always knew it was a risk,* and *no one will hurt you like that again.* No, Raphael was a black hole, absorbing his pain in silence without trying to convince him to do anything more.

For the first time since their binding, Connor found sleep.

# 17

Clara dreaded the morning and everything it would mean.
One of the last things Hephaestus had mentioned before
turning in for the night was *axe training.* Something about
how he wanted her to learn how to defend herself better in case they
were ever in another situation where she'd need to fight. The Nemean
vest beneath her jacket would not solve all problems, especially in
battle.

On a normal day, that would be the most intimidating thing she'd
have to face. But there was something worse waiting for her: having
to look Aphrodite in the eye after she'd seen them embracing the
night before and having to explain that no, it wasn't what it looked
like, even though that's definitely what someone says when it *is* what
it looks like.

So how could she convince the goddess of the truth? What Clara
shared with Hephaestus was certainly intimate. They were two
broken bodies, barely patched together by their own curiosity and
ingenuity. Their souls were in a constant dance as well, sharing and
receiving each other without complaint.

But attraction wasn't something Clara felt toward anyone, let
alone a married god. Especially when said married god spent half his

waking hours pining desperately for Aphrodite to the point where Clara felt like banging on their mental bond and telling him to quiet the hell down.

She just had to convince Aphrodite of that, using words instead of feelings, and damn if words were not Clara's strong suit.

Clara managed to avoid the goddess for most of the morning, until she finally walked into Raphael's backyard for axe practice. Aphrodite idled in a chair on the back portico, fingers laced over her lap and the wind brushing through her hair.

"Good morning, Clara."

Clara swallowed, and it stuck in her throat. "Morning," she squeaked.

The next words rushed out of her mouth like a projectile.

"Aphrodite, I need to talk to you about last night. I just need to tell you that me and Hephaestus, we weren't...it's not..."

"Shh, Clara." The other woman laid a slender hand on Clara's shoulder. "I know. He told me everything."

"H-He did?"

"Yes. And I'd be able to tell if he was lying, so, even if I didn't trust him already..." She smiled, a little sad. "I'm so sorry you've felt so much pain before. But I think it's good for him, for both of you, to have someone to share that with. You're his ward. You're meant to be close."

Clara could breathe for the first time since waking. Had this weight really constricted her chest so much?

"I'm glad you know what's up," she said. Even the muscles in her face seemed to unwind, relax.

Aphrodite hummed, a little somber. "You know...even if you did desire each other, I suppose I would deserve the rejection. It would not surprise me if he preferred you over me."

It seemed impolite to laugh when Aphrodite sounded so serious, but a nervous bark escaped from Clara's throat anyway. "Um. *What?*"

Aphrodite blinked. "Is that so hard to believe? You're young and beautiful and so much like him."

"I..." *I am really only two of those things,* she wanted to say, but rewrote those thoughts as soon as they emerged. Cognitive Behavioral Therapy was second instinct when it came to the self-esteem monster after the many years of practice.

She shook her head, restarting with a purer truth. "Aphrodite, it doesn't matter what I am. He loves you so much it physically hurts him. I can, you know, feel it in the bond. It's almost scary. I mean, I never understood what that kind of love felt like before I saw you through his eyes."

Aphrodite's eyes seemed to sparkle, just for a second. Her lips parted in wonder, and that, it seemed, made her appear more beautiful than ever.

"I never knew that..." she whispered. "It's hard to tell what's caused by my abilities, and what's real."

"Believe me. He's real."

Clara couldn't help but wonder whether Ares had been real too. Just as soon as she tried to vanquish her flash of shame at the thought, Aphrodite looked at her with an arched brow.

"Something wrong?"

"No," Clara replied quickly, her back stiffening—an old habit from childhood. Whenever she was in trouble, Dad had made her stand at attention to hear his chastising lecture. Over time, it became reflexive to associate that posture with guilt.

"You're nervous...or maybe curious? I can't quite tell. It's a dull yellow for you. Most people are more of a dark orange."

"Yellow?"

"I can see people's emotions...in a way. Everyone has a glow that changes color depending on their mood. Blue means fear, terror, or anxiety. Red is usually rage, arrogance, spite—the incensed emotions. The yellows and oranges are usually shame, but they can also be curiosity. I suppose those go together, in a way."

"So that's what you meant, when you said you'd know if we lied?"

"I try not to pay attention to it. People deserve privacy." Aphrodite sighed, hugging herself. "Really, in this place, I don't think I want to see how people feel about me. It's always some shade of contempt."

Clara's shoulders folded inward. "Why would anyone care about that after all this time? That was thousands of years ago, wasn't it?"

Aphrodite made a humorless noise in the back of her throat. "Sanctines never forget. My presence alone is enough of a reminder. And I'm sure they're shocked to see Hephaestus at my side. I'm surprised I don't see contempt from you, now that he told you the truth."

"I know you're a good person. The only thing I don't understand is why you stayed together. If you loved Ares, couldn't you have...?"

Aphrodite lifted a shoulder. "Ares was not my husband. Nor did he love me. After the affair, I told myself I would work on the marriage I had. But it wasn't easy. I didn't choose to marry Hephaestus. Hera offered me to him."

Clara's eyes widened as her mental portrait of Aphrodite and Hephaestus filled in. It was a question she hadn't wanted to ask so openly: how had the most beautiful woman in all Olympus end up with a surly, limping blacksmith? In hindsight, an arranged marriage seemed the only reasonable explanation.

Not that she needed to offend Hephaestus by admitting that.

"I can't imagine getting married at all, let alone to someone I didn't love."

Aphrodite hummed, pulling at a sandy curl. "It was not bad at first. I found him handsome and charming in his own way. He wasn't raised by the gods. He lacked their pettiness and vanity. And he constantly gave me trinkets he'd made by hand. Jewelry, baubles, furniture. He built a home for us on Mount Etna. The sight of the sea makes him ill, but he still designed our bedroom to have the best view of it. He knew that it's the closest thing I have to a home, and that I loved watching the sun set over the water. I...I thought he was quite wonderful."

Her face fell, emphasizing the scant age lines at her eyes and mouth. "But he would never touch me. I tried so many times, but he always untangled from my arms. Enough time passed and I realized that while we were married by law, we were not husband and wife. We were two lonely people occupying the same space."

Clara frowned. The Hephaestus she knew—the Hephaestus whose heart she shared in her chest—yearned for his wife with every glance at her. A painful, guttural need that burned as bright as his fire. But if this was accurate, perhaps it explained Aphrodite's soft surprise at hearing how Hephaestus truly felt.

"If he chose you, why would he reject you?"

"Over time, I learned where he came from and about Hera...how she threw him away the day he was born. If his own mother couldn't love him, perhaps he assumed I couldn't either."

*No one wanted me,* he'd said to Clara, drunk and vulnerable. Despite plenty of evidence pointing to the contrary, he wasn't convinced otherwise. Nothing was enough to rewrite the scars Hera left on his heart.

"Sounds like Hera's a bitch," Clara said.

The goddess laughed, the sound like a wind chime. "I hope you never have to meet her. She's the worst of all of them."

Aphrodite rose from her chair, gesturing toward the axe harness hanging from Clara's shoulders. "Hephaestus mentioned that he'd like to spar with you today. I can help you get started, if you'd like. It'd be better to fight me than to fight Hephaestus. If you injure him, you'll feel the pain reflected back at you."

"Huh. Guess that's true. Sure, then."

Aphrodite moved down the portico and positioned herself about twenty feet before Clara, twirling her chain belt around both slender hands.

"I can start with just the chain. Once you get the hang of that, we can move up to the swords."

Clara's voice wavered as she took her own position. "Are you sure it's okay if I hit you?"

"I'll barely feel it, Clara." Aphrodite readied a running stance. "Are you ready?"

"Ready as I'll ever be."

Aphrodite darted forward, her chain whipping through the air. Clara yelped, flailing wildly, tossing one axe toward the goddess.

When it sailed past Aphrodite's hip, barely nicking the fabric of her dress, Clara groaned.

Aphrodite stopped short of colliding with her, and Clara lifted a hand to summon the axe from the dirt. It hit her palm and she turned away, trying to quell the bubbling burn of failure in her veins.

A gentle touch to her arm beckoned her to turn. She swallowed, willing her pulse to slow.

Her frustration fizzed right back when she faced Aphrodite's considerate features. Clara started to sweat, the moisture collecting on the back of her neck.

"What's wrong?" Aphrodite frowned. "You won't hurt me."

"It's not that. I'm just...not good at this. I don't think I'll ever be ready to fight you. And, no offense, but you're not exactly a warrior. What happens when I have to face someone who can really fight?"

Aphrodite smiled grimly. "You're right. Rarely have I been in real battles. Ares taught me to spar. But that was a long time ago."

Clara sensed Hephaestus before she heard his cane, clopping with each step. She watched as he finally emerged from Raphael's house, a broadsword in each hand, seemingly unaware of their conversation.

"Ah. I see you've started without me." Now at Aphrodite's side, Hephaestus extended one of the swords he retrieved from Raphael's house. "Feel free to use one of these, if you'd like."

The goddess strutted forward and plucked the blade from her husband's hand.

As Clara watched Aphrodite take her stance, she swallowed hard. "Not sure I'm ready for that yet..."

"I won't hurt you, Clara. This is just about strategy. I know that's natural for you."

Her comment did make Clara smile, albeit marginally.

Still several feet away, Aphrodite raised the sword, pointing it toward Clara's sternum. Hephaestus circled them both, one hand on his hip.

"It may be tempting to rely on the axes' distance abilities," he said. "But they're equally useful for close combat. So bend your knees, slightly. Keep your body fluid. This time, use the left arm to throw and the right arm to block."

Clara complied, taking a crouched stance with both axes elevated. Her arms bent, one arched back to throw and the other curved toward her to fight Aphrodite directly.

Aphrodite attacked in a blur, arching the sword at Clara's throat. Instinct took over with no strategy behind the wheel. Clara lifted both axes over her head, crisscrossing them in an X-formation to awkwardly block the attack.

Aphrodite did not bring the sword all the way down, thankfully, for both Clara's wrists and eight of her fingers lay completely exposed to the attack. In a real situation, she would have been lucky to get away with both hands. She cowered like a mouse beneath Aphrodite's blade, her eyes closed and her face turned away.

*What made me think I could do this?*

"Don't feel like that," Hephaestus chided, mortifying her further with his recognition of her shame. "It takes warriors decades to become master fighters. I just want you to be good enough to keep yourself alive. And these axes were for you alone. Remember that. They'll listen to you. Let's go again."

Clara lowered the axes and filled her lungs with air. She steeled herself for the next attack, imagining Connor's face. Imagining the rugged eyes looking down the tops of his golden guns, as he fired them effortlessly. Once upon a time, he was like her. Just a young person who'd never touched a weapon. If he could become what he was today, she could become good enough to survive.

Hephaestus pointed to each of them as he spoke. "Aphrodite, go slowly this time. Clara, pretend the tree behind her is a spectre, and use your right hand to block her."

*Come on, you can do this. It's just physics. Just forces meeting and opposing.*

The goddess lunged with her sword aimed at Clara's ribs. Aphrodite moved purposefully slower, but Clara's mind worked at breakneck speed, calculating that a pinwheel arm movement was enough to knock Aphrodite off the war path. At the same time, Clara hauled her left arm forward and tossed the axe toward the tree. The axe missed the trunk, but Aphrodite's impending attack distracted her from the disappointment.

Clara hooked her right axe-head onto Aphrodite's blade and yanked it sideways. Aphrodite fell askew, her sword sliding under Clara's armpit. With the goddess off balance, Clara reared back her left hand, open palm waiting for her returning weapon. When the second axe returned home, she hacked it down toward Aphrodite's throat, stopping an inch before it hit the skin.

"That would be a hit." Aphrodite laughed softly, untangling from Clara. "Well done."

"Well, of course it's better when you guys give me time to think."

Hephaestus hummed. "It won't be so easy in real life. But this will get it in your muscle memory. You're a fast learner."

"Maybe…"

The back door creaked and an unfamiliar man stepped through. He was decked in golden armor, his face rugged, and an elegant hilt made of ebony hung at his waist.

Clara lifted an axe, but Aphrodite seized her wrist. "Don't. It's General Michael."

Clara breathed. *Just Raphael's brother. Their swords look alike. And well, so do they.*

"We're gathering our reconnaissance team." He looked directly at Clara. "Your brother wishes to say goodbye before he leaves."

"Leaves?"

"Come. We're departing soon." Michael beckoned, and returned to the house.

Clara looked to Aphrodite and Hephaestus, gaping. Hephaestus nodded, filling her with a burst of strength. She nodded back, and followed Michael into the house.

Connor paced Raphael's main room, his body draped with an armory's worth of battle weight. As soon as the war guild showed up at the door, they had showered him with leg knives and swords, armor for every inch of skin, gauntlets and throwing stars. He had stood stretched like the Vitruvian Man as a warrior from every pantheon patched him with something of use. The only thing he turned down was a bow and arrow from Hachiman, Michael's second-in-command, as archery was one combat skill he never picked up in the Navy.

He paced despite the weight, creaking the floorboards with every step. He had never liked goodbyes, and he had had to say an abnormally high number in his life. They never got easier.

As he waited for Michael to return from the backyard with Clara, he took a closer look at Raphael's stuff. You could tell a lot about a person from their belongings. And in this case, Raphael's lack of possessions was most telling. Connor had never seen a residence so lacking in personal effects. Even the Navy barracks he spent many years in had more personality, as cadets pasted letters from home or pin-up posters by their bunks.

Still, one curio cabinet in the corner held some semblance of character, although judging from the layer of dust on everything, it wasn't touched often. None of the mementos seemed connected by personal taste or aesthetic flow. Many looked like artifacts from millennia ago —pre-Israelite vases, hand carved idols and jewelry, a few bronze weapons and beeswax candles. More mysterious were the innocuous modern items like lighters and cheap costume lockets displayed as artistically as the others.

Raphael appeared at his shoulder, quiet as always. Neither one of them had been particularly talkative all day.

Earlier that morning, when Connor had awoken, Raphael remained in slumber. The angel's emotions becalmed in his sleep, and his position never altered through the night. He could have been a pale corpse, hands gently folded over his chest as he lay on his back.

Connor's own mental wall had fallen while they slept. Rather than rebuild it, he'd stepped over the hurdle between them, peeking inside Raphael's heart. Stealing far-too-long glances as he watched the angel sleep.

*Do angels dream?*

And for the first time since their bonding, Connor recognized some small beauty. Because yes, angels did dream, and he *felt* it. When he closed his eyes, he could almost see it spread behind his eyelids. Colored, intense flashes of memory. Fleeting sounds and faint smells.

Raphael had stirred then, revealing a faint smile. And of course, Connor wrenched back as if burned, returning to his side of their union before Raphael caught him.

It was exhausting to keep blocking Raphael out. Connor knew it was absurd, knew that he was useless to their team if he kept spending half his energy inside of his own head. Maybe, he hoped, the wall could become second nature after a while. Maybe, Raphael could do the work keeping it up instead.

*Maybe,* the quietest voice in his head said, *you can let him in.*

But he didn't do that. Instead, he locked all those thoughts in a nice little box, and asked Raphael, who lingered by his side in the present, "What is all this stuff?"

"From my wards, across the centuries. They were parting gifts."

Connor smirked. "Have to think of something to give you before I bite it."

Raphael smiled back, somewhat bashful, which widened Connor's smirk. "It's not mandatory, of course. But hopefully, you'll have a long time to consider it."

The back door groaned as Michael returned, with Clara not far behind. As she approached, Raphael faded away to the corner of the room, leaving them with some privacy.

Standing before him, she filled his view. Of course, he was responsible for the surprised distress on her face, but this was inevitable. Neither one of them had become wards to sit on the sidelines.

Clara's gaze roamed across his overstocked body. He teetered from the lopsided weight, and knew his dark skin was pallid. As much as he'd done this before, it never became fun to walk into a place that could kill him.

He waited for her to speak first.

"You look ridiculous." The comment seemed light, but her voice wavered with worry. "They gave you a sword?"

"Yeah." He humored her attempt at breaking the ice with a tight smile. "We all need a last resort. Maybe I'll get in a bind and need to whack someone over the head."

Her charade broke apart with a stifled noise. "Why you? Why Raphael? You don't need to be at the Embassy with them. Stay here with us."

"They need all the help they can get. Most of them have never stepped foot in there. And I think they want Raphael to play medic for them, in case someone loses an Icon mid-battle."

"Then I could come with you, too," she choked. The statement was obviously more out of camaraderie than actual desire; it was a sense of duty to remain by his side. Clara had never liked idling. But Connor lifted a solemn, dismissive hand. *I know you're trying to do the right thing. Don't.*

"No. The only reason they're letting me go is because I've been in combat—real combat where one wrong move can kill you. That's not your life. You've got better things you can give."

"So what am I supposed to do while you're out there?"

"Now that you mention it…"

He glanced over his shoulder. Raphael and Michael chatted quietly on the other side of the room, oblivious to his conversation with Clara. Still, he guided his sister to the far end of the room, a gentle hand on her elbow.

"Michael told us some stuff about Set, but…I've got a bad vibe. Like he's not telling us the whole story. They have a history together, but Michael wouldn't go into details."

"Why would he hide something from you?"

Connor blew out a heavy breath. "I don't know. But if you try and find more information about Set and Michael, and why the hell they were working together in the first place, it might help me feel better about all this."

Clara sniffed. "Fine. I can do that."

Connor engulfed her small frame in one motion. The armor must have felt rough against her face and chest, and it was too thick for him to feel her warmth. He could barely feel her at all.

Pulling away, he rested a hand on the back of her head. "I don't know when I'll see you again. But if you need to reach me, they say you should try to find a herald. Then you can contact me anytime, anywhere I am."

"You, too. Be safe, okay?"

"Yeah."

He kept his stare locked on hers as he backed away. But when he finally turned to follow Raphael and Michael, he did not look back.

W hile no soaring skyscrapers or humanoid architecture filled Concordia's skyline, the capital's energy buzzed like a busy metropolis. Sanctines of all walks of life passed by in a full rainbow of clothing and adornments. Many eyed Clara suspiciously as they passed, unabashed in their confusion at her humanity. Some were excited or interested, but a handful turned their noses up.

She looked to Aphrodite for an explanation, but the goddess's hazel gaze stayed glued to the cobblestone path. And it dawned on Clara that she was not the one people were glaring at. She heard their whispers too, about the *whore of Olympus*. The *bitch who ruined Ares.* Aphrodite refused to lift her gaze.

As they passed a disjointed row of buildings, Clara's gaze traveled over the runes and symbols accompanying every sign. Although the language was foreign, most symbols were obvious: fire, music, hunting.

"What are these places?"

A pace behind her, Hephaestus replied, "Guilds. They've been around since the unity. I suppose they can be useful, but they mostly just argue with each other."

The last building on the left was actually a tent with a sword and shield emblemized onto its red banner. After it, the alley opened up into sprawling courtyard, easily as large as Piazza Navona. Perhaps even larger. It had been awhile since Clara toured Rome.

A pulsing green portal hovered in the center of the square, standing on a short dais and housed within an elaborate stone archway. Sanctines casually strolled through it alone, or arm in arm with another, as if moving their way through a shopping mall door. The colors shifted with every walkthrough—a flash of green, sometimes red, then green again. The foot traffic was light here, hardly anyone around aside from the occasional portal travelers.

Beyond the portal, on the north side of the square, a blue mosaic building reflected the shifting light.

"That's the library," Aphrodite said. "Come on."

They walked around the portal arch and ascended several dozen marble steps to the library's entrance. Clara's neck craned as she absorbed the intricate façade. On the portico, a chandelier supported three iron rings filled with candles. The fire reflected off blue tile made from natural shells. Clara ran her fingers across the mosaic, the stone smooth and cool.

The interior of the library appeared warped and sepia through the front door, which was nothing more than a thick slab of amber. Aphrodite pushed it open, and the *smell* hit Clara before anything else. The overwhelming mix of dust, paper, and something...ancient.

The three of them shuffled inside, sheltered beneath a dozen levels of balconies and a domed ceiling. A broad spiral staircase, which started on the opposite side of the main rotunda and spun upward to the final story, connected each of the balconies. And in the center of the ceiling, a glass oculus allowed in dancing purple light from Paradisa's evening aurora.

The only décor of note in the first-level foyer was a perimeter of bookcases near the walls, and a semicircular desk stacked with ancient tomes and candles, behind which a muscular woman in a white sari puttered around. A golden crown held back her black hair, and a lotus flower rested behind her right ear. Most strikingly, two extra arms sprouted from her waist, and she held books in each of the extra hands.

As Aphrodite, Hephaestus, and Clara walked to the desk, the four-armed librarian looked up. "We're not open to visitors right now. You'll have to come back tomorrow."

"We'll only be a few minutes, Saraswati," Aphrodite crooned in persuasive tones. Clara's focus contracted, and she shook her head. Even listening to Aphrodite mesmerize other people could screw with her head.

Saraswati snorted. "You'll have to do better than that. Your charms won't work on me."

Aphrodite's displeasure showed on every pore of her flawless face. Saraswati's hawkish gaze landed on Clara next. It pierced and dissected her, crawling under her skin. Clara shivered, silently wishing for Hephaestus's warmth to envelop and shield her from this invasion.

Hephaestus shouldered his way forward. "It's alright. She's my ward."

Saraswati barked a laugh. "You want to bring a ward into our library, too? Who do you people think you are?"

"We're here to save the world," Clara said, smiling. "Well, kinda. At least it'll help."

"Oh?" A snort. "As much as I'd support the idea of books saving the world, I doubt two Olympians and their ward coming into my library after hours is a life or death situation."

Aphrodite lifted her chin. "Does the word *Inquisitor* mean anything to you?"

All the snark drained right out of Saraswati's warm face. "Well, it's a broad term, Olympian. It has a multitude of definitions—"

"What about as a title? A title that Athena wore, supposedly?"

"You should ask the War Guild, if this is—"

"The War Guild sent us here," Aphrodite interrupted. *That's not exactly true,* Clara thought, *but close enough for library work.* "But they're busy at the moment. The least we can do is get information for when they come back."

Saraswati sucked in a breath, glancing to each of them in turn. Two of her arms were clasped together in front of her waist, while the others wrung together before her chest.

"Ack! Fine. Come with me."

---

The war guild spread out across a carriage the size of a bus, most of its members occupying benches alone. In the farthest row back, Connor peered at the glass ceiling, perplexed by the chromatic swirls in Paradisa's night sky. Splashes of purple, green, and blue backlit the overcast clouds. Occasionally the colors exploded, lighting up the fog.

After nearly an hour of traveling, their carriage slowed to a halt, and their comrades rose. The heavy clanks of shifting armor rebounded through the cabin. Connor's arm hair fluffed up beneath his chainmail. Badb shambled in front of him, nearly as tall as him, her red mane tied back with a Celtic knot comb.

They disembarked from the carriage in single file and converged on a rocky foothill with the Embassy perimeter about a half-mile ahead. Michael scanned their crew of seventeen before he was satisfied with everyone present.

"Listen closely. The Embassy is large, and spectres will be on patrol throughout the entire city. Stay close to me and follow my lead."

A gravelly voice rumbled behind Connor. "Sticking together means we may never find them in this maze! On my own, I can tear down a hundred spectres!"

Connor turned, noticing this long-haired man for the first time. He was so pale his skin seemed transparent. And unlike most of the war guild, he wore no armor. His shirtless white body nearly provided its own luminescence, and a gnarled stump remained in place of his left hand. He must have ridden in the other chariot, because there's no way Connor could have missed seeing him before.

Beside Michael, decked in leather armor and gripping a wooden longbow, Hachiman lifted his chin. "The general would prefer for us to stay together. When we will encounter spectres, you will have your taste of their flesh."

"Indeed," Michael murmured to his second-in-command. "Follow me."

Michael led them down the cliff toward the perimeter of the Embassy villas. Connor and Raphael drifted to the back of the group again, out of earshot.

"Looks like we've got a few hot heads around," Connor muttered.

"This guild is on an unsteady truce," Raphael said, "like most of Paradisa's unity. Some of these gods are not tactical warriors. They're only bloodthirsty. But Michael would not have brought them if he didn't trust them. These are his best allies."

*And that would be why Ares isn't here,* Connor noted, recalling the tense words between Michael and the Olympian brute.

Connor craned his head back, peering back at the kaleidoscope sky. "I meant to ask you before...what's up there?"

Raphael cast a casual glance upward. "Just the sky."

"No stars? No moon?"

"Earth is a planet with stars and a moon. Paradisa is...different."

Even when Raphael's explanation was murky and irrelevant to what they were walking into, it gave Connor an additional sense of preparation. Truly, this strange new environment brought out his keenness, and it was the one thing he could ask Raphael about that always had answers.

"Well whatever it is..." Connor's mouth twitched in a solemn smile. "...it's really something."

"I think I prefer the stars." Raphael's shoulders twisted. "They make me feel insignificant."

Connor bumped his elbow against Raphael's. "And that's a good thing?"

"You worry about Clara when you're away from her. You're worried about her now."

"Yeah..."

"I can only imagine that you worry because of your mortality. She's probably just as worried about you for the same reason."

Raphael cast a forlorn look toward his brother, who walked at the front of their party. "But we are not fragile. Michael and Gabriel could go years without seeing me and not waste any moments on concern. At any point, they would still know exactly where to find me. So when I go to the Earth, and I stand beneath your stars, it's as close as I ever get to...being mortal. Because the universe is so vast and so much older than me."

It wasn't about the vastness of space, or the sense of being small. It was about hearing honesty from those who Raphael desperately desired it from. Without deathbeds to confess on, or words of love exchanged in the wake of tragedy, a compassionate angel had to wander with perpetual longing. Perhaps on Earth, surrounded by creatures who understood fragility and emotion, Raphael did feel more at home.

It shouldn't have surprised him, as Raphael's age had to be unfathomable, and the only way to sanely cope with an infinite lifespan was to feel time at an accelerated pace. For all Raphael had done so far to change his life, Connor's name might not linger in Raphael's memory. Eventually, when Connor lived out his own infinity in the Embassy of Wards, his closest celestial friend could forget he ever existed.

Such concerns must have projected from him like electricity, for Raphael laid a hand on his shoulder. "That's not to say we can't appreciate the people in our lives, of course. Even Michael admired Jeanne, you know. She was his favorite ward."

"Admired her?" The notion struck him as odd. Raphael previously said he was the only angel capable of such emotion. "I thought you were the only one with...feelings?"

Raphael took back his hand, crossing his arms over his chest. "He must be capable of something. If it wasn't possible, we wouldn't have laws against mating with humans."

Connor twisted, glancing to other members of the war guild, hoping no one overheard Raphael's blunt talk of interspecies mating.

He darted a sidelong look at his companion "Mating? What, through virgin birth magical stuff?"

"Angels are not celibate." Raphael sighed, his eyes dodging Connor slightly. "Nor can we lie, which I hope you don't take advantage of now."

The revelation nagged him, but he couldn't bring himself to ask Raphael the questions burning in his throat. Such as, *what if you were with a human you couldn't get pregnant?* Or *what about you, Raphael? You ever hook up with one of us?*

"I just didn't think you could see us that way. Humans, I mean."

"The union of humans and angels often resulted in feral offspring called nephilim. We finally outlawed it. It was getting too dangerous. Even then, it's rare for anyone to romance their ward. I suppose you would call that more of a professional relationship. You're probably the first ward who's known anything about me beyond my name and intent."

Connor's body temperature surged upward. Out of thousands of years and an unknowable number of wards, he was the first to know Raphael as more than some divine spirit or stranger with a message. Surely Raphael had protected others before, guided others, and maybe even loved them. Why did Raphael choose to reveal so much to him?

He would have to add those questions to his "post war conversation" list. Their party slowed to a halt. Badb stopped short in front of Connor, and he nearly got a face full of her heavy red mane.

A brick wall surrounded the Embassy, stretching fifteen feet tall and capped with iron spikes. It was the same décor as the one near the front entrance—perhaps it encircled the entire villa. But as Connor's eyes adjusted to the darkness, the small, iron wrought side gate shifted into focus.

As they neared the gate, Connor slipped his hands under his arms, grazing his golden guns. Raphael's gaze flickered to him for a second, and the angel's hand fell to his own sword.

They weren't alone. Every Sanctine in their crew withdrew their own weapon of choice: the feather-haired god Anhur held a crooked staff, the Avalon goddess Badb wielded a silver broadsword bigger than herself, and Hachiman slipped an arrow onto his bow. Connor flinched when a lion jumped into his peripheral vision, but it was Sekhmet in her lion headdress.

Michael pulled the gate open with a soft *creaaaak*. Connor and Raphael brought up the rear together, which didn't do much for Connor's wariness. He had never had to worry about that sort of thing in the SEALs. But then, he had always known he had a faster gun than his enemies back then, always had a sniper watching his back, and he had always known what his team was getting into.

Before progressing through the gate, Michael paused, turning to address his soldiers.

"Sekhmet, Kartikeya, Neit, and Badb will follow me in the front. Hachiman will lead the rest of you in the back. Once we confirm the perimeter is clear, I'll lead us all to the common temple." His gaze fell to his dutiful brother with a bit more softness. "And Raphael, take care of any fallen, should that happen."

The other angel nodded. "As you wish."

## 19

---

Michael and his four chosen soldiers led their invasion through the Embassy perimeter. Connor and Raphael passed through the gate last, following their group into a village of narrow streets and buildings no higher than two stories. It was the least magnificent area Connor had seen in Paradisa; it was congruent, too amalgamated from everything else in the world. There was nothing unique about the neutral colored shops and residences, or the pebbled sidewalks.

Michael raised a fist, and their entire company jerked to a halt. "Listen."

It started as a rumble—a thump of footsteps in a stampede from all four directions. Then came the growls.

Spectres swarmed in by the dozens, crowding them in from every street corner. Michael engaged them with the first strike of his flaming red sword, the fiery blade cutting through a spectre's neck. With Hachiman's battle cry, the war guild roared to action. Badb and a half-dozen other gods broke off from the group to challenge the spectres one-on-one, but Connor stayed by Raphael. And Raphael ran, skirting the edge of the battle.

Connor kept up the pace, his torso twisting as endless bullets ripped from Pollux's chamber. Blackness curled around him and Raphael, a thin miasma to hide beneath as they continued to run through the streets of the common village.

The sword and chainmail and other war guild donations weighed down Connor's body. It made his arms too heavy, threw him off balance. He wasn't hitting anything worth a shit.

"Ugh! Watch my six!" he groused to Raphael. With the angel defending their perimeter, Connor hid behind a pillar and untied gauntlets from his arms, shrugged the sword off his back, and pulled the chainmail vest over his head. There. Light and lean, just like he was used to.

The battle still raged, loud and mad, but spectres were the least strange thing about it. As Connor elbowed his way through the crowd, a red armored lioness ripped open the throat of a spectre with its teeth. When the creature turned to smoke, she leapt to her next prey with a bone-rattling roar.

*Must be Sekhmet. Avoid...*

He and Raphael circled the battlefield again, Raphael's sharp eyes looking out for the fallen. Connor's trigger fingers moved fast enough to ache, providing support from the sidelines, when a spectre launched itself between him and Raphael.

The angel spun backward, ripping his sword through the creature. Connor halted, teetering as Raphael's sword hovered near his gut.

"Sorry," Raphael said breathlessly.

"Some reflexes you've got there, Ninja Turtle."

Connor's smile snapped back into a scowl when a spectre pounced on Raphael from behind, one pale hand on his throat and another restraining his armed hand.

He jerked his gun up, aiming it over Raphael's shoulder. It was too close a shot; too complex, with the spectre wrestling Raphael to and fro so quickly that Connor couldn't focus on its face.

*He's immortal. But he won't be if that spectre takes his Icon.*

He pulled the trigger. Pain exploded below his collar as the bullet whizzed through Raphael's flesh. But the shot hit the spectre where its heart should have been, and the resulting explosion of smoke knocked them both into the nearest wall.

Connor's pain ebbed with agonizing slowness as Raphael's wound closed itself. Raphael waved away the smoke and started running again, not bothering to thank Connor audibly. But if there was anything he'd learned about Raphael, the angel was in a perpetual state of gratitude.

They ran near the wall of the common temple, beneath indigo-stained windows. Connor continued to fire Pollux, hitting far fewer spectres than he should have. Hephaestus's weapons were great, but these bastards moved quickly. With every nonfatal wound, they tore into smoke and reformed unaffected. Only deadly shots nabbed them for good.

"Look out!" Connor yelled, barely audible over the clank and roar of battle. Two spectres cornered them, out of Raphael's sword range. Connor grabbed the back of Raphael's coat and yanked him to a halt, lifting Castor over the angel's shoulder.

Before he fired, one of Hachiman's arrows shattered the stained glass above them. Connor ducked, covering his head as the shards descended. The spectres screeched as a monsoon of colored glass rained upon them, scratching their undead flesh.

Connor grimaced, firing Castor aimlessly toward the two distracted spectres. The gunshot threatened to pop his ears. But after a breath, the kiss of smoke stroked his face. Castor had done its job.

He opened his eyes in time to witness Badb flying into the temple wall behind Raphael, her armor clanking and crushing bone. She collapsed, red hair falling over her face like tendrils from Raphael's weeping willows.

Connor aimed Pollux at the spectre who had thrown Badb, but it evaded his bullets with her Celtic hair comb in hand. He swore, lowering the pistol.

When he turned around, Raphael was kneeling at Badb's side. She groaned through gritted teeth, a hand clawing at her chest plate. The faint cuts on her forehead didn't heal as they should have.

Raphael's hands fell upon her. "Stay still. I'll heal you."

Badb squirmed in her armor. "I don't need your help, angel."

"You have multiple broken bones, and your Icon has been taken." Connor had been around Raphael long enough to sense a note of impatience. "If I heal you, you can fight more."

The goddess from Avalon huffed, but protested no more. *War deities and their pride. God forbid anyone keep them from collapsing upon the battlefield with a war cry and some gushing wounds.*

The spectres seemed uninterested in Raphael's healing work. Connor stooped beside Raphael, crouched in a safe position to shoot from the cover. In his shooting spree, he was momentarily distracted by Michael who mowed down spectres with his red sword and raw power. All that skill and grace, thousands of years of battle painting his movements. Fucking epic.

But in a moment, everything shifted.

The spectres exploded in one unified burst, casting a blanket of smoke across the battlefield. The shift from roar to silence lurched Connor's gut. No, this was *wrong.*

Something was coming.

Footsteps. The cackle of low laughter. And through the scattering darkness, a lean figure with a jackal headdress. Set.

---

Clara's hand slid along a banister made of marble, cool to the touch. Saraswati occupied much of the space before her, tall and lean and with four arms in constant motion. She led the way up the library's grand staircase, while Aphrodite and Hephaestus brought up the rear.

At the fourth-floor landing, a marble statue of a woman held a wooden sign. The letters were initially foreign, like all Sancti runes. But as Clara stared, they rearranged and blurred into focus. *Level Four —Amaravati, Tian, Avalon.*

She blinked, rubbing her head. "How can I read that?"

Saraswati shrugged. "The Guild of Words and Wisdom enchanted every word in the library to shift into the reader's native tongue."

"Neat. So that's who runs this place?"

"We founded this library shortly after the unity. Every kingdom donated copies of their histories, discoveries, culture. The Guild prescribed that to have a truly united Paradisa, information must be transparent and accessible for all."

"And from what I've heard," Hephaestus added, stopping on a higher step, "not everyone's history agrees."

Saraswati tutted, not unkindly. "Those rumors are quite true. Although, our histories agree more than you may expect. Through my reading over the centuries, I've found that many kingdoms have different words for identical concepts."

As they meandered through the maze of shelves, Saraswati casually plucked a half dozen tomes off the shelves and cradled them in the crook of her arm. At the end of the stacks, she pulled open a door —amber, like the front—and ushered them inside.

"Whoa." Clara craned her head back. The private study room was no less modest than the rest of the library. A painting of the Concordia lagoon shined on the ten-foot-high ceiling. Every kingdom had its spot around the lake and a bridge leading to the central capital, just like she'd seen when walking into Paradisa for the first time. Of course, she hadn't seen it from above, as it was presented here. Every kingdom around the capital like spokes on a wheel...

Saraswati dropped her books on to one of the wooden tables with an inelegant slam. The noise was enough to sober Clara's awe and drag her back to the task at hand.

"Are you sure you want to open this dialogue?" Saraswati asked, brushing a lock of hair out of her face with one hand. Two others rested on her hips, and the fourth gestured to Aphrodite.

The goddess of love straightened her posture. "We're certain. We need to know. The fate of Paradisa depends on it."

Saraswati sighed, pulling one large green tome off her stack and laying it open on the table. "As you wish."

A beam of light shot up from the book, filling the room with a jade hue. Clara blinked away stars. The color morphed quickly until it divided and shaded itself, and figures formed from the light.

*This,* she had to mentally laugh, *is going to be a picture book.*

Hephaestus pulled up a chair and plopped down in it. He rubbed his bad knee, sucking his teeth, and Clara's own knee spasmed. Sometimes she was able to block it out or suppress the secondhand pain. But after a long day of walking, the pain was hard to ignore.

She remained standing. It gave her a better view of the majesty floating at waist level.

Saraswati rounded the table and pointed to the moving images before them. "Before there were humans, and before there were Sanctines, there were only Ascendants."

A mountainous landscape grew from the green light, and with it, life. Something walked beside the cliffs, their exact appearance obscured by darkness.

"What did they look like?" Clara asked. "I can't tell."

Saraswati shrugged. "We do not have record of that here. But all our kingdoms point to similar ideas. The Asgardians called them frost giants. The Avalonians thought of them as Fomorii. In Amaravati, we call them Asuras. But they are all terms for the same creatures—leviathans who ruled the cosmos. Their power was limitless. Some accounts say they could swallow the whole sky."

The green projection morphed again. A blurry scene came to life, its visuals as obscure as the Ascendants, but Clara could *smell* the scene—burning, split flesh, pain. Saraswati's skin looked dull in this hue, and half the scene's shadows obscured her face.

"It wasn't long before the Creators learned they'd made a mistake. That the power the Ascendants held had driven them mad."

Clara's brows rose. "Creators? Plural?"

Hephaestus smirked. "I thought you said you weren't...what were those fancy words again? Singularly dogmatic?"

She lowered her chin. "I know. That's just...there are *some* things I thought I could trust."

"Don't have a crisis about it. Eden still insists there's only one. Actually, we think there was one as well. So, you're in good company. None of us really know, so no use speculating."

"Speak for yourself." Saraswati cut her eyes at him, before continuing with her story. "The Creators, or Creator, devised a plan to destroy the Ascendants and bring peace back to the universe. But they knew they could not kill their once-beloved creation. Ascendants can never die...unless they are used to create new life."

A green hand reached up from the center of the imagery, holding a golden sword by the hilt. The blade turned, thrust into one of the shadowed Ascendant creatures, and beams of light exploded from the wound.

"They used the Sword of Creation, the tool originally used to forge the Ascendants from soil, to split the Ascendants into two new races."

*Holy crap.* Clara took a step back into the study table where Hephaestus had taken a seat. She lowered herself into the chair beside him, watching helplessly as the Ascendant ripped down the center, each of its halves writhing until two new shapes emerged.

"Sanctines and humans," she whispered, before Saraswati continued the lecture. The Hindu goddess looked upon her, with a terse nod.

"Indeed."

Clara glanced to Hephaestus and Aphrodite both, looking for any evidence that they knew about this. Hephaestus's jaw had grown slack while Aphrodite wore a pensive frown.

Saraswati pointed to the two new actors in her story. "This event was known as The Fissure. And the Creators were merciless. Using the Sword of Creation, they fissured every Ascendant in existence to create their new species. And to ensure that humans and Sanctines could never again reform into these monsters, they split our people between three realms. Humans, to the corporeal Earth, and us, to the spiritual realms of Paradisa and Abyssus."

"Is that when they hid the Sword?" Hephaestus asked.

"Correct. So that it could never be used again to create life."

Clara wiped her fringe out of her eyes with a shaky hand. "Is that what the spectres are, then? They're these...Ascendants? But that doesn't make any sense. Spectres are totally mortal. They're tough, but they're nothing like what this story says."

"I know of these spectres. Athena has spoken of them in the Guild of Words and Wisdom." Saraswati closed the green tome, leaving the room dark and quiet now. "Whatever they were made to do, it was not to be Ascendants. I don't believe they can be reformed into the sum of their parts. Even the demi-gods and nephilim, our offspring with humans, are not Ascendants either."

"This is fascinating," Hephaestus said, "but what does this have to do with Michael and Set? And Athena? Sure, we can see why Set was interested in the Sword, but..."

"Patience," was all Saraswati said as she opened a purple book next.

This projection filled the room with cities and life: pyramids, temples, mosques and towers. Kings sat on thrones, angels wielded swords of fire, and deep within a hidden valley...

Shadowed creatures.

Saraswati walked around the room, two hands clasped behind her back while the others gestured to the scene. "What the Creators did not realize is that not all Ascendants were killed in the Fissure. A small handful had escaped and had hidden for thousands and thousands of years."

"These buildings are from our time," Hephaestus murmured.

"The Inquisition was from our time," Saraswati said. "It was a secret movement, led by Michael of Eden, to investigate the chance of Ascendants having infiltrated Paradisa. There was suspicion that Ascendants could change their form and take the identity of Sanctines already living."

In an Egyptian-looking temple, a mass of dark purple smoke transformed into a regal-looking man with an Ankh staff.

"Osiris," Aphrodite said, almost sounding forlorn. Clara couldn't blame her. She herself waited for the other shoe to drop.

"Osiris was the king of Aaru, and beloved by all his people." A magenta crowd of gods surrounded their leader, lifting their staffs and cheering. Osiris nodded humbly to them, one by one. "But for reasons known only to him, Michael thought differently. Long before the unity was even a thought, he asked Set, Osiris's own brother, to be Inquisitor of Aaru and to vanquish the Ascendant who'd replaced their king. And in an unusual show of solidarity, Set said yes. Their orders came from the Creators—a higher power than either of them."

"Was he right?" Clara gulped. "*Was* Osiris an Ascendant?"

Saraswati took a deep breath, watching the grisly scene unfold before them. "Yes. Set must have known for sure when Osiris refused to die."

The imagery turned violent. Set's curved sword flashed through sprays of red, until Set stood blood-soaked and surrounded by a dozen dismembered pieces of his brother's body.

"Set scattered the remains of Osiris across the universe so that he could never be reassembled into his Ascendant form. It was the best he could do, for Ascendants cannot be killed, only Fissured, with the Sword of Creation.

"But as far as Aaru knew," Saraswati continued, as the scene fast-forwarded into an angry mob of hands pulling on Set's clothes. "Set had just murdered their beloved king. They thought he was vying for the throne. Michael had sworn him to secrecy and had known society would upend if we knew Ascendants had infiltrated our kingdoms. So, they cast him out as a pariah. And when he asked Michael to intervene on his behalf, the general refused. Set followed orders to save his kingdom, but his leader betrayed him."

She closed the purple book, and the ambient lights in the study room returned to normal brightness. Somberly, she said, "I'm afraid that's all I have."

"If all of that was secret, then why was it in a book here?" Clara asked, reaching for the purple volume. Maybe she was a child of the 21st century, but *check your sources* had been ground in her head since grade school. When you grew up with Wikipedia as your go-to information source, it was a given.

She cracked open the pages. Green-ink hieroglyphs morphed into English as she flipped through. Several pages were just rants—paragraphs and paragraphs with no punctuation, no breaths taken, of rage against dynasties and betrayal.

"It seems to have been a diary of Set's," Saraswati explained. "It was only recovered a few hundred years ago, somewhere in Concordia. It was before we'd enchanted it to be universal, so whoever found it couldn't read the hieroglyphs, and they donated it to us. When I first deciphered it, I...I thought it might have been the rantings of a madman. But I started to wonder if it was true. You are the only ones to ever come here mentioning the Inquisition."

"Set called Athena an Inquisitor," Clara said. A shaky, clammy feeling like a fever clung to her skin. "But if they were both on the same side, why would he want to kill her?"

A booming voice broke through the amber door, cutting the conversation short.

"HEPHAESTUS! I know you're here, you coward!"

Clara rushed out the door and to the fourth-floor railing. In the center of the lobby stood a burly man. His white teeth glinted in the dim light, large like tombstones. Black leather armor shielded his body from head to toe, and his hand rested on a large sword against his hip.

Clara retreated to the study room before the man saw her. She glanced between Hephaestus and Aphrodite, who had both grown pale.

"Is that who I think it is?"

Hephaestus closed his eyes. "Ares. He's found me."

---

There was nothing comforting about a silent battlefield, for any reason. In Connor's many years of experience, it was always the aftermath of brutality or a harbinger of doom.

The spectres that had vanished reformed from the smoke on the eaves of surrounding buildings. They crouched like gargoyles, looking down onto the square, waiting for Set's command.

Set circled their party, spinning his klopesh sword with a casual flourish. "I'll admit, Michael...you've always been clever. How did you know I wouldn't flee the Embassy as soon as your brother found me here?"

Michael never left his defensive stance, with knees bent slightly and shoulders hunched. "Because you have nowhere else to hide."

Set stopped, and pivoted toward his rival. "We followed the same masters. The same orders. And while I became the Pariah of Aaru, you rose to General of the War Guild? Fascinating, how that worked out."

"You were never promised glory. You were never promised anything, except the continued survival of our world. Be grateful Paradisa is still standing because of your sacrifice."

The Egyptian god threw back his head, barking a laugh that sounded almost like a wolf's howl. "You think being able to accept your definition of peace is enough, when my entire country has been taken from me? You think I care about the continuity of our world when I have been banished from it? Oh, Michael. By Ra's eye, I am finished accepting your excuses. Why not end this, once and for all? One-on-one."

Raphael grabbed Michael by the arm, yanking his brother to face him. Panic sunk into Connor like cold rain.

"Michael, don't do this. We have a small army with us. We can take him together!"

The General took a deep breath, and reached up to cover Raphael's hand with his own. For a split second, it looked like a tender gesture. But soon Connor realized, he was merely prying Raphael's hand off his armor.

"I accept his challenge. I won't put the rest of you at risk, not when I can end this myself."

"This is suicide, please!"

Michael looked over Raphael's head to set his steely gaze upon Connor. "Keep him safe."

Connor nodded, their locked gaze lingering for a moment too long. Michael broke it apart with a fist in the air, turning to enter the arena.

Connor didn't need to be told to protect Raphael; it had become his rightful place. Michael probably knew that, but perhaps he wanted it stated aloud from his own mouth. For Raphael to know that he was the same sort of older brother as Connor, and not the heartless statue he pretended to be.

Raphael radiated with dread. It practically pulsed off his skin. Connor did his best to repel it, keeping the bond between them firm as always, but maybe he should have been absorbing it instead. Maybe sharing the burden instead of rejecting his partner.

Connor settled for resting a hand on Raphael's shoulder and refusing to move. He couldn't force himself to be ready on the inside, but hell, he could do this.

Michael and Set faced each other. The spectres leapt down from the ledges at once, half-turning to smoke to make a gentle landing around the dueling opponents. Almost peacefully, they scattered into an evenly-spaced ring, forming a perimeter fence of cold bodies between the onlookers and the fight. Raphael tensed under Connor's hand.

"It'll be okay," Connor whispered. "He can take him."

Empty words, of course. What the hell did he know? Even if they weren't bonded, Raphael could probably sense the bullshit platitude. But Raphael, the literal saint, still managed a weak, grateful smile.

"It's time to remove our Icons," Set said, lifting an ankh necklace over his head. "We fight as mortals today."

"My Icon is my sword," Michael retorted. "What shall I fight with, then?"

A spectre stepped out of the lineup to pluck Set's ankh from his hand for safekeeping. Set glanced back to Michael, smirking. "I'm sure your war guild has something more than capable."

Athena broke through the barricade of spectres to join Michael's side, and unsheathed her impressive blade. "Let mine serve you, General. I've longed for his blood on it for centuries."

"Well, well…" Set sneered. "As if I needed more motivation to win. I certainly won't be dying by your blade today."

The goddess of war narrowed her eyes. "How certain were you of victory when you sent the spectres to kill me the first time? Or the second?"

184

"Spectres can only do so much." He twirled his klopesh. "I'll be doing this myself."

Athena retreated to her original spot, and this time, the ring of spectres interlocked arms after she passed. The motion went around the entire perimeter, until none would be able to penetrate their barrier without a real fight.

Michael lifted Athena's sapphire sword in Set's direction, his eyes narrowed.

"Let us begin."

Set leapt into action first, running full sprint at Michael. He raised his klopesh above his head with both hands and jumped ten feet, a carnal roar escaping him as he embodied death from above.

It was a stupidly aggressive move, and Michael clearly knew it. The archangel dodged it easily, leaving Set with nothing but friction sparks as his klopesh hit the cobblestones.

Michael circled him on the balls of his feet, crouched with the grace of a predator. Set straightened his back and stormed forward again, the klopesh curved in a defensive barrier across his face. Their blades struck together with a clank that made Connor's teeth hurt.

The fight extended for minutes until Connor had to actively remind himself to breathe. Every time the klopesh sliced a small nick into Michael's arm or leg, a gasp tore from the crowd. Near-misses on Set were cheered for, which only seemed to spurn the pariah into harsher attacks.

But unlike before, when his aggressiveness made him messy, he now crossed into the territory of dishonorable rage. The klopesh swung relentlessly from arms that never seemed to tire, and Michael stumbled with the effort to block every attack.

Connor looked down at Raphael's hands. One gripped his sword hilt, as if expecting to draw his weapon at any moment. But the other found itself buried in the fabric of Connor's jacket, knuckles stark against the black denim.

He looked back up at the angel's tense profile, tight as a guitar string. "Hey, it'll be o—"

And in one merciless, painfully unsatisfying instant, the klopesh curved across Michael's throat, cleanly separating his head from his body.

It was over, just like that. One missed step, one unpredictable strike, and they'd lost.

A strangled noise tore out of Raphael's throat. "NO!"

The entire world continued around them, but Connor's focus locked onto the general's crumpling body. The brutality of the scene – Michael's wide-eyed face rolling across the stone, the stump of his neck pouring blood onto Set's leather boots—remained mercifully brief. Michael barely went limp before his body faded into golden particles and rose to the sky, taken by the wind to wherever dead angels assumed.

The square erupted into war cries and the slick sound of unsheathed swords. The perimeter of spectres roared in return, stepping back to tighten their ring around Set and Michael's remains. Set reclaimed his ankh necklace from an outstretched spectre hand and casually lowered it over his head, the godhood returning to him with an all-body glow.

Raphael sprinted in a blue blur, sword already lit, ripping through the nearest pair of spectres like tissue paper. The sheer force of his movement was enough to knock others halfway across the square. As soon as he was within arms-length of Set, he swung recklessly toward the Aaru god, his fury asphyxiating all senses. It gripped Connor's lungs, rose up through his veins, and replaced his own emotions.

Connor rushed toward the center of the arena too, the world falling into one piercing note ringing in his ears. He focused long enough to nab headshots with the remaining spectres Raphael missed, but the creatures continued to emerge from every nook and cranny of the Embassy.

But halfway to reaching Raphael, sharp pain ripped across his thigh. His leg crumpled beneath him, and his body fell ungracefully onto the stone. Immediately, he twisted and shot a round behind himself for the spectre that had scratched him. Craning his head, he caught sight of blood gushing from Raphael's leg, and Set's klopesh sword pulling away from the angel. *He did this.*

Set placed a firm kick across Raphael's face – *fuck, Connor's jaw burned* – before fleeing with four spectres shielding him on every side.

"No!" Connor shouted, lifting Castor from the cold ground. He unloaded the bottomless chamber toward him, but hand shook too hard to aim properly. Set ran unaffected, bullets easily whizzing past him.

Connor swore, pushing himself up. Someone else would have to chase that bastard; he had a far greater cause to take care of.

He ran backwards, shooting at the fleeing spectres until he collapsed next to his wrecked companion. Raphael's white knuckles gripped Michael's vacant breastplate, his shoulders wracking.

"Michael..."

The rawness of Raphael's despair crushed him. Connor's eyes swelled as the pain of loss hollowed him out.

Connor pulled Raphael away from Michael's armored shell. Rather than responding to the comfort, Raphael trembled more violently. His eyes glowed with supernova light. Soon, there was nothing but the rumble, and the internal wailing of Raphael's pain.

Connor peered up, stunned to see the rest of their company frozen in place. He scanned the crowd for Badb, whose arms were raised with her broadsword in one grip. She wasn't stopped in time, as her eyes flitted with frustration, but not a muscle twitched.

Raphael's body pulsed with heat. Air rustled around him, blowing dark hair back from his forehead. Connor continued to cling to him, pulling the angel closer to his chest and ignoring how Raphael's skin nearly burned him.

Connor gritted his teeth while Raphael's hate and horror poisoned him. The painful sensation pulled at his navel as though the cord between them was snapping. It was almost as raw as their binding ceremony, but in an entirely different way. That was physical pain. This was mental pain: a rushing, tingling wave roaming over the back of his skull. Like a tumor had grown and was about to rupture.

*I have to push back.*

He struggled, clenching everything as if he could physically push his heart into Raphael's chest. What could Connor give to soothe the sting of losing a brother, a brother Raphael had struggled with until the last moments; a brother he was never sure loved him?

*He has me.*

He wasn't Raphael's brother. He wasn't divine. But he'd had an unusual connection with Raphael from the moment they'd first met. And from the moment he'd gone from being a human to being a ward, when his hand had been clasped in Raphael's. How bizarre, what he had done—giving a piece of his soul to this man, a man he hardly knew, but whom he trusted. And Raphael, whose lonely posture seemed to strengthen ever since that moment, filled with newfound purpose.

All across the temple, gods and spectres levitated off the ground. The spectres whined with a high-pitched vibrato. Smoky tendrils escaped their pores as their loose facsimile of life threatened to unravel.

Connor hurt down to his molecules, too. He grabbed Raphael's face and pressed their foreheads together, forcing himself to peer into those blinding white eyes.

"This isn't you! You don't want to hurt anyone!"

Screams rose from their army. Connor would never forget the heartbreaking wails from the war guild, as Raphael's chaos slowly tore them apart. Connor dug deeper, calling more intimate memories to his mental viewfinder: standing in Raphael's common room before leaving, discussing his collection of ward tokens. Laying in the dark, talking about Lucifer, the first time he'd heard anything about Raphael's life before they'd met.

Raphael smiling at him in Hephaestus and Aphrodite's parlor —*"perhaps it is you that could not resist me"*—and the warm flush crawling over Connor's skin at those words.

"I'm not going to let you do this!" He buried his hands into Raphael's hair, clinging tighter. He struck a mental sledgehammer into the barricade between them. His pleas would never work with inhibitions. And so long as he held himself back, he wasn't truly being a ward.

As Connor prepared himself to fail, to be ripped apart by the invisible force along with the rest of the war guild, the manic glow in Raphael's eyes drifted away. White faded to make way for aquamarine, glossy with stunned tears.

The temple windows shattered in unison, raining upon them with colored glass. Raphael collapsed against Connor's chest, but nothing was visible through the dark mist. Connor bowed his head, holding his friend until the smoke subsided. *Please tell me you didn't kill our team. I don't know how to tell you if you did.*

Hachiman and the others hit the ground with a unanimous cacophony of metal hitting stone. Then, voices—stunned, concerned, and pissed, but alive.

Raphael stilled, unconscious against Connor. Although Connor's emotions were his own again, they didn't fit correctly back into his chest. Some felt new, uprooted, or exposed like a raw organ.

Despite Raphael's lack of consciousness, his expression retained tense exhaustion. Connor gently touched Raphael's tight brow, his jawline, admiring the sharp curvature of his face. Connor hated when men were called beautiful, but Raphael was something close. Lovely. Lovely and terrifying.

His thumb grazed downward, barely brushing the corner of Raphael's parted lips, while his other fingers moved over his black hair. If only his touch could buffer the angel's stress away, relax the muscles beneath it. As it was, caressing Raphael only calmed himself.

Badb's heavy footsteps stormed closer. "What the hell was that? He could have killed us all!"

"He just saw his brother murdered!" Connor snapped, his embrace tightening around Raphael. "Have some fucking respect!"

But he couldn't blame her, not really. Not when he looked down at Raphael with a heavy sense of horror. Not when this gentle being, asleep in his arms, almost ripped apart an army by the atoms.

## 20

Ares was everything Hephaestus had described, and worse. Clara flinched with every decibel of his voice echoing through the library. Perhaps some of it was Hephaestus's own terror drowning her, but she had plenty of her own reaction to the rage of a man like that.

Saraswati pushed her way through the study room door, and spun to face her visitors. "There is only one entrance out of here. You will have to go past him to escape. But if you stay quiet, I can go down there and distract him."

Hephaestus clutched his hair. "No, no. It's too close. He'll see us."

"There are shelves down there." Clara gripped Hephaestus's arm, shaking him slightly. "We can hide behind them, get to the front, then make a run for it."

"And if he sees us, I could persuade him not to follow," Aphrodite pointed out. "I won't let him touch us."

Saraswati gestured to the far wall of the level. "There *is* an alternate staircase. Take it down, and I'll take the main. Hurry!"

That seemed to sway Hephaestus enough, for he moved past them and headed toward the outermost wall. They traced the wall and found an alternate staircase, much less majestic than the one spiraling up to the oculus. It was narrow, tucked behind a simple archway, with marble steps and a walnut railing. Clara and the gods rushed down all four flights, slowing when they encountered the first-floor landing. Clara moved herself to the front and craned her head to look through the dividing archway. Through the rows of shelves, she could glimpse Saraswati creeping closer to Ares in the rotunda.

The Hindu goddess grabbed Ares' shoulder with two hands and jerked him to face her, merciless.

"What are you doing here?"

"I know he's in here."

"I have no idea what you're talking about, and I will not let you bring your petty vengeance into my library." Saraswati pulled a jagged dagger from the corner of her desk. She lifted its tip to the man's throat. "Get. Out."

"Let's keep moving," Aphrodite whispered against Clara's ear. "Quietly."

Clara tiptoed ahead, using the brawling voices of Saraswati and Ares as her guide. With the gaps between the stacks, she made sure their backs were turned before she dove behind the next shelf. Aphrodite followed as silent and swift as an assassin, but Hephaestus moved painfully slow, too carefully buffering the noise of his cane. Clara's breath stopped every time he crossed the two feet of empty space between shelves.

They passed five shelves in the outer ring before arriving at the last one, where nothing but empty space waited between them and the door. *Ten, thirty, sixty feet?*

Sixty feet they had to cross without Ares catching up.

Her pulse pounded so loudly that Ares could probably hear it. He was a war god, which could have meant any number of powers. Heightened senses, brute strength...whatever he had going for him, the receiving end would be unpleasant.

She bent her knees and peeked around the bookshelf corner. Saraswati and Ares circled each other in the central pavilion.

"Get out, Olympian. You know you can't harm me."

"I'd have a hard time killing you." Ares smirked, all teeth and wild

191

eyes. He crossed the rotunda to a wall-mounted candle lantern. "I can harm you plenty."

In a swift movement, he ripped the lantern off the wall and hurled it at the nearest bookshelf, which happened to be the one Clara stood behind. She shrieked and fell backward as fire exploded inches before her face, engulfing the shelf in flame. Gentle hands caught her before she hit the hard floor, but she thrashed on instinct.

She was blind. All she could do was feel the heat from every inch around her, and hear Saraswati wailing over the burning books. Aphrodite moaned her name, shaking her.

Then, the scariest sound of all: Ares's guttural, triumphant, voice.

"Hephaestus! I see you!"

Stomping footsteps. Clara blinked as fast as a hummingbird's wings, struggling not to whimper. Some light blotted into her vision, but the rest remained shrouded.

She stammered, "Oh God. Oh God, he knows! We have to run!"

A hand firmly wrapped around her wrist and pulled her up. Aphrodite's blurry outline looked toward something, and she spoke with a voice drenched in fierce harmonics. "Stay back!"

Ares' voice drew close, so close. "I know better than that, Aphrodite!"

Clara looked everywhere, *anywhere,* to find Ares, but her surroundings remained like melted watercolors. She followed the sound of his voice, and her slowly restoring vision landed upon a far too close silhouette, with his hands raised around his ears. *If he can't hear her, he doesn't have to obey her. Oh no, oh no...*

Her logic had fried. Running from killers and demons was something Connor could stand up against. Connor was bad at puzzle games, but at least he could be brave. Without an answer to find or something to build, with nothing but the last minutes of her life flashing before her in a storm of fire and danger, she was nothing more than an anchor of meat.

"Run!" Hephaestus shoved Clara with an iron-hot hand. "Run! Go!"

Aphrodite's grasp found hers and pulled her toward the entrance. Clara pushed her way through the amber door and separated from the other woman, teetering as her vision returned enough to regain balance.

A pang hit Clara's hip, bowing her over. Beyond the amber door, Hephaestus was still in the library with his cane spear in one hand and a fistful of fire in the other. The world seemed to disappear as she watched Hephaestus and Ares circle each other. Golden blood leaked out of her companion's side.

She had to go back in. She couldn't stand around and watch him fight a monster. If Hephaestus died, she would die anyway.

She unhooked one axe from her back harness and darted toward the amber door. But Aphrodite's strong arms engulfed her, lifting her off the ground.

"Clara, don't!"

"He's going to kill him! I can't leave him!"

A pulsing throb of pain snaked from the back of her knee to below her calf, sharper than Hephaestus's normal leg pain. Clara refocused on the library, her eyes stinging as she searched for Hephaestus. Beneath Ares's smug smirk, Hephaestus was curled on the marble floor, a hand on his knee.

*Stand up. Please stand up!*

He never had the chance. Ares held him down with a booted foot and a bloody scowl.

"NO!" Before her feet could move, Ares slashed at Hephaestus's throat, spilling golden blood across the tile.

"No..." Clara choked, her voice stolen. She collapsed to her knees, clutching her stinging throat while Aphrodite screamed Hephaestus's name as if in a tunnel.

With Hephaestus's first wound nearly healed, Ares struck the flat side of his sword against Hephaestus's temple. Consciousness vanished from her friend's eyes, and he slumped onto the library floor completely limp.

Clara's head pounded. Her vision realigned enough to see Ares throw an unconscious Hephaestus over his shoulder and grab his cane.

*Saraswati! Aphrodite, somebody. Somebody do something!*

The door opened, and Ares sauntered through. Aphrodite rushed up to him with her dagger already in hand and got in one violent swipe to his face. He yowled, staggering backwards, his face a mess.

Aphrodite approached for a second strike, but all Ares had to do was lift his sword.

She took the attack full on, gasping as the blade sunk between her ribs. Ares smirked with indifference as he stabbed his former lover. Aphrodite slumped against a column with the sword still buried inside of her. When Ares yanked it out, she slid to the ground, leaving a golden streak on the column behind her. Clara watched him from the ground, her hands curling into fists.

Clara's entire body groaned as she forced herself to her feet. She ran down the steps, unhooking her other axe along the way. At the base of the stairs, she hurled one axe to spiral clumsily at Ares's back.

Ares snatched the handle as it sailed by him. His teeth glinted in the glow of the red portal, and for a moment, he looked like a vampire.

Clara gaped. As she leaned back to hurl the other axe more furiously at the war god, Ares opened his fist, releasing the first one. Reflexively, she lifted a hand to catch it.

Ares shouted, "I've heard it's terribly painful, when we leave our wards in other worlds." He edged his way into the portal, Hephaestus still unconscious on his shoulder. "Enjoy your death, human."

He turned to cross the crimson glow, and Clara's legs moved faster than she ever thought possible. Despite her speed, she was hit with the separation as soon as it occurred. Her insides gnawed worse than the bonding ceremony, igniting her nerves in shock. She stumbled, but tightened her fists to cling desperately to her weapons. Ares had been gone a half second, and she had four more feet to cross. *I'm going to make it.*

In that brief span of time, perhaps from the drunken flash of pain, she imagined Connor standing on the edge of the portal, his hands outstretched toward her. If he had been there for real, he would have watched her with the most helpless, exhausted face. Because Ares was right. She would die if she did not go through this portal. She could already feel it happening.

So she went, replacing the plaza with red nothingness, immersing herself in blazing heat.

---

C onnor paced the Embassy's common temple. Every step was a new balancing act on piles of rubble. Some of the towering statues of kings and saints had fallen and had cracks in their faces big enough for Connor to slip a hand into. Their white marble eyes stared blankly upward as he climbed over their broken bodies.

Over a half dozen familiar faces remained intact around him including Badb, Anhur, and Hachiman, although their expressions had lost all arrogance.

Who could blame them?

Raphael, now conscious, stood over the altar with his arms crossed over his chest. He stared through the remaining war guild members and ruined brick. Connor ascended the steps leading up to him.

"I'm so sorry, Raphael."

What else was there to say? No one had ever said the right thing when Eric died. He wasn't even sure what they could have said. Grief was an inconsolable thing.

"He told me to take care of you." Connor's voice hollowed out as he remembered Michael's enigmatic eyes—the eyes of a brother whose emotions were foreign, but present.

Raphael pressed his hands onto the altar's surface, hunching forward. His sleeves had rolled up to the elbow, revealing pale forearms that flexed under his weight. "He didn't want me in the way."

"He didn't want you to get hurt. Straight from his mouth. Why do you think I try to keep Clara out of all this shit? I'll always worry about her, even when I know she can take care of herself." His heart hurt. Although his soul was bound to Raphael, sometimes it felt like Clara owned a piece of him too, and it ached when she was too far away. "Can't hold people back just because you love 'em, though."

*And you can't hold onto them when you lose them either.* Death had stolen Eric from him, but he'd long acknowledged the senselessness of hate crimes, and his helplessness in the face of them. At least those criminals served time. Roger ratting out his love for another man had been the singular ruinous choice of an individual, though, and it was a choice with no punishment to the perpetrator. All it had stolen was *Connor's* control; had robbed him of his dreams and created a void of unresolved business. And in that way, he had never related more to Raphael.

Connor licked his lips, rambling to fill the void. "You know I can feel your pain. And I've felt loss before too, okay? I know how it feels to look down and see someone you love just lying there—"

"I've lost plenty!" Raphael whipped around, cutting him with the sharp, cold, biting words. "But it wasn't supposed to be him. He was the one person I could never lose."

The temple rumbled, just slightly, and pebbles echoed as they fell from the damaged pillars. Connor extended his hands, drawing closer with tentative steps, as if approaching a wild bear. He dared to lay his hands on Raphael's shoulders, and the rumbling subsided.

"We're going to find Set. We're not going to let him get away with what he's done."

"But can I rest if someone else has the satisfaction of killing him?" Raphael grimaced, the anger looking so out of place on his peaceful features.

"Hey, don't talk like that. That's not you."

Raphael untangled from him, eyes narrowed. "And what do you know of me, Connor?"

Perhaps Raphael's meltdown was too fresh in Connor's memory, but the reality of those words physically chilled him. He wasn't sure how to describe what Raphael had done to the temple. It had been complete abandonment of control. The horrified moans from their comrades as Raphael ripped them apart at the atoms...

Connor spread his arms wide, then let them fall limply back to his sides. "You're right. I don't know much. But I know you're a good man. You cared about me and Clara before you had any reason to.

You've never given me a reason not to trust you. So, let me save you for once. I don't understand what you did to this place, but I don't *care.*"

Raphael's mouth tilted. "I already know what I did. Angels have the belief of over two billion people behind us. It makes us...immensely powerful, even among Sanctines. My brothers aren't bothered by the possibility of destruction. But the power always frightened me too much to experiment. I've always been content being this way, so I never tried to learn."

"I like you this way, too." *Like* was an understatement, but, no time for thoughts like that. "And if you don't learn to control it, something a lot worse could happen."

Raphael let out a breath, finally unburdened from anger. "If it weren't for you, something a lot worse would have happened, Connor."

The statement wrapped around Connor's heart, pulling snug. It was nice to hear that Raphael found him useful, but the gratitude Raphael sent to his chest was even better.

"I'm human. I've lost people before, in ways that weren't fair. And I am *here for you,* okay?"

The crush of boots over wood and dust drew closer. Hachiman approached, with his bow slung across his back. That set Connor's worries at ease more than anything in the past ten minutes.

"All the spectres have gone, along with Set," Hachiman confirmed. "We don't know where they headed."

Raphael rose with Michael's breastplate in hand. He delicately offered it to Hachiman, reminding Connor of military funerals where they handed American flags to widows.

"We yield to your command," Raphael murmured. "You're the general now."

Hachiman's face tightened. He seemed like a quiet soldier, not a violent one, always buffering Michael's aggression with whispered advice.

After some pacing and stroking his chin, Hachiman came to a decision. "Our primary mission should be to return to Concordia and report this to the Guild of Law and Justice. Set has declared war on Paradisa, and we will need to gather troops. But I will assign someone to stay here and look after the Embassy. They may alert us if Set or spectres return. I don't want this area under enemy control again."

"We'll follow, but Connor and I must leave you once we reach the capital." Raphael glanced to Connor, sucking in a breath. "We have business in the Claustrum."

Connor had only heard that word in reference to one person. "Lucifer?"

"What I know, and what everyone has always known, is that Lucifer wants Michael dead. Perhaps this is what Set could offer, in exchange for the Sword's location."

"So you think Michael was right, about them working together?" Connor ran a hand over his hair, blowing out a harsh breath. "Wouldn't Lucifer want the satisfaction of killing Michael himself?"

"That's why we need to speak with him. At best, perhaps he knows where Set is headed to next. If we go through the omniportal in Concordia, I can take us there."

Connor tilted his head. "Who's to say that he'll be honest with us when we get there?"

"Angels can't lie, even him. He may not be forthcoming, but if we are careful, he cannot lead us astray." Raphael attempted a smile, but it came out as a grimace. "Maybe he'll respond well to me. I wasn't the one who put him down there."

Connor snorted inside his head. As much as he respected Raphael's knowledge of this world, Lucifer was probably called *the great deceiver* for a reason.

---

The Concordia portal dumped Clara at the top of a rocky hill inside some kind of cavern. She keeled over with her hands on her knees, gasping. The phantom pain of separation ebbed, but its sharp effects lingered. They hadn't been apart long, so Ares couldn't have gone far.

She mustered the energy to run, following some torches to a nearby archway. Beneath the arch, a trail twisted downhill to a deteriorating town of charred, broken buildings. Corinthian columns were among the toppled ruins, but the town was too dilapidated to reconstruct in her mind.

A murky green river cut through the town, lacing the air with briny acidity. Jagged boardwalks lined each side, occasionally branching off into small piers. Clara stumbled to the shore, scanning this strange town for any sign of the burly Ares.

A splash near the boardwalk shot an unneeded jolt into her overworked soul. The god of war, with Hephaestus lolling across his back, stepped up to a canoe roped to a wooden stump. He hacked the tether with his sword and pushed the boat off the banks with a strong kick. Carelessly, he tossed Hephaestus's unconscious body into the boat and jumped into the buoyant cradle with him.

"No!" Clara ran, arms pumping with the weight of her hatchets in each hand. Ares' boat drifted toward the center of the river, but that was plenty close for her weapons. She heaved one furiously from her right hand.

Ares ducked as the axe whizzed past his neck and splashed pitifully in the water. Clara didn't wait for it to return, leaping off the pier and into the icy river. The weight of her own body dragged her beneath the surface where no sandy floor met her feet.

While her arm stretched upward, she barely managed to catch her slick-handled axe. It hit her palm with a wet *smack,* and she hacked into the rushing river with its broad blade.

"Hephaestus!" Water clogged her sinuses, drowning his name in her mouth. Her friend was sprawled across the back of the canoe, his limp arms hanging over the sides. His blackout left nothing on his side of their bond. There was just her own despair as Ares's boat shrank away from her swimming range.

Clara huffed, resigning herself to return aground. She had never been great in the water, but she was fit enough for a sprint. If she made it to the shore, she could beat Ares to his next dock.

A corpse-white hand erupted from the water and dug fingers into her Nemean leather vest. Clara screamed, twisting to hack her offender in the face. It was a bald facsimile of a human, its eyes and mouth sewn shut, and she splashed away in repulsion. One axe head splashed into the water, cutting through the current while more hands emerged and grabbed at her clothing.

Clara thrashed, kicking against a tangle of other limbs. With the river so deep, all she could do was flail against the rushing water and determined monsters. But with every inch gained, another hand tugged her back to the center of the river.

She hacked in every direction. While the ghouls fell victim to her blades, they always whirled back, yanking on her hair and unraveling her ponytail, tearing at her skin with their overgrown fingernails and carving scratches into her jeans.

Five feet from the shore, Clara gurgled as a dozen grabbing hands pulled her beneath the surface. Their sharp nails cut through her wet skin, spitting the flesh with a dozen scratches, but her lungs burned far worse. Her breath and hearing washed away, muffled by the abyss.

Had she died from the spectre in the hotel, Mam and Dad would have had the peace of knowing their daughter was no longer of Earth. At least if she died at the library, or at the Embassy, it would have been for the fate of the world or her friends.

But she was here, sinking into blackness, about to succumb to a pointless death. Her corpse would remain a mystery to all, and her bereft brother would spend the rest of his days watching every door with a trace of hope, wondering if she might come home.

Pink light flashed above the water, and the hands tugging at her harness and shirt and pants abandoned her. The grotesque monsters floated away until their white eyes were the only things visible in the black water.

The water still played its own game of chicken, holding her down with its airless might. She flapped her arms, but empty lungs no longer kept her buoyant. Within a meter of the surface, her muscles fell limp, refusing to function without oxygen to fuel them.

A hand reached into the murk and grabbed her wrist, yanking her free of the icy embrace. Her lungs exploded when she hit oxygen, her limbs weak and immobile. She dropped both axes on the lip of the shore and collapsed against the wooden planks, groaning as someone's hands dragged her out of the water.

She blinked the water from her eyes. Aphrodite's face was above her.

"They listened to me." The goddess panted from the effort of dragging Clara across the pier. "I didn't think they would…"

Too labored to ask what that meant, Clara turned onto all fours, insides burning as she coughed up water. When her lungs and stomach finally relaxed, she crawled closer to the splintered boardwalk and collapsed on her back. She'd survive.

"What were those things?" Clara moaned, soaked and spread-eagle on the dirty ground.

"This is the River Styx. They're departed souls imprisoned between worlds."

"Grabby bastards." She pressed a hand over her eyes, trying to rub out the remaining blurriness. "Guess this is Hades, huh?"

"Yes. Our Olympian corner of Abyssus."

Clara's heart clenched, but not from the near-death experience. "Ares took Hephaestus. They got away, and I didn't see where. God, why not kill him in Paradisa if he wanted to?"

Aphrodite crossed her arms, somehow looking small despite her height. Her cheeks deadened with pallor.

"He wants to humiliate him first."

## 21

Clara and Aphrodite ran with the river as their compass. Despite the burning of Clara's muscles and the tightness in her chest, nothing revealed itself through the thickening fog of Hades.

Aphrodite swore in Greek when they reached a dead end—the outskirts of the city where Styx curled beneath a stone tunnel and the sidewalk ended.

Aphrodite tugged at her braid. "Where would Ares take him..."

Clara scrunched her eyes shut. "I can sense him a bit. I think he's still unconscious."

"The other side of the river still has a path, and we can cross that bridge a block back. We can keep following the river, and maybe we'll catch up to them."

Clara nodded, following her back to the wooden bridge. Perhaps disassociation kept her calm, like the severity of the situation had not hit her clearly enough. With Hephaestus in danger, she could have dropped dead at any moment. But it was a waste of time to dwell on hypotheticals anyway.

She and Aphrodite backtracked to the bridge and crossed it. After a half mile sprint alongside the shores of Styx, the river split into an intersection.

"Hold on!" Aphrodite threw out an arm, blocking Clara's path. The goddess approached the river, and the white surface reflected her slender body. The water looked different from the murky swirls of Styx. Silver fluid, almost as light as smoke, flowed where there should have been water.

Aphrodite spun, her face as white as the river. "This is the River Lethe. This is what Ares is going to do."

"Drown him?"

Hazel eyes glistened. "No. Touching this river erases a person's entire memory. He would be a shell. He wouldn't recognize either of us. He wouldn't remember his name."

Clara shook her head. An empty Hephaestus? One without all of Hephaestus's flaws, all of his tics and joys and humor? A man who would no longer make jewelry and weapons to show he cared? A man who could no longer joke darkly about his mother throwing him off a mountain or the scars etched into his skin?

*That's even worse than us dying together.*

Aphrodite grabbed Clara's hand and pulled her down the road. The goddess glanced back only once to say, "We can follow it from here! And whatever you do, don't touch the water."

Clara ran along the river's edge, blindly following wherever Aphrodite led. She heard the roaring yells before anything—the same guttural anger that turned her blood cold in the library. She and Aphrodite rushed in tandem, nearly stumbling across each other to turn the street corner where the Lethe twisted west.

Ares towered in the fog with a sword in his fist, and he paced the planks of the river dock. Hephaestus knelt before him, arms tied behind his back. His shirt had been ripped off, allowing his fractal scars to reflect the dim light. Hephaestus's cane was tossed onto a pile of smoldering rubble, too distant from its host to heal him from anything Ares would do.

Aphrodite yanked Clara backwards, pulling her tight against a wall. "Can you hit him from here?"

"What? I don't know. Why?"

"I can persuade him to stand down, but only if he doesn't know I'm coming. I need eye contact for it to work. If you hit him, he'll be distracted long enough for me to get close."

"He's a god of war, I don't think I can—"

"He won't expect you to be strong. But I do. Come."

Clara reached for her axes, weighing one in each hand. She rounded the corner, staying behind Aphrodite as they crept closer to Ares. His back was turned to them as he continued to circle and gloat at Hephaestus.

Aphrodite stopped, extending a hand beside her. "Now."

Clara moved around her with one weapon raised over her head and heaved it with the fury rising from the base of her gut. The axe head imbedded itself between Ares's shoulder blades and ignited a shout that echoed across Lethe.

Ares grabbed the axe handle and ripped it out of his back with a roar. As he turned, he spied Aphrodite nearing.

"Ares!" she said. "Sta—"

Bellowing, Ares threw Clara's axe at the goddess. It sunk into Aphrodite's throat, dropping her to the ground with a choked scream.

"No!" Clara yelled. She forced herself to look away from Aphrodite and refocus on Ares. His armor was too solid to penetrate, and his skin was a self-mending canvas. She couldn't kill him without separating him from his Icon, and she had no clue what it was. But he was not hers to kill anyway.

Ares's sword arced towards her throat. Clara lunged backward, watching wide-eyed as the blade swept over her face, centimeters from slicing off her nose.

Ares wasted no time lunging towards her, aiming a jab to her stomach. The blade hit her below the ribs, knocking the air out of her. Yet no blood seeped from her waist. Ares's blade had sunk into her tan vest, but it didn't pierce the fabric. *The Nemean vest.*

Just as Clara's heart swelled with newfound confidence, Ares exploded with rage. He backhanded her across the forehead with his free hand, knocking her to the stone ground.

Clara groaned, her sight blurry. Past Ares's boots, Aphrodite struggled to get the axe out of her neck with no success.

One of Ares's feet flew at Clara's face, and everything turned black.

———

Connor held his breath, still not used to the watery sense of going through a portal. His eyes were clenched shut, and only Raphael's hand tugging his arm gave him any sense of direction. As he was told, the Concordia portal could take them anywhere they desired across all three realms. Raphael had to do most of the desiring because Connor had no idea how to picture this...Claustrum.

Concordia itself had been magnificent, but he didn't have much time to dwell on its beauty. Between their current mission, and his idle thoughts of Clara—*where the hell is she now?*—he could barely keep his own head on straight.

He tried not to think of her as lost, but was reminded of one of his worst moments, the type of moment that still made his face hot ten years later. Tween Clara had wanted to go to the mall, and Connor, despondent in the first month home after the discharge, had nothing better to do than to take her. It had taken about six minutes for him to lose her in JC Penney, and he had nearly had a heart attack as he ran through clothing racks looking for his five-foot-tall sister.

That was a shopping mall. Now they were across dimensions from each other, probably.

As Connor sensed Raphael's bond reaching out with a hand of sympathy, he once again threw up the mental wall. *It's just temporary. Just so I can hear myself think.* It would be too much to feel Raphael's problems swirling around when he was set to burst with his own. At the same time, a small voice reminded him that Raphael's pain was from certainty—a terrible, irreversible certainty of a dead sibling—while his was from mere speculation.

*Trust Clara to stay safe. Raphael needs me more right now.*

He shook off the sensation when they arrived on the other side of the red portal. The stench of tar swooped in to replace the airless, tasteless nothing they'd just stepped through. He opened his eyes, and the sight was enough to open his floodgates for dread.

A network of dark rivers extended in coils beneath their feet, stretching from the gloom to the distant glow of civilization. It looked like night, but when Connor looked up, there was no sky. If it weren't for the oil lamps scattered every ten feet, they'd be in total darkness.

Raphael glanced over. "Welcome to Abyssus. I had hoped you'd never see it."

He approached the bridge before them. Connor trailed behind, following Raphael across the bridge to the face of a toppled boulder.

"Don't feel bad. I always thought I might end up in hell."

"If you did, this would be the worst part of it. The Claustrum was built on the outskirts. These criminals are too dangerous to be kept near the districts, even in Abyssus."

"What do you have to do to end up here?"

Raphael shrugged. "All kingdoms have our own prisons, but the Claustrum is reserved for the worst traitors and tyrants in history. Men whose crimes were so universally damaging that their punishment belongs to everyone. If they are human, they're forbidden to progress to the astral. If they're Sanctine, their Icons are confiscated and destroyed. Regardless, the Claustrum is an eternal sentence. No one is ever released."

Connor shuddered. It was hard not to empathize with an eternity in a hell pit. "How are any of them still alive without their Icons? You said Lucifer's been here for centuries."

"We're naturally slow to age. Icons just protect us from injury. I'm sure many of the prisoners have taken their lives in the pit, but Lucifer has far too much he'd like accomplish."

The bridge ended at a narrow crack where two towering megaliths leaned against each other. A hundred feet deep into the cave, they approached a spiked, wrought iron gate. Behind it, a dark, wet hallway stretched into a silent abyss. No sign, guards, or anything suggested the biggest night terrors in the universe resided beyond this gate.

"This is where the Claustrum begins." Raphael wrapped a hand around one of the grated bars and yanked, pulling the gate from its frame.

Raphael paused, staring down the dark hall. He sucked in a breath, but did not move. Connor felt stuffy with the angel's reluctance and the fear of truth they could discover.

"Hey." Connor bumped a gentle elbow against his arm. "We're in this together. Okay?"

He used to throw that phrase around in the barracks, sometimes as a platitude. This time, he wholeheartedly meant it. Ever since bringing Raphael back from the nuclear edge, his purpose seemed clear as polished silver. *Protect Raphael. Not from death, but from those who wish to break his heart, to manipulate his good nature. Protect him from the man we're about to meet.*

Raphael's brow twitched. After a few seconds, his expression settled upon gratitude.

"Thank you, Connor."

Connor crossed the gate first, instinctively wrapping his hands around the handles of his guns. "Where are the guards?"

"The Claustrum is said to be guarded by several things." Raphael glided in behind him, closing the gate. "But I'm not sure any are people."

They descended together into the dimly lit dungeon, which sloped downward into more dampness. Connor twitched when a drop of water hit the back of his neck. His grip on Castor and Pollux remained tight despite the sweat collecting on his palms.

The dark hallway finally opened into a dim rotunda lit by torches on the perimeter walls. Connor craned his neck, looking through a cracked, dusty oculus in the domed ceiling. "Maybe there's nothing left anymore. If there was something here to stop us, it would be here by now."

"Are you sure about that?"

Connor shrugged, turning back to Raphael. But where Raphael had stood, with the same guarded expression and earnest blue eyes, was Eric.

# 22

Clara groaned, blinking. Pain flared indecisively between her eye sockets and temples. She tried to bring a hand to her cheek, but a rough cord tied her wrists behind her.

The blurry world shifted into focus. She sat propped against a wall with Aphrodite beside her. Aphrodite was less fortunate, as her mouth was gagged in addition to her bondage.

Ares paced before them with a shining silver blade in his hand. He twirled it end over end, walking back and forth on the Lethe's shore while Hephaestus knelt behind him.

"Good. You're awake," Ares said, giving Clara that vampire smile. "Wouldn't want you to miss the show."

"I have no interest in whatever you have to show me," she said under her breath. Beside her, Aphrodite made a noise beneath her gag, her eyes wide.

"Let them go, you bastard!" Hephaestus bellowed. He squirmed against the ropes tying his arms, thrashing back and forth. "They haven't done anything to you!"

Ares barked a cruel laugh. "Your whore wife is just as responsible for my situation as you are. And I'm not to blame for a stupid girl being foolish enough to bind herself to you."

He grabbed Hephaestus's hair and yanked his head back, exposing his throat. Ares dragged the dagger along Hephaestus's jugular, just light enough to avoid cutting him. Clara almost felt the sharp chill running across her own neck.

And then the agony came.

Pain knocked the wind out of her in a swift punch, enough to make her sight shimmer in a cascade of grey stars. She fell sideways, scraping her face on the hard ground, but that pain was nothing compared to the phantom blade on her skin. The cuts snaked from her left collar bone to her wrist as Hephaestus screamed, distantly, beneath the exact same sensation.

She opened her mouth only to gasp. She swallowed the hurt and the salty phlegm building in her sinuses as the pain finally drooped into a dull ache.

On the edge of the river, Hephaestus hunched over with his face against the ground. His fractal scars, which Ares artfully re-carved into the smith god's skin, seeped golden ichor. Clara dug her fingernails into her palms. Maybe she could distract the mental pain with real pain.

Aphrodite squirmed, whimpering as the gag muffled her protests. Clara managed to right herself against the wall again, arching her back to flex out the persistent sting. She was barely upright before Ares resumed his sick torture, and the slicing pain regained its fervor. Her body buckled, and she bit her lip hard enough to skin it.

"See, ward? Look at how pathetic he is. You gave your soul to this?" He sauntered over to Aphrodite next, spitting at her feet. "And you... you gave your bed to this."

Clara spoke through gritted teeth. "He's a thousand times the man you are. Only a coward needs to tie our hands to fight us."

"I know war far better than you, girl." The red-faced god sneered. "War is never fair. The only thing that matters is who is left standing at the end of the fight."

*And it won't be you, you son of a bitch.* Every turn of her head set Clara's nerves alight. The pain came in quick lashes and ebbed, but it never fully abandoned her. It remained sheer under her skin, pulsing and confusing her muscles. It took every thread of will and focus to keep herself from collapsing into fragments.

But through her blurry haze of pain, she remembered how good Connor was at handling injury. She was tired of being the girl on the sidelines letting grown-ups do the heavy lifting. She couldn't be a child anymore, depending on caretakers and heroes to sweep her responsibilities away. One day, she would have to fight to save another person. *She* would have to be the one spitting fire and bleeding from wounds as she crawled across the pavement to save a loved one, not stopping in their defense until she took her final breath.

May as well start today.

She stilled herself against the ongoing torture, forcing herself to look away from Hephaestus's increasing wounds. In the quiet of her mind, she shielded herself against the storm of anguish. It helped, surprisingly, to block Hephaestus out. Her sense of him reduced by pushing out his pain but wasn't gone entirely.

*My axes. I need my axes.* Hephaestus's screams filled the air as Ares began cutting his shoulder blades. But fifteen feet away, her weapons glinted on the ground.

She glanced back to Ares. He circled Hephaestus gleefully, slashing in no real pattern. But his focus was entirely off Clara and Aphrodite. Could her axes move fast enough to avoid his attention?

Clara took a deep breath and nudged Aphrodite with a knee. She jerked her chin toward the axes, winking. Aphrodite slowly nodded, shifting slightly to expose her open palms behind her back. It would take both of them to untie Clara. There was no way to maneuver herself to cut her own bonds with her hands tied behind her back.

Clara shifted herself, angling her hands to face her axes with no obstruction in between. She watched every degree of Ares's movements, every step as he circled Hephaestus with his tormenting laughs. When his back was completely turned away from her, she finally opened her hands.

One axe handle hit her palm, and she clamped her fingers down like a vice. Nerves surged up through her chest, prickling across her ribcage and lungs. *Yes. We're so close. Now give it to Aphrodite.*

Carefully keeping the axe behind her back, Clara scooted back in position against the wall. She angled herself toward Aphrodite's back, and their fingers brushed against each other. With a few seconds of fumbling, Aphrodite held a firm grip on the axe, and Clara began sawing her ropes against the downward facing blade.

Ares abandoned his torture of Hephaestus, sauntering closer to Clara and Aphrodite, twirling his dagger in his fingers. Clara leaned closer to Aphrodite, masking what they were doing behind their backs. Maybe Ares would think her a cowering woman. Let him.

"You haven't been screaming, ward," he observed, dragging his gold-soaked blade gently across her face. "Am I going to have to carve into you, too? I'll mark into that pretty face that Ares was here."

Clara squirmed under the knife, allowing herself the pretense to rub her bindings harder against the axe head. With the tip of the Ares's dagger pinpointed into her cheekbone, the rope behind her snapped.

Aphrodite opened her fingers, allowing the axe to fall into Clara's right hand. Clara smiled, knowing her eyes were cruel to match, and she cast that gaze right into Ares's eyes.

"Fuck off."

She kicked him in the chest, barely hard enough to make him stumble, but enough to catch him off guard. As he struggled to right himself, Clara leapt to her feet and sank her axe into the back of his neck.

He roared, falling to his knees. Golden blood leaked from the wound as the war god collapsed, his neck taking the axe with it. Clara left it in; it would be awhile before he'd maneuver that out of his flesh. It might not have killed him, but it would buy them time to escape. Clara reached toward her second axe, summoning it with an open hand.

First, Aphrodite. Clara chopped at her wrist bindings, severing them in one movement. Aphrodite waved her away, grunting against the cloth in her mouth and pointing to Hephaestus. She reached around the back of her head and started untying her gag as Clara crossed the pier to help her companion.

"Hey," she murmured, kneeling beside him. She placed a hand over his, steadying her grip as she sliced through his bonds. His golden blood utterly soaked him, and it spread between her fingers on his arm.

"Clara, I'm so sorry. Are you o—"

"Stop. Don't do that. Let's just get out of here."

Ares rolled his neck as he returned to his feet, shaking off the axe wound. He lumbered toward Aphrodite, still gushing golden blood, withdrawing his sword from a hip sheath. As his sword slashed through air above her, Aphrodite dropped her gag and called out with layers of persuasion.

"Stop!"

Ares obeyed, his limbs locking into place. His eyes flashed through a rotation of emotions, from confusion, to anger, to dread.

"You should never mess with a woman's heart, Ares." Aphrodite circled him, never letting him escape her judgment. "Especially when she can control yours."

"I should have known you would cheat." Ares narrowed his eyes, knuckles going white around his sword hilt.

Aphrodite stopped in front of him. Her nose scrunched. "And I should have known that you would prey upon those weaker than you."

"Most people are weaker than me. I know I've made you weak plenty."

She trailed her free hand across his studded armor, smirking. "Tell that to me when I take your Icon."

Ares glowered. "You won't find it."

"Ah, but isn't it funny," Aphrodite whispered, "how Hephaestus's defiance exposed you for the world to see? But I would have known anyway."

She plucked his abandoned dagger from the ground and slipped it beneath his collar. A moment later, she pulled it away to reveal a silver chain with a black tooth pendant. With a fierce tug, she ripped the chain from his throat.

Despite being stripped of all power and position to argue, Ares seethed, "You wanted everything I did to you."

"I wanted love." She lowered her voice. "You took advantage of me when I was too desperate to say no to you. You used me as a trophy over him. I didn't even know he wanted me until the day he caught us."

She backed away with his Icon in her grip, pulling his immortality away. The more distance she put between them, the more Ares grimaced.

Within a few feet of Clara at the river's edge, Aphrodite stopped. "I'm no girl anymore."

Ares's Icon hit the fluid of the Lethe without a splash before drifting to the infinite bottom.

She returned to Ares but did not come within arm's length. About ten feet separated them, and she raised the dagger toward his heart.

Ares scowled. "You won't kill me. You don't have it in you."

"You're right. I'm not going to kill you." Layering her voice, she beckoned, "I'm going to offer you a chance for redemption. Perhaps this way, you will have the chance to become a person worth living. I want you to drop your weapon and walk to the edge of the river."

Ares's face was the canvas of a man who knew his fate and feared the inevitability of it. His sword dropped, clanking, and his body lurched with robotic movement. With every step, he bent away from the river as if that could prolong his fate.

Hephaestus's breath hitched as Ares drew nearer. Clara squeezed his arm, extending a wave of calm through their bond. Although the god of war was a few feet away, all danger had been drained out of him. His only weapons were his words now.

Ares looked back at the goddess. "You won't be able to live with this, Aphrodite. You'll hate yourself. And we both know you can't afford any more of that."

Aphrodite steeled her voice. "Keep walking."

His feet shuffled as if chained to the ground, every muscle taut. Beneath the beard, his cheeks strained with a flush. "This will do nothing. I will burn your face into my memory, and when I come back up, you will suffer. I will take you in front of him until you die of shame!"

Aphrodite glared from under furrowed eyebrows. Her lips tightened.

"Bathe in the river, Ares."

There was no apology there. This despicable man—once a lover, now a captor—became nothing. The River Lethe bathed him of all memories, leaving him nothing more than a shell floating across her rushing surface. He floated on his back, expression glazed and catatonic, as the wispy white fluid carried him away.

Hephaestus groaned against Clara, shaking. Quick footsteps shuffled beyond them as Aphrodite reclaimed Hephaestus's cane from the other side of the pier and rushed back. In the meantime, Clara rubbed her companion's back, trying to ignore the ruined flesh.

"It's over," she murmured.

"You found me," he gasped. He pressed his forehead against hers, a hand on the back of her hair. Every iota of his gratitude dumped into her chest, and she joyfully opened herself to it.

She had no words. She had nearly lost him—not to death, but to extinction of memory. For those few heartbeats, after she realized where he was and how to find him, she had been terrified he wouldn't recognize her when they reunited.

Aphrodite fell to her knees beside them, thrusting Hephaestus's cane into his hand. With the cane restored to its maker, the god of fire's skin shone in its original pattern of lightning scars, healing as red sparks of light cascaded across his back. The ichor remained though, painting him in a golden sheen of his own courage. When the healing was complete, Clara felt his energy sapped, but fire had reignited in his gut.

"You're incredible. Both of you." Hephaestus rose, shaking his head. Aphrodite's breath wavered at her husband's tilted smile that matched his tilted posture.

Aphrodite cupped his face in her hands. "I'm just glad you're alright."

He let out a weak laugh. "I'd be better if my wife and ward didn't have to save me."

Aphrodite smiled. "And I thought Ares was prideful."

Clara looked away from the couple, giving them a moment alone. Well, as alone as she could with Hephaestus bouncing around in her chest. Besides that, she could hear them embrace, along with whispers of Greek she couldn't decipher.

It was hard to remember where they'd been before Ares stole them away. The library. Set. Ascendants…

"Connor," Clara said aloud in a squeaky voice. "Connor needs to know what Set's really up to. We have to find where he is and get him that message!"

Hephaestus's hand fell upon her shoulder. When she looked into his eyes, they burned with pure flame. "Then we'll get you a herald."

## 23

Connor rounded on Eric with Castor and Pollux drawn. There was a narrow exit ten feet behind him—a tunnel leading away from the rotunda and deeper into the Claustrum. But no matter how much curiosity was known to kill, he had to have an answer for the phantom in front of him. More than that, he had to get Raphael back.

"Where's Raphael? What the hell have you done with him?"

Eric stared at him with too much familiarity. This hellscape wasn't allowed to pull that vulnerability out of him. Connor's fingers tightened on each trigger, but his fists trembled.

Eric lifted a hand. "Connor, please…"

Despite hearing his name, soft and calming in Eric's voice, Connor didn't lower the guns. But he couldn't bring himself to shoot either. If this was an underworld, could it have been the real Eric? Or was it an illusion cast over Raphael, tempting him to hurt his friend?

"Put those down." Eric gestured to the golden guns, hands raised in surrender. "Let's just talk."

Connor ignored the suggestion, despite his desire to listen. The intuition buzzing the back of his neck wouldn't let him.

"Connor. It's *me*."

"The hell it is!" Connor shook Castor, taking an uneven step forward. "You're gone."

"No, no. I'm not. I'm here, standing right in front of you, begging you just to listen. Please, Con. Trust me."

Acid rolled in his stomach at the old nickname, at the mannerism, at all of it. If the Claustrum had created a mirage, it created a damn good one. God, his hair even fell in his eyes the same way. His eyes were still perfectly dark blue, like the darkest depths of the sea. Navy eyes for his Navy guy, Eric used to joke. This wasn't the warped memory of Eric shaded by ten years of absence and regret. This was the spitting image of the man in Connor's wallet—the real Eric, as he had actually been.

Eric continued, spilling memories only he would know. "I never thought we'd be in this situation, you know. I mean, you did tell me you'd shoot me if I left my clothes in the dryer one more time, but I never thought you were serious."

"Shut up," Connor whispered, but his trigger fingers held much less conviction. Both guns trembled in his grip as Eric pleaded, his soft face begging Connor to listen. Begging Connor to believe him.

Connor closed his eyes. "Those aren't your memories. They're mine. Whatever you are, you're just pulling from me."

It wasn't smart to keep his eyes closed in a volatile situation, but he couldn't look at Eric anymore. Listening to the voice was bad enough. Maybe this was a trick or a ghost or some sick coping mechanism, but it hit him exactly where it tried to.

*Focus. Where is Raphael? I need Raphael.*

The bond was murky, hard to locate. Raphael remained on the other end of it, but Connor couldn't decipher where.

He opened his eyes to Eric. "If you want me to trust you, then tell me where Raphael is."

"I see how you'd think this was fake, Con, but how about one of *my* memories? How we spent that night at East Bay and Market, hopping from bar to bar until we found that one remodeled church...and when you said that it seemed kind of blasphemous to put a bar in a church, that's when I knew you were the one."

"Shut UP."

Eric continued his insistent rambling, taking step by step closer. "I never laughed as much as I did with you. I've missed you and...and goddamn, I can't believe I have you back."

Connor dropped his arms and stopped breathing. The world melted from his knees to the walls. He tightened his eyes shut again, for maybe when he opened them, everything would make sense. Maybe standing before him would not be a facsimile of Eric.

In the hotel, he had thought it was Eric sitting at the bar. A few days before, such a revelation may have been pleasant. Now, he missed Raphael instead. Just when their bond had opened up, just when he started to separate the angel from the man, just when he'd given Raphael a moment of respite in his lonely wanderings...

As Eric drew closer for an embrace, Connor wiped his mind of everything except Raphael. He recreated the angel's face—everything from his tender eyes to his sharp cheekbones, his soft black hair and the faint age lines, his shy smile and averted gaze every time Connor cracked a joke. The way he turned his face away after healing Connor, like that link left them too vulnerable to each other. And most importantly, he focused on Raphael's immaculate heart, which still ached in mourning.

Eric stepped into Connor's arms, but Raphael felt immensely far away.

Connor's stiff arms returned the embrace of the Claustrum's morbid mind game. Part of him yearned for the illusion of Eric pressed against him once more in a goodbye Connor had never gotten the chance to give. But now, he wondered why he had ever wanted such a thing. Eric was dead, and Raphael was in trouble somewhere else. The wish seemed trivial.

"The first time I saw Raphael, I wanted more than anything for him to be you." He tightened his grip around the fake Eric, sucking in a breath. He exhaled, using those two seconds to center his focus. "But it wasn't. And I'm okay. Because now I have him."

With a swift movement, he pulled away and grabbed Eric by the collar. His arms twisted, pushing Eric as roughly to the ground as his strength could manage. Before Eric had time to react, Connor put a Castor bullet through his forehead.

Eric's body dissolved into colored sand, then reformed itself into a new silhouette, this one far larger and more fearsome than the lithe human ghost. Connor lifted Castor toward the humanoid shape, already retreating into the rotunda's narrow exit.

"Connor Bishara!"

The sand formed a furious face, and a mane of white hair floated weightlessly around the deviant. A brown leather vest and green tunic formed from the particles as well, but they never took shape beneath his waist. The giant torso with a tail of pixels and light hovered in the air over Connor with a finger pointed firmly in his direction.

Connor fired with abandon, but every bullet phased through the giant. Each hit scattered colored grains throughout the rotunda without harming the malevolent god.

"All break under the illusions of Gwydion!"

Connor glared and, accepting that his guns were useless in this contest, casually tucked them back into his harness.

"Sorry, you bastard. I don't break."

With a roar, Gwydion swooped toward him with outstretched arms. Connor sprinted toward the dark exit crevice, instinct taking over before thought. The cave was just wide enough to accommodate his broad frame as he descended deeper into the Claustrum's embrace. Without the heavy golden guns in his fists, Connor pumped his arms as he ran, fueling himself further down the damp, winding corridor.

The deeper he ran, the tighter the cave crowded in. The sharp, sticky walls brushed against Connor's arms, cutting at his shirt fabric and the top layers of his skin. But it was better than feeling Gwydion's breath down his neck.

The rocks around him rumbled and dust trickled upon his hair. *Oh hell, not a cave-in. He better not cause a cave-in!*

His heart pounded in time with his feet against the uneven cave floor. As his surroundings grew tighter and tighter, he peered desperately ahead, hoping for it to end with every winding turn.

*There!*

With any luck, the small square of dim light thirty feet ahead was not one of Gwydion's illusions. With the ground shaking so hard that it nearly unbalanced him, and baseball-sized chunks falling all around, there was no time to consider another option. Connor propelled himself to the end of the tunnel in one fiercely-held breath.

He exited the cave with a lunge, grunting as his elbows took most of the ground's impact. As he escaped, the cave walls collapsed upon themselves, leaving nothing but a pyramid of rubble.

Connor turned on his back and scrambled away, anticipating an explosion of rocks to rain upon him or for Gwydion to erupt from the trap and drag him back to the rotunda of illusion.

After an eternity of bated breath, nothing came. All was still. There was only the gentle trickle of a nearby waterfall into a shallow basin.

He groaned and sat up, collecting himself. These new surroundings calmed him with their tranquility. The top of the waterfall was obscured, rising above and beyond the hanging ceiling of crystal stalactites. Dim lanterns throughout the chamber served as light sources, and the crystals scattered light evenly throughout the room.

The adrenaline dwindled, and he became cognizant of blood dripping from scratches on his arms. He moved his focus back to the bond and to the pain pulsing from Raphael's broken heart. A myriad of memories ran across his senses—Raphael's and his own—but they all linked back to pain. To regret. To not being sly enough, not being fast enough, to letting someone else determine their fate. The ache burned through Connor's chest like acid.

And still, he welcomed it with open arms. Because for better or worse, binding to Raphael was the first thing he'd done in his life that was purely for himself. As much as he loved the SEALs, Dad had undoubtedly influenced that path. As much as he loved Clara, too, much of his life had been lived for her.

Raphael didn't care about any of that. He came to Connor with no expectations and with no strings attached to acceptance. Raphael was the first person he could ever be entirely himself with. With Eric, he still lived two lives: the civilian and the soldier. Raphael had seen all of his faces and demanded nothing from any of them.

Connor jumped up at the sound of his own name, gentle and familiar. When he laid eyes upon the man who'd said it, he was too relieved to consider the possibility of another illusion.

"Holy shit!" Connor stared at Raphael, ten feet away. "Is it you?"

Raphael's shoulders slumped with relief. "Yes. Yes, of course."

Connor reached out with his soul, into the space that Raphael occupied and all the emotions that swirled within his divine body. It was impossible to process mentally, but Connor allowed it to wash over him and mingle with his own core.

The bond pulsed. *Raphael. Yes, it's really you. I can feel it.*

He surged forward, and they were soon in each other's arms. Connor wasn't sure who reached out first, but they stood in a messy embrace anyway, all tangled and haphazard.

Raphael's voice ghosted quietly across his ear. "I thought I'd lost you."

"You're not getting rid of me that easily." Connor pulled back from their embrace, both his hands rising to cup Raphael's face.

Raphael's breath stuttered. Connor could hardly breathe at all. Back in that cavern, all he'd hoped for was Raphael in his arms, and now he *was*. Their bond ached, and he wasn't sure whether it came from his side or Raphael's or both. All he knew was the swelling need between them, the regret of: *what if I hadn't gotten out of that place and never got the chance to...*

He surged forward to press his lips against Raphael's.

A shockwave pulsed through their bond, tingling down his neck and spreading across his chest. Connor clamped his eyes shut, focusing not on the stony stench of the prison or the horror picture show he'd just escaped, but on the warmth of Raphael's mouth moving in response to his, on the impossible softness of it. Raphael's serenity blanketed him through the bond, reducing his trepidation to nothing.

Raphael gripped his shirt, pulling him tight and close, and by God, if that wasn't enough to make him *want*. Connor parted his lips to take him deeper, to taste him and share his warmth. He slid his hand upward, sinking into Raphael's smooth black tresses, spreading his fingers across the base of the angel's skull. Something seemed to thrum beneath his palm where Raphael's head met his spine, and a phantom tingle echoed in Connor's own neck.

Finally, when they parted to breathe, Raphael's lips spoke against his own. "Connor ...I..."

Connor froze, inching back to look at him. "Shit, was that not—?"

"No, I..." A reciprocated kiss, then, Raphael's fingers spread across his jaw. "I wanted that. I just, probably shouldn't take advantage of my ward like this."

Connor pressed their foreheads together, meeting Raphael's gaze a mere inch away.

"No, hey, look at me. Do I look like anything other than a grown ass man who can decide shit for himself? You are *not* taking advantage of me."

Raphael turned his head, kissing the side of Connor's thumb, and *shit,* it was hard not to shiver at that. "Okay, Connor. I accept your affection."

Connor wanted to snort, but with the relief of being alive, with the warm weight of Raphael in his arms, wanting him back, he let out an honest-to-God giggle instead. "Well you don't have to sound like such a robot about it."

Raphael idly rubbed his arm, his tone sobering. "Where did you go, before?"

Connor relaxed, one hand still cupping Raphael's cheek. "I don't know. This guy Gwydion made me see shit that wasn't there before chasing me to here. I guess I lost him after he caved in the exit."

"Oh, Gwydion," Raphael pulled back, holding him at arm's length. "A trickster from Avalon. No surprise he'd be a gatekeeper for the Claustrum."

"So what happened to you if you didn't see *him?*"

Raphael stepped away fully, dodging Connor's scrutiny. "Something similar enough. Illusions, tricks. One of the many ways this place keeps out visitors."

Connor's ears burned. A cold wave of nausea rose in his throat, either sick with the Claustrum's methods or sick with himself for wondering what Raphael saw.

"Hey, it's all over now. You remember what I told you, right?"

"Yes. We're in this together."

Connor forced a smile. "Exactly. Now where is Lucifer?"

"I passed the cell block on the way back to you. Follow me."

The Claustrum crowded in on them, a dark network of increasingly chilly tunnels. At least the blue light of Raphael's sword cascaded over Connor's skin, offering some comfort. As the angel used it to light their path, a blue glow flickered across the walls, giving them the illusion of being underwater.

His lips still tingled from their kiss. Even more gut-lurching was the memory of Raphael's words: *I wanted that.* Because...fuck, Raphael wanted him? How was that even possible? Sure, Connor wasn't blind to the angel's smiles, his reciprocated flirtation. Their bond was a warm and honest trail between them, open and tender, without secrets. Still, proof didn't equal sense.

Suddenly, he was less certain of things. He'd crossed a line that he couldn't walk back. And as much as that glorious kiss was worthy of elation, his heart flooded with doubt. They would need to talk about this, when they weren't jailbreaking the devil out of the world's worst prison. He needed to hear, in Raphael's own voice, why the angel would ever want him back.

They walked past the first cages of moaning inmates who rotted beneath dribbling rocks. The captives did not shuffle when they heard visitors approach, but they followed Connor's movements with unblinking yellowed eyes.

Raphael pointed to a rotted oak door at the end of their path. "There."

All other cells were gated by slotted bars, allowing the prisoners to peek into each other's cages. Lucifer's began with a door.

Connor crept up to the wood, inspecting the bent iron nails sticking out in all places and the rusty doorknob threatening to crumble off. He frowned, expecting something beastly to strike the moment he opened the door.

"You know, there are all kinds of stories about people making deals with the devil. It usually doesn't end well for them."

Raphael assured, "Lucifer cannot do us harm, so long as we don't allow him to."

Connor turned the knob and pushed inward. Raphael slipped inside first with Connor close behind. A turn of the corner revealed another cell barred by an iron grate. The gaunt figure inside sat on damp ground with his back to them. Lucifer's shoulders were broad, hunched as he sat with his knees against his chest, his willowy arms wrapped around them. Short black hair covered the back of his head, chopped at unusual angles as if sawed with a sharpened piece of stone, and, in this state, it probably was.

They approached the cell, and Lucifer's shoulder blades slid beneath his tunic.

"Who visits me today?"

His words rumbled Connor's bones with darkness. Raphael moistened his lips.

"I don't know if you remember me." Raphael's voice, although low, sounded abnormally serene compared to the prisoner's. "It's been so long, and I was just a boy…"

Lucifer stood with the faintest rustle of cloth. He turned, pressed his face against the rusty metal bars of the cell. His thin eyes narrowed, as pale as ice.

"No mistaking a brother of mine, Raphael."

While his gray skin, stained teeth, and thin hair betrayed the abysmal time he'd spent in his cell, it remained obvious that Lucifer had once been handsome. He was a faded glory shrouded beneath suffering and punishment. All of his beauty rotted, left in the past where he'd envisioned his brave new world.

Despite Lucifer's tarnished persona, Connor was left disturbingly star-struck to lay eyes on the world's greatest bogeyman. The night terror, the great beast, the prince of darkness. The physical embodiment of all evil in the world…and he looked like a mere man.

Normally, the humanity of angels reassured Connor to some degree. But he couldn't feel at ease when Lucifer, aside from his towering height, could blend into any crowd as a sinister puppeteer.

Lucifer pulled away from the wall of his cage. He paced with his hands clasped behind his back, spine erect and chin held high. Madness radiated from him; the madness that being alone would do to any man. Connor imagined the many arguments Lucifer must have had with himself here. Perhaps winning arguments with himself all day was what fueled his remaining pride.

"You know why we've come," Raphael said. "You've aligned yourself with Set."

"Set?" Lucifer sing-songed, directing his crystalline eyes to the leaky stone ceiling. "Clearly not much, as I'm still here."

"It was enough."

Lucifer batted his lashes in mock sympathy. Still, Raphael's voice replayed in Connor's head—*angels cannot lie*. Despite Lucifer's sardonic tilt, the words coming out of his mouth had to be true.

"I swear, brother. He came, bled me for information, and left me here."

Connor stepped forward, half a foot from the cell door. "What kind of information could you have? We hadn't even built the pyramids when you were put here."

Lucifer stopped, setting his wicked stare upon Connor. He leered, tilting his head like talking to a child.

"Human time means nothing to me. But I imagine you humans tend to forget history after a few thousand years. You hunt down relics to tell you of what already passed." His voice sharpened. "Well, so do Sanctines. I'm the relic."

Raphael crossed his arms over his chest. "You're hardly older than I am, and I have a reasonable memory. There's nothing from your past that I wasn't there for."

"Oh, brother, you may be as old, but are you as wise? Were you paying enough attention? Did you run in the right circles?" Lucifer shook his head, snorting. "I don't think you did. I remember you being a carefree naïve boy completely willing to accept anything you were told."

"And you find Set wise?"

"Set offered me something I've pined for a long time in this hole. I'm an easy friend, I promise. My loyalty can be entirely bought."

A muscle twitched under Raphael's eye, but he showed no sign of defeat. They hadn't marched all the way down to the depths of the Claustrum to leave without answers.

Lucifer leaned forward into the bars and gestured to the ebony hilt hanging on Raphael's hip. "You could buy me, too. Just have to meet my price."

Raphael's hand fell to Michael's former Icon, gripping it protectively. "Michael's sword no longer functions as an Icon. He was murdered by Set. You have no use for it."

Lucifer's eyes glimmered, the jaundiced sheen clearing from them. Crazed glee bubbled beneath his expression while boiling rage buzzed down Connor's bond with Raphael.

"Not what I'm asking, brother. Michael put me down here," Lucifer whispered. "Only Michael could let me out."

He kicked at the iron cage, and the bars crackled with red electricity. Connor jumped back from the magical force field jumping across every bar.

Raphael's voice eclipsed the zapping noises. "Why should we let you out, Lucifer?"

*No, we are not letting him out. How could you even consider it?* A few years in the Navy had given Connor a lot of things, like good stamina, that had long faded away. One thing that stuck around was his intuition, and it was almost never wrong.

And if anyone needed that intuition, it sure as hell was Raphael.

The bond was not a mental link, but Connor could forecast his doubt. Sometimes it was easier to pass a feeling off to Raphael than it was to confront him with words. Moreover, it was good to have a communication method that Lucifer could not eavesdrop on.

Lucifer wrapped his hands around the gate. "Set wants to use his spectres to kill off all those old Inquisitors he hates so much. We could stop them, together. All I need is that sword to break these bars."

Connor shoved himself between Lucifer and Raphael, grunting. "No deal. We'll take our chances with Set."

It didn't matter if Lucifer said his information was invaluable. It didn't matter that they had almost been swallowed by the Claustrum to reach this point. Releasing a mad criminal who wanted to destroy humanity was not worth any answer.

"Fine," Lucifer drawled, traipsing away from the bars. "Sacrifice the lives of your friends as clueless simpletons and regret for the rest of your days how you had the chance to make a difference…but you chose not to."

Connor frowned at Lucifer's back. Reverse psychology. Perhaps the great deceiver thought he was a master of it. But plenty of myths he knew about the fallen angel suggested that the devil always had to honor his debts. Sure, there was always a back door or a loophole to screw over the naïve human. Perhaps that made Lucifer predictable, though. Perhaps they could beat the devil at his game.

Connor glanced to Raphael, whose hand still rested on Michael's Icon. Raphael's plea was evident in both the bond and his gaze. Connor chewed his lip, brimming with reluctance. They were too desperate to make this deal, and no deal ever went well for a desperate party. But as much as it pained him to admit, he needed this, too. Letting Lucifer out had the potentially deadly consequences for Paradisa, but letting Set proceed with his plan would surely destroy it. Never before had such a literal lesser of two evils presented itself to him.

He nodded at Raphael, sighing.

Raphael exhaled, watched Lucifer through the prison bars. "We agree, under the following conditions. You will lead us to Set and the spectres. You will help us fight them and do your best to ensure our survival and the survival of our allies. When that's complete, I will appeal to the Guild of Law and Justice for a pardon. If they agree, you will be transferred to Cocytus. I can do nothing else for you. Your crime is unforgivable, and it's not my place to decide your fate."

Lucifer gave an oily smile. "You have a deal. I only want to stretch my legs."

Raphael stepped back, unlatching Michael's sword from his hip. Gripping the sword in both hands, he ignited it, and the crackle of electrical interference buzzed between the cell and the fiery blade.

"Stay back."

After Connor moved out of the blast radius, Raphael slashed Michael's sword into the prison bars. Light and force exploded from the collision, blinding Connor with pure whiteness. The sound overwhelmed him, rattling his ribcage to the point of nausea. He latched both hands over his ears, but the waves still penetrated his flesh.

Finally, the energy directed itself back into the cage. The iron bars dissolved, and Lucifer stood up from his protective crouch. Slowly, he took his first step out of the cell, and the snark vanished. Lucifer looked at the ground, at his worn soles on muddy foundation, seeming to realize that he'd waited millennia just to walk on this side of the gate.

He glanced up, regaining his smirk. "Follow me."

Lucifer lifted his chin and straightened his back, sauntering to the cave's entrance with a bizarre aura of authority.

Before following Lucifer, Connor reached for Raphael. He leaned close enough to whisper, despite Lucifer already out of earshot.

"We have to stay one step ahead of him. You know you can't trust him. Not after all he's done."

Raphael sighed. "He never got along with Michael, but he always liked me. The brother I knew has to exist in there still. It never made sense to me why he turned. I've always...I've always wondered if maybe he was put down here for the wrong reasons."

"That would mean Michael lied."

"Which is impossible, of course. I know. But nothing else explains Lucifer's behavior."

Raphael shook his head, moving away from him without further words. Composing himself, Connor followed Raphael and Lucifer through the old oak door. But instead of a twisting path of deteriorating prison cells, they were met with an empty, circular room.

"The hell?" Connor froze. "This isn't the way we came."

"The prison is changing," Raphael murmured. "It knows."

"Wonderful." Connor's hands flew to his guns, unsheathing them from the harness with a fluid movement. Darkness enveloped the far half of the room. Connor trained both Castor and Pollux toward the mysterious black.

The sound came first: a guttural growl like magma churning beneath earth's surface.

A bloom of weightless whiskers rose from the gloom, perched above a row of carnivorous teeth. A reptilian face fully emerged behind them. Yellow eyes and crimson scales.

The creature slipped across the stone floor with a sickening wet slosh. Its large, menacing body stretched for dozens of feet, supported by four thick legs. Its razor talons could slice a man in half with one swipe, and its eyeballs rivaled the size of Connor's head.

"Fucanglong," Raphael said under his breath.

Connor didn't care about that mouthful of a word, or what Raphael meant by it. He already knew the slithering creature, its nostrils flaring with hot smoke, was a dragon.

## 24

Connor's thoughts slurred to a stop. Of all the weird and wild things he'd seen on this journey, of all the factors he'd been forced to re-evaluate about reality, this was now the strangest. An honest to God *dragon*.

He lifted both guns before he had time to think about it, unloading three shots from each barrel. Pollux's bullets targeted the dragon's head while Castor's zoomed toward the throat and front legs. Beside him, Raphael ignited both his own sword and Michael's, launching himself toward the creature.

The dragon's glowing eyes locked upon Connor. His bullets ricocheted off the reptilian scales and sparked when they hit the surrounding walls. But judging from the smoke billowing from the dragon's nostrils, it wasn't immune to pain.

"Shit!" Connor yelped as a swell of fire exploded from the dragon's mouth. He ducked and rolled, barely escaping the heat by crouching into a crook in the wall. As soon as the fire abated, he was on his feet again.

With a yell, he unloaded three more shots from Pollux's chamber. They skimmed the dragon's side, but the monster remained unfazed.

"For fuck's sake! This guy has to have a weakness!"

Nearby, Lucifer stayed tight against the wall. "It's clearly not you."

Blue and red fire flashed between Connor and the monster, followed by the dragon's throaty screech. Raphael fought somewhere within the brightly colored arc of fire, his arms moving too swiftly to perceive.

The dragon retreated, swatting at its seared nose with a clawed hand. Its jaw dropped with a bone-shattering roar, followed by another swell of fire aimed toward Connor. He barely managed to duck behind a pillar before the dragon fire followed him, close enough to singe his skin with proximity burns. Connor wheezed against the pillar, holding his breath and clenching his eyes shut until the heat dispersed.

Finally, the fire stopped and oxygen swooped into the vacuum. When he rounded the pillar again, Raphael was on the other side.

"There's a passage behind it! Let's go!"

"What?"

Raphael declined explanation, instead opting for a vine of *trust me* through their bond. Connor clambered to his feet and ran after the angel. When caught between a fire breathing dragon and Raphael, there was no question who he'd side with.

Of course, that hypothetical assumed he was running away from one and into the arms of the other. That was not the case, as Raphael's iron grip led him directly *beneath* the belly of the beast, toward a tiny black passage on the other side of the cavern.

Lucifer ran alongside him, close enough to bump shoulders. The passage beneath the fucanglong was wide enough to accommodate two of them side-by-side. Lucifer fell back a few steps to hobble behind Raphael and Connor. Connor was too frenzied to decide whether that was a good thing. Sure, Lucifer was closest to the jaws of death, but turning his back on Lucifer made the hairs on his neck stand up.

Not to mention, if Lucifer died, this was for nothing. And they would be no closer to figuring out what Set planned to do with the spectres.

It physically pained him, but Connor holstered one of his pistols and offered Lucifer his free hand. "C'mon! Faster!"

"It's been a while since I had to use my legs, human!"

It took every ounce of will to not retract his hand. The only thing that enforced his charity was the burst of dragon fire exploding down the tunnel, which nearly grazed Lucifer's back.

Lucifer leapt forward to avoid the flames, crashing into Connor's side. Connor stumbled, and his opposite shoulder smashed into the tunnel wall.

"Raphael!" Connor cradled his injured arm. Combat and fear were old friends, but no one ever got used to pain. Especially the sudden, sharp pain of a four-inch gash splitting open his flesh. Blood leaked down and coated his entire bicep, already curving across his elbow.

Raphael moved further down the corridor, only glancing back. "I know it hurts, but we can't stop."

Connor gritted his teeth, rolling through all the mental exercises for pain management. *Breathe in, breathe out. In, out. Pleasurable, happy things.* Of course, Raphael's face filled his mental flipbook, which was both good and bad.

"C'mon, Raphael, that dragon isn't getting in here."

"It's not just a dragon. The Claustrum is a living prison. It will keep sending reinforcements. We have to keep moving."

The walls and floor groaned. Lucifer pushed between Connor and Raphael, running until he left them behind in the tunnel's dark void. Raphael stashed Michael's sword and grabbed Connor's good arm. A faint blue glow emanated from the angel's fingers.

*Oh thank God,* Connor thought, expecting the sweet relief of healing to buffer away his flesh wound.

Before Raphael's powers reached his broken side, a wave of water rounded the previous corner, hitting them with a waist-deep torrent. They broke apart from one another, flailing to stay balanced against the powerful surge. Ahead, Lucifer lost the same battle, falling beneath the water's surface and splashing to stay afloat.

The water level rose from seemingly nothing, escalating impossibly fast to their chests. Connor's feet scraped stone as the tide pushed him, but he lacked any power to anchor himself to the ground. He thrust himself upward and gulped in air, barely missing the droplets of water slapping him across the face.

Raphael's black hair streaked across his face. He extended an arm. "Connor! Take my hand!"

Another rumble from the Claustrum's creaky structure, and the floor vanished from beneath their flailing feet. The rushing water tilted, and Connor's back hit the floor at a forty-five-degree angle. The floor had not disappeared—it sloped, downward, into a black gorge.

His nails scraped against moist brick, desperately searching for purchase.

He slid past Lucifer, who had somehow managed to find a single uneven brick to cling to with both pale hands. Less fortunately, Connor slipped into deeper gloom.

"Connor! Catch!"

Michael's red sword tumbled toward him, flaming blade over ebony hilt. Connor's fingers expanded, hopeful and fraught and...

Yes! His left hand wrapped around the warm hilt. He jabbed the blade into moist brick, jerking his body to a halt. Water rushed past, the sword's fire lighting a small radius around him. His good arm ached with the weight of his body dangling beneath it. Still, he'd hold onto the sword until his arm ripped off, if that's what it took.

A few feet above, Raphael caught himself with his own sword. His shoes dug into the wet rock, but there was nowhere to climb.

"Lucifer!" Raphael hollered upward, but no one answered.

Connor looked below his feet, and two red orbs flickered in the rift. And, sinister beneath the sound of rushing water, Connor heard a hiss.

"Raphael! There's something down there!"

Raphael looked around. "I...I might be able to move this platform we're on."

"Be my guest!"

Raphael pressed a flat palm to the rock. As he heaved with focused breaths, the platform growled. Connor relaxed slightly as the angle grew less steep, and the floor rose up to support his body.

A sharp noise that had nothing to do with Raphael rocked the platform. Connor's body twisted, and his lame arm flopped helplessly to his opposite side. He looked down and saw that Pollux's barrel lined up with a blue claw the size of a sedan.

He pulled the trigger and a golden bullet struck the claw. One large talon shattered, but the scaly hand hung on. Another claw joined it on the platform, a snakelike tongue flickering between them.

*I just made it angry.*

As the creature clawed its way upward, fighting against the rushing water, Raphael reactivated the platform's movement. Something solid jutted out above them—the rest of the floor, where the piece they laid upon had separated. Connor swallowed hard, glancing between the upper platform and the creature as Raphael brought them closer and closer to escape.

The creature lurked near enough for Connor's firelight to illuminate its face. Much like the fucanglong, it had the vague appearance of a dragon. But instead of scales, its skin glowed as blue blubber embellished with purple script. Sancti script.

The floors converged, crushing the monster's skull between two layers of brick. The cobalt glow drained from its skin and turned to a latent black sheen. Both claws loosened from the brick and slipped, leaving nine long hatch marks all the way down to the edge of the platform. The creature, just as much a prisoner as Connor, vanished into the blackness with a heavy splash. Raphael lifted their platform into its final realignment.

Connor groaned, spread-eagle on the wet floor, every muscle throbbing. It all hurt so much that he'd nearly forgotten his broken shoulder.

"You made it." Lucifer approached, soaked with what was probably his first bath in several millennia.

Connor sat up, not sure if Lucifer looked happy to see them or not.

Beside him, Raphael jerked Michael's sword out of the rock and lifted its light toward their enigmatic companion, gauging Lucifer's expression.

With his free hand, Raphael hauled Connor to his feet. Connor leaned into the touch, not bothering to cover his zeal, because the water drenched him so cold, and Raphael's body radiated heat. The angel reclaimed Michael's sword, and the fire and mystical blade both faded. Raphael pocketed the sword, urging Connor back into motion.

"We're not safe yet. Come on."

Connor forced his joints to run, keeping both Lucifer and Raphael in his peripheral vision. Within moments, his footsteps turned to *clanks* instead of the moist thud of rubber on brick.

The floor was no longer stone. Instead, beneath his feet spanned a network of rusted iron grating. Green, scaly imps latched to the underside of the floor grates, using clawed hands to reach up and scratch at their feet. Dirty, curved fingernails caught on the bottom of Connor's jeans, ripping the denim. The spitting hisses hit his ankles with acidic saliva that burned through his skin layer by layer.

Luckily, the floor turned to cobblestone a few feet later, but they continued running. The walls exploded on both sides as something broke through, scattering bricks and dust across the corridor. As Connor passed, a pair of hunched greenish humanoids clambered amidst the miasma of dust.

Connor grabbed Pollux from his now-bloody hand and pointed it back to the lumbering silhouettes. Barely looking, he fired off as many rounds as his trigger finger could manage, all while running blindly behind Raphael and Lucifer.

"You have to do something!" Connor insisted. "You're the only one who's strong enough. I saw what you did at the Embassy!"

"No, Connor. I had no control. I could kill all of us if I do that again."

"Would you rather run from this shit until we die anyway?"

Ahead, Lucifer ducked into an alcove with a wooden door. He held it open, gesturing impatiently. "In here!"

Raphael and Connor rushed into the room, and Lucifer slammed the door behind them. As soon as he secured both chain locks, something hit it from the other side. Hard.

Pressing his back against the door, straining to keep it from buckling, Lucifer managed a sneer. "I'm flattered the Claustrum thinks I'm worth all of its defenses."

"You better be worth it," Connor grumbled. His shoulder throbbed too badly to bother enforcing his brain-to-mouth filter.

His gaze darted, searching for another passage, but a few seconds of investigation revealed a complete dead end. Only a circular glass window in the ceiling allowed in a strip of light. Judging from a broken chain on the ground, the stench of animal feces, and the buzz of flies around a few rotten corpses, this room was once a cage for one of the Claustrum's hell beasts.

Connor rounded on Raphael, whose complexion could not be paler. The angel's eyes, usually enlightened with optimism and valor, stared vacantly. The chase had broken him, sucked the hope right out of his soul, as he seemed to realize they were out of options.

Connor reached for Raphael's cheek and forced Raphael to look at him. "We're stuck in here, and you're all we've got. I can help you control it, like last time."

"That was once. Just because you did it earlier—"

"Raphael, I like you, but shut up. Nothing you can do is more dangerous than what the Claustrum is already doing. And if I had to choose, I'd rather have you kill me than whatever's waiting for us on the other side of that door."

Raphael stayed quiet. Connor sensed the fear twist inside of him, as fresh as when he had knelt over Michael's abandoned armor. It had never been about his mortality. As Raphael had told Connor on the carriage ride to the Embassy, Sanctines had no concept of fearing death. No, he feared *Connor's* death; feared failing to protect his sworn ward. He feared loneliness in a world with one less brother.

Connor couldn't find the words to convince him, so he pushed something through the bond instead: hope. *Let me help you. We can do this together.* Then, something he needed to say aloud.

"You aren't alone."

The light returned, along with the goodness and empathy that had prompted Connor to become Raphael's ward in the first place. The light that made sharing his soul with someone else bearable. That light shone in Raphael's eyes, dissolving the cataracts of despair, and permeating through every tendril connecting him to Connor.

Raphael nodded. "Get back from the door, Lucifer."

Almost appearing relieved, Lucifer moved to the far side of the room without further retort. Raphael lifted a hand toward the door, where the iron frame bent from outside force. The wood between beams splintered outward like teeth.

Connor squeezed Raphael's shoulder. "Do it. I'm with you."

He refused to look at anything but Raphael. If this was his last moment, he wanted his final sight to be of the angel.

He focused on their connection, clearing his mind of all pain and panic, imagining himself as a rock of serenity for Raphael to adhere to. After a deep breath, Raphael's eyes filled with white light. The glow spread to his skin, steaming through every pore, almost making him too warm for Connor to touch. But Connor held on as he had in the Embassy, clinging to the idea of control in a sea of chaos.

The room shook. The jagged dome overhead leaked streams of dirt, pouring upon them like sand in an hourglass. Pebbles the size of hail broke loose from the ceiling, *clip-clattering* with each impact. The more violently the room quaked, the harder it was for Connor to remain standing. Raphael was slipping from him, his control teetering on a steep cliff while the ground dissolved beneath it.

"Hey! Focus!" Connor's grip tightened. He closed his eyes and mentally poured white light from his chest into his companion. Controlled, steady, ready to be reeled if needed.

Connor heard the door fall. He heard Lucifer screaming, heard the growls of a thousand night-creatures crawling toward them, and heard the scrape of claws against stone. And from within, he surged all his strength to Raphael, both mental and physical, for their final moment.

"Now!"

The ceiling imploded as if a giant had stepped into it, raining dozens of tons of solid rock upon the horde of evil bursting through the doorway. When the boulders hit the floor, enough dust exploded to blot out the scant ceiling light, blanketing Connor and Raphael in obscurity.

Silence.

The glow receded from Raphael's body, and he slumped like a rag doll against Connor, who caught him and gently lowered them both to the ground. But the dust settled, and he smiled up at Connor. Grinned at him. With the bond wide open between them, the relief was too much to contain without beaming, laughing. The thrill of still being alive after a torrent of death pushed them to the edge of oblivion...that was worth at least a smile.

Connor leaned over him, a hand resting on the side of Raphael's throat, laughing in return. Buzzy elation danced between them, almost intoxicating. Perhaps it was the fact that Connor had never seen Raphael smile so genuinely, beyond mere politeness. A smile that highlighted the subtle age lines in the corners of his eyes and that almost pronounced the dusting of freckles across his nose. It flipped Connor's gut, and if Lucifer hadn't been standing so close...

Then Raphael's smile dropped, and he rubbed his own shoulder. He sat up on his elbows. "Sorry I had to push out your pain before. We didn't have time to stop."

Connor gave a laugh, still alight from the experience of pure entwinement. The shoulder almost didn't hurt. Everything just felt tingly, from the tip of his nose to his fingers and feet.

"I don't mind you pushing it out before, but it would be nice to have it healed now."

Raphael fingers brushed his elbow, and cobalt light spiraled from the contact. It washed over and through Connor's skin, knitting up every deformation it discovered. Connor exhaled as his pain evaporated.

"Thanks," he said.

"Connor..."

Lucifer rose to his feet, snorting. "Spare me your ardor. We should go before they send something else."

Raphael's face tilted toward the mountain of rubble that buried their predators. The rocks sloped upward to the fractured ceiling where the strip of dim light had returned.

"And now there's up."

## 25

"Ah, sulfur and ash. I've missed the outdoors." Lucifer strolled out of the Claustrum cave with his hands on his hips. His clothing hung tattered and half soaked, his hair was a knotted mess, and dirt caked his skin despite his trip through the river. Though he looked like a most unfortunate beggar, it put no damper on his proud posture.

The bleakness of Abyssus was a comparatively welcome sight once they climbed out of the Claustrum. Despite that, Connor's hands hadn't moved more than two inches from his guns since they'd emerged from Lucifer's prison. After ten minutes of downhill wandering, they found their way back to their starting path. They crossed the bridge that had led them to the godforsaken prison, and God willing, they would never have to return.

They traveled over cliffs in silence until Connor's legs strained. Abyssus was a labyrinth of bridges and rivers, nooks and caves that somehow all led into other, larger caverns within the vast underground web. The deeper they voyaged into Abyssus, the more lost he felt. And a part of him wondered if Lucifer wasn't leading them to wander in permanence, blind and helpless, while he snuck off cackling. Did the devil really have to keep his word, or was that wishful thinking?

"Where are you taking us?" Connor asked uselessly. Surely Lucifer wouldn't give him an answer, particularly one he'd understand. But maybe Raphael would be able to make sense of it.

Lucifer replied over his shoulder, "Graveyard of the Gods!"

Aphrodite had mentioned that place. *Where old, powerless gods go to die.* Where the Sanctines becoming spectres ought to have gone.

Raphael cleared his throat, trailing behind Lucifer. "Why there?"

Lucifer glanced back "It started as Set's recruitment base. He'd see the old and the weak standing on their pedestals, ready to become stone. He approached them and offered...an alternate ending. I imagine if he's in Abyssus, there's no more suitable place to start his war."

Raphael frowned. "You *imagine?* You're not positive?"

Lucifer stopped and turned, his arms crossed. He arched an overgrown brow, the edge of his lip curling upward. "Give my charm some credit, brother. He came to me for a little bit of advice, and in return, I asked the right questions. My speculation is incredibly informed."

Connor snorted. "From what I've heard, you failed *your* world domination plan. Why would he possibly want your advice?"

"Because I knew where to find the Sword of Creation."

Michael had been right. Maybe he hadn't been fully forthcoming with every piece of information, but he'd known exactly what demons from his past longed to conquer him.

Lucifer continued, shrugging. "And now my bargain with Set has been met. I owe him nothing more. And look at you, having brought Michael's Icon to me and breaking me out. I must say, I couldn't have planned that part. A nice bonus to what I asked Set to do to him."

Connor stared, so much coursing through him—some emotions his own, some Raphael's —like a crowd of voices speaking over each other.

Raphael knew. Connor knew. Even Michael himself had known, before the fact. Yet Connor shared a single thread of hope with Raphael, that perhaps it wasn't true. That perhaps the Lucifer who had become their grudging ally, who Raphael struggled heroically to understand, was not the mastermind behind Michael's death.

That thread of hope snapped and left Raphael a bit more broken, with a rawness Connor wished he could reach in and patch up.

"It's been thousands of years," Raphael whispered. "You rebelled. You committed an unforgivable crime. And you think he deserved to die for upholding justice?"

Lucifer grabbed the hem of his tattered shirt and lifted, revealing the skin and bones of his starving torso. A thick, knotted, unmistakable scar curled from his bottom rib to the top of his pants, pink and raised against pale skin. A stab in the gut from Michael and a permanent sentence in the Claustrum for attempting to overthrow humanity—that's how Raphael had described it before.

"He did deserve it." Lucifer glowered, yanking his shirt back down. "He was anything but a white knight. And since Set took great delight in killing him as well, rest assured I was not his only enemy."

Connor gently grabbed Raphael's shoulders, holding him back. On the surface, it was to physically restrain his partner from snapping Lucifer's neck, which Raphael would undoubtedly regret later. Beyond that, maybe his touch could be as calming to Raphael as Raphael's was to him.

Lucifer turned away, thank God, leaving them to continue on their path in silence. After much stumbling through rocky crevices, Connor and the angels found themselves kneeling on a particularly high cliff, looking down at what looked like an outdoor museum of statues. An uneven scatter of effigies—not all humanoid or human sized—occupied most of the plateau, stretching for almost a mile north and east. They were frozen in stone with their heads bowed, a final gesture of subservience to humanity before nature reclaimed them.

"This is it," Raphael murmured.

"Shit, it's huge," Connor said. "How're we gonna find Set in this place?"

Lucifer pointed to an empty patch in the far left of the Graveyard. The plateau was clean and empty, somewhat acting as a pier. Beyond the edges of the jetty looked like a three-hundred-foot drop into inky water.

And in the middle of the jetty stood Set and innumerous spectres.

There must have been as many, or more, as at the Embassy. When Set fled after murdering Michael, every spectre in the vicinity had run with him, some of them transforming into their smoky forms to slip away even faster. How they'd found a portal to get through to Abyssus, Connor had no clue. Either there was a secret portal Set had known about, or a herald guarding a portal was lying dead somewhere.

Either way, Set had made it to the Graveyard with his army, and he seemed poised to take things one step further. Most of the spectres slinked in the shadows, crouched against the cliff walls. Six of them stood in a circle in the center of the plateau as Set paced around them.

"What do you think this is about?" Connor muttered close to Raphael's ear.

The angel turned his face, nose bumping against Connor's cheek. The warm intimacy was a small comfort

"I don't know," he answered. "Maybe that's his personal guard."

A slick *shink* of metal, and the Sword of Creation was in Set's hand. All six spectres were facing each other in the ring, their backs to their master. So, Set's first unlucky victim had no way of anticipating the blade shoving straight through him.

Connor's mouth dried out. "I didn't think he'd stab his personal guard."

This, however, did not seem to be an act of murder but perhaps an act of suicide. For one by one, the spectres obediently impaled themselves onto the blade, and golden light burst from every one of their wounds. The Sword was barely long enough to fit all six bodies, but the spectres squeezed together, trying to occupy the same space.

Maybe they *were*.

As Set began a foreign incantation, the spectres twisted and squealed. Their white flesh bubbled beneath the surface, seeming to melt. In the fires of that moment, the skin met and merged, binding them all into a writhing, squealing blob.

The light pouring from the ritual became too bright to look at directly. Connor shielded his eyes with a hand and waited for the screaming to stop. The longer this secondhand torture continued, the more nausea swelled in his throat. *Please make it stop, dear God...*

As if his prayers were answered, the sounds did stop, and the light dimmed. Left in its place was a towering, barely humanoid figure, lumbering far above the Graveyard statues.

Set withdrew the Sword and took a step back, craning his head to marvel at his latest creation. The monstrosity let out a roar that shook the mountains and Connor's ribs. A dusting of loose gravel descended upon his head from the cliffs above.

"Holy shit. What is that thing?"

It really didn't matter if that thing had a name, though. Connor was all-too familiar with what it meant. This was Set's nuclear option. His final weapon to wipe out his enemies now that his stealthy assassin plan had failed. And in his lust for revenge, suddenly his targets had become far less specific. This monstrosity would not be picky about who it crushed beneath its feet. Maybe Set had been concerned about collateral damage before, but he'd clearly moved past that.

Even Lucifer looked less than enthused. A crease formed deep into his forehead.

"This better be a good cause to die for," he said dryly. "Because we're not getting out of this alive."

---

Clara emerged through the omni-portal, greeted by fresh Paradisa air. She drank in a deep breath, embracing the clean smell. A gust of snowy wind cut through her, but anything was preferable to the rancid humidity of Abyssus.

She needed a herald who could convey a message to Connor wherever he was. And the thing about heralds, Hephaestus had said, was that they usually held the dual role of portal guardians. Generally, they stayed put at their home portals, which made them exceptionally predictable to find.

In their case, the most friendly and predictable herald they knew was at the top of Mount Olympus. She glanced left and right, searching the nearby perimeter of the portal. Sure enough, a skinny man with a snake-engraved staff hanging from his hip idled at the base of the portal dais.

"Hermes!" Hephaestus called, brushing past Clara to lead the way.

The portal guard whipped around. His winged shoes flapped and lifted him into a defensive hover. His dark hands reached for his staff, just before he caught sight of who his visitors were.

"Oh! Hephaestus. Dangerous to sneak up on me, you know. Could have blown your head off. I'm pretty tough, you know."

Hephaestus snorted. "I quiver in my boots."

"I mean it, really! Aphrodite, you wouldn't want me killing him on accident, would you? I don't think my conscience could take that... leaving Aphrodite all lonely like that. Guess I'd have to keep her compa—"

Aphrodite herself cut him off with a stern, "Hermes..." And probably for the best, as Clara distinctly felt a flash of frustration spike in Hephaestus's heart.

"Ay, forgive me Dite, you know I'm a joker. So, what brings you back here? You didn't bust up your carriage, did you?"

Clara stepped forward, looking up at the hovering god. "We need to send a message to our friends. My brother is Raphael's ward, and they're...well, we don't know where they are. But it's urgent we get in touch with them."

Hermes lowered himself back to the ground. With a smooth movement, he unhooked the compact silver staff from his belt, and held it out to Clara.

"What would you like to tell them?"

his is really bad." It felt superfluous to whisper such in Raphael's ear, but Connor couldn't stop himself from vocalizing it. Perhaps voicing his dread expelled some of it from his chest, although he couldn't say he felt much better after.

"You're not wrong," his companion murmured.

*"Connor? Connor, can you hear me?"*

Connor grasped at his skull, nearly toppling from the sudden voice in his head. Clara's voice. But not the part of his brain that thought in Clara's voice; this was *actually* Clara's voice.

"Wha...? Clara?"

Raphael frowned, touching his shoulder. "Connor? What's wrong?"

"You can't hear that? Clara...I heard her voice," he stammered. "I heard it, I sw—"

*"I'm inside your head with a herald. Hermes."*

"She says she's with Hermes," he blurted to Raphael. The angel's eyes widened. Connor covered one ear with a hand and returned to Clara. "Yeah. Yeah I hear you, Clara! You're okay, right? Are you?"

"I'm fine. Where are you?"

"We're in Abyssus, at the Graveyard of Gods. We found Set."

"Connor, before you do anything...we went to the library to look up what you asked, and...you were right about Michael. He was hiding *everything* from you. Michael asked Set to kill Osiris. They thought he was some kind of elder god thing posing as the king." She recounted a brief story that opened his eyes. "And now that he has his army, he's been going after Inquisitors. He feels like they all went home heroes, but he got kicked out of Aaru, and they never vouched for him because their mission was so secret. There's probably more, but that's all we could find in the library. Maybe now you can confront Michael about it though."

"Yeah, well...Michael's dead now. So, I guess whatever else he wanted to keep went to the grave with him."

He braced himself for Raphael's grief to spike at those words. As anticipated, Connor's chest tingled, and a swell of cold brushed down his spine. The more frequent these moments became, the more it struck him that the effect of grief on Raphael's body was different than it'd been on his own with Eric. Connor had always felt it as nausea, panic, heat. Raphael's lurched as this numb void. An emptiness that couldn't be filled.

Clara's voice softened. "Oh, no...that's...God, is Raphael okay?"

Connor glanced at his companion, noting the way his cheeks sagged. Raphael was always handsome to him, but there was no denying the hollow glaze in his eyes.

"Been better. But we've got a bigger problem than that, Clara... Set's here, and he just merged about six spectres into this big fuckin' monster. It looks like it crawled out of the ass end of a sewage pipe, and it's big as a house."

"Excuse me? He *merged* spectres?"

"Watched it with my own eyes. Guess the Sword of Creation can be pushed pretty far."

She sighed, muttering, "Dammit. You *cannot* let him take that thing to Paradisa."

"Wasn't planning on it. But we're a little outgunned right now. It's just us and Lucifer."

"*Lucifer?*"

The limits of Clara's incredulity were probably being pushed. He couldn't see her, but somehow felt her gaping at him.

"It's a long story."

"Fine. Let me see what I can do about backup. Don't try anything stupid until we get there!"

"W-Wait, until *you* get here?" If he hadn't been laying on his stomach, he would have thrown up his hands. "Oh, no. You do *not* need to come here. You stay up there with Hephaestus and Aphrodite, do you hear me?"

"No promises. Love you!"

"Clara!"

He felt her vanish and muttered a swear under his breath.

Clara's palm collected sweat around the caduceus. If Hermes could hear her conversation with Connor, his expression betrayed nothing.

Clara's throat tightened, and she withdrew into her own mind as the line between her and Connor broke. She knew it not by the silence, but by the empty ache his absence left behind. When Clara released the snake staff, severing her connection to Connor for good, a hot tear escaped her left eye. It was strange to be so close to him and suddenly ripped away. Strange to have taken him for granted for so many years, only to be thrown into a situation where she didn't know if she'd see him again.

The feeling dissolved when she heard her name announced in the real world. Aphrodite's hand fell upon her, turning her around.

"Where are they?" Aphrodite asked.

"The Graveyard of Gods." Clara shook her head. "Set is using the Sword to merge multiple spectres together and..."

Hephaestus leaned closer. "And?"

"It's monstrous. It would take a small army to destroy, they said. That, and uh...he said they have Lucifer with them. He's the one who led them there."

Hermes let out a low noise. "What are they thinking, breaking that monster from the Claustrum? I've never much liked Edenites, but I'll never forget the day Michael spoke of what happened. He said his brother tried to conquer all three realms. That he wanted to kill all the humans and take Earth for us."

Clara pursed her lips. "I don't know how much we should trust Michael's word, anymore. But either way, Raphael made some sort of deal with him for a less secure prison when this is all over."

Hephaestus crossed his arms. "So they've got Lucifer, but who else? There's no way they can take that thing on just the three of them."

"Right," Clara said, turning back to Hermes. "Which is where I need your help."

The herald jumped slightly, his winged shoes flapping to keep him afloat. "Oh? Wow, I'm never pulled into these kinds of things. Exciting!"

Clara closed her eyes, rearranging the facts in her head. First, they needed to call upon some help. There was the war guild, of course, but who knew what state they were in since Michael had been apparently murdered. There was Athena, who probably wanted nothing more than to drive her sword through Set's heart.

Contacting them with Hermes' powers would be easy enough. Getting them all in one place and transported to Abyssus? Maybe less easy.

"I have a list of people I want to ask to help us," Clara said, her brow tightening. "But...is there a way for you to get them here?"

"Of course! I can make portals at will. I can bring anyone anywhere or take you to any place you'd like to go." Hermes beamed, and thrust his caduceus into the open air beside them. White light spun out of the end and looped into an oval-shaped portal. Unlike most, it did not shine with colored light to indicate a destination, nor did anything appear on the other side of it except for smoke.

"You'll need to choose your location first, though," he added. "Who are we going to pick up first?"

———

As they descended the mountain and crept discreetly through the Graveyard rows, Connor tried to quell his distrust roaring toward Lucifer. Their only ally in the field of withered stone gods was someone who had tried to destroy humanity. What could possibly go wrong?

Although he stayed tight at Raphael's side, he always kept Lucifer in his peripheral vision. At least Raphael had finally come around to cautious realism. The earnestness in his heart regarding his brother had almost been nauseating.

Maybe he'd talk to Clara about all this ward codependency, if he ever saw her again.

*When you see her again.* He glanced up, admonishing his own brain. *Have a little faith.*

They ducked behind a few stone effigies, far enough not to be detected by Set. Connor rubbed his scruffy jaw. "What's the plan? Do we want him dead or alive?"

"I would prefer if Set survived long enough for a trial with the Guild of Law and Justice. There's a lot we don't know about him. It would be most just to hear his whole story and punish him accordingly."

Lucifer's nose wrinkled. "Well if we're going to get started, I'll need a weapon, won't I?"

"Find a stick." Connor deadpanned.

"We're not fighting sheep, human. I need a *real* weapon." When Lucifer's gaze landed on Raphael's belt, his expression morphed into sly content. He gestured to the ivory hilt. "That one, perhaps."

Raphael didn't blink. "That's my Icon. No."

*Hooyah,* Connor thought, broadcasting his pride loudly to Raphael. *Don't let him push you.*

Lucifer stepped forward, his face inches from Raphael's. "The other one, then."

Raphael's hand fell to the other hilt attached to his belt—the one with ebony and rubies.

A hint of a threat crept into his voice. "You're not wielding Michael's weapon."

"Why? Because I killed him? Then I'm particularly entitled to it."

In the jetty beyond, Set yelled out to his spectres. Luckily it startled Lucifer enough to shut him the hell up.

Connor leaned into his companion. "It's just a sword now, Raphael. Let him have it."

Raphael hesitated, running a thumb over the black engravings on Michael's hilt. Finally, as Set's voice grew louder, he tossed the sword to Lucifer with a disgusted grunt.

Raphael rubbed the spot between his brows, clenching his eyes shut. Connor offered a small smile that Raphael didn't see and touched the angel's wrist.

"Hey," he muttered, turned away from Lucifer. "Let's get through this. He'll go back to prison. It'll all be over soon."

"I've been so foolish." Raphael sighed, his words barely above a whisper. "I knew he was behind Michael's murder. That's why I went all this way to find him. But I still didn't want to believe it."

"Of course you didn't. He's your brother. No matter what Clara does, I will never stop believing in her. I can't expect you to do any differently."

Raphael opened his eyes. And the gaze he granted, sparkling with awe, filled Connor with warmth. "I've lived a long time, Connor. Thousands of years. And I'm suddenly unsure how I made it this long without someone like you."

Connor let out a quiet laugh, rubbing the back of his neck. His hand brushed against the chain of his Saint Olivia medal. That medal had followed him around for decades, reminding him of his family, his heritage, and a facsimile of his faith. But he didn't need an amalgamation of holy books anymore. He had Raphael.

"This could go bad. Battles always can. There's never a guarantee. So if I don't make it out of this," he said, unhooking the chain from his neck, "add this one to your collection."

He dropped the medal into Raphael's hand, and the angel stared at it with glassy eyes. Raphael pursed his lips, bringing the medal close to his chest. "Nothing is going to happen to you. Not if I'm here."

"I regret nothing." Connor smiled with real authenticity for once. "You've already saved me from myself."

Connor watched the small details, from the crinkle in Raphael's eyes to the white knuckles wrapped around the medal. The moment dilated, and Connor simply stared at Raphael's lips. He sucked in a breath, having momentarily forgotten to breathe.

Raphael leaned in, slightly. But his feet stayed rooted on the stone, one hand holding the medal over his heart.

"Good luck to us both, then," Raphael whispered.

An elbow jabbed Connor in the ribs, rudely popping the bubble he occupied with Raphael. Lucifer muttered, "Look at what just opened."

At the edge of the jetty, a green light sparked in mid-air. It spun around itself, expanding with every rotation, until it was nearly seven feet across and ten feet tall. And in the murky glaze of the portal, reflected like an underwater mirror, waited a small army of familiar faces. Hachiman, with his bow already strung, led the front of the pack. The newly appointed general crossed over into Abyssus with two silent steps.

"Let's go," Lucifer said, and they were on the move to meet their allies.

As Lucifer led their attack with Michael's sword raised, Raphael and Connor running behind him, Connor couldn't help but watch where the Raphael's hair curled at the nape of his neck. *I've got your back, Raph. Hell, I've got your everything.*

# 26

They emerged from the Graveyard into the jetty clearing, where a dozen of Paradisa's strongest warriors poured in from Hermes' green portal. Some were familiar, like Sekhmet, the lion goddess, and Athena, running around with her blue sword. So many more were wild and unknown, a variety of garb and weaponry. War calls shouted in every language. Connor watched the world itself come together in this tiny sliver of the universe.

The fighting occupied land and sky, surrounding Connor from every angle. His guns were futile in comparison to the fire swords and lightning arrows whizzing around him. Past Lucifer, a towering god slashed at a half-dozen spectres with his scythe. That alone was enough to keep a fifteen-foot radius clear around him.

As Connor ran closer to the portal, he glimpsed a flash of Clara stumbling out of it. He thought she met his eyes for a moment, but the glance ended in a blink. Behind her, Hephaestus's fire bloomed to engulf three spectres, which haloed his sister's silhouette.

Connor found himself smiling, proud of her in the most detached sense. Like it was the first time he could be proud of what she was doing without taking some form of credit for it.

Raphael was a fucking sight, too. The wind swept his hair off his brow, and adrenaline flushed his lips into a deep red. He spun grace-fully, the blue flame sword creating a halo of light around him until his eyes seemed to glow. A carnal, uncompartmentalized part of Connor longed to grab him in the middle of battle and kiss him right there.

"Connor!" shouted Lucifer. "Have you fallen asleep?"

*Well at least that's the first time he's used my name,* Connor thought wryly. But maybe the prince of darkness wasn't wrong. He needed to focus. He shoved his desire into a box to save for later and put himself back in the fight.

He shifted his attention to where the pale, massive spectre and Set had converged. Sekhmet lunged for the creature in her lion-headed form, teeth bared. Her claws sunk into its chest, but it batted her away like a ragdoll. Meanwhile, Set stood barricaded by a few armored spectres and the big one itself, so the only person who'd made it to his proximity was Badb. The spectres swarmed her almost immediately, ten hands ripping at her clothes and tugging at her hair, forcing her to retreat.

Connor ducked behind one of the effigies at the perimeter. The thick stone pedestal buffered some sounds of the battle, isolating him enough to think.

He closed his eyes, sucked in a deep breath, and tightened all the loose screws within himself. His bond with Raphael, once a source of strife, now became an anchor of healing. The tendril danced around him. *Follow Raphael's path.*

Soon, that tendril came within a few feet of him, along with the scruff of shoes on stone. Raphael plopped down beside him, sharing the cover of the pedestal.

Connor cracked open an eye. His companion looked a little worse for wear. Never had Raphael sweat in his presence before, but his forehead shined with it now.

"Starting to think we need to use your supernova mode to take this thing out."

"Absolutely not. That's far too unstable. I could easily hurt someone."

Connor sighed. Deep down, he knew Raphael was probably right. The only reason it had worked in the Claustrum was because it was just them and an immovable object to focus on.

He poked his head over the statue's pedestal, sizing up their current status. Most of their army remained—only a few had succumbed to the creature or Set—and the spectres were culled. Still, there was that damned monster casting a shadow over...

Connor froze. He thought he had seen Clara running headfirst toward the big one.

Shit. That was Clara running headfirst toward the big one.

---

The Graveyard of Gods was an arena of blood and magic. Clara danced between the violence—*ha, never thought I'd use gymnastics for this!*—and her arms burned with every hack of her axes. In the corner of her vision, Hephaestus battled with fire, dousing spectres effortlessly with its majesty. At his back, Aphrodite slashed her brass dagger across the faces of monsters and shoved the knife between their ribs in the seconds between.

One particularly burly spectre made the unwise choice of charging at Aphrodite, his arms outstretched.

She saw him before Hephaestus did, but she didn't run. Rather, she dropped her dagger and took a defensive stance, her hands readied before her. When the spectre was in arm's reach, Aphrodite sunk both hands into his leather armor and hammer-threw him right off the cliff.

Hephaestus looked back and stared, his mouth agape. Aphrodite caught his lopsided gaze, let out an exhausted little laugh, and brushed her wild hair behind her ear. "What?"

He didn't sputter out an answer—instead, he crossed the distance between them and grabbed Aphrodite by the waist. He kissed her, firm and fierce, like he'd never get the chance to do it again. Clara's head spun with it, hit like a brick by his reflected passion. She couldn't help but stare, transfixed by the divine couple, as Aphrodite grabbed Hephaestus by the collar and pulled him closer.

A spectre leapt toward them with a sword lifted to kill. Clara threw her axe with all the power she could muster, and it thumped the spectre into smoke before the kissing couple noticed.

"Can y'all save that for later?" she shouted, raising a hand to reclaim her boomerang axe.

Hephaestus smiled sheepishly, waving her over. "Clearly you have things handled!"

Clara joined them, but kept her eyes darting around in search of enemies. "Yeah, well, doesn't hurt to have a firewall."

"Not a bad idea."

At Clara's back, Hephaestus conjured a blaze from his palms, lacing it around himself, Clara, and Aphrodite in protection. Clara's palms sweat around both her axes, but it had nothing to do with the heat of nearby flames. To her right side, Aphrodite brandished her dagger and belt, spinning the chain in a lethal lasso.

"Ready?" Hephaestus hollered, glancing over his shoulder. Distracted, Clara caught his orange-rimmed gaze.

"I don't know!" she screamed, watching a barrage of god-on-spectre fights through Hephaestus's flames. A few brave souls made a dash for Set, but they barely managed to make it through his personal ring of spectre guards. Most were occupied with the behemoth at the center of the battle.

"Just don't let anyone kill you!"

Hephaestus lowered his fiery barrier and activated the spear-end of his cane. Within moments, every spectre who'd lurked around the fire waiting to strike swarmed them at once. Yet they stood firm as a resolute triad, back to back with one another.

Clara kept one axe in her right hand to hack at Spectres within her reach. With her left hand, she hauled the other boomerang axe across the jetty. The flying axe struck a female spectre in the back, right as the spectre was making a move to crush Athena's skull.

The goddess of war stumbled, wide-eyed, before watching the axe make its return trip to Clara. She arched a brow, with a curious blend of respect and concern across the fire of battle, before resuming her own decimation of spectres.

As her axe cartwheeled across the Graveyard, Clara's vision filled with the silhouette of a particularly nasty spectre, its eyes jaundiced and hair gray.

She swung with her remaining axe, but it dodged too quickly, bending inward to avoid being disemboweled. Clara stumbled, and the spectre rushed in as she fought to regain balance. Yet, as it lifted its clawed hand to strike her throat, Clara couldn't help but grin.

It barely had time to display shock before her returning axe tore through its body. By the time the axe hit Clara's palm, the smell of ashen smoke brushed over her face.

"Oof!"

She sensed the pain before Hephaestus hit the ground. A pulsing throb echoed from the back of her knee and down her calf, although nothing personally struck her.

Her instincts kicked in before her mind, and her arm swung in an arc toward Hephaestus's attacker. The axe struck spectre flesh and clanked against Aphrodite's dagger as the goddess arched the same motion from the opposite side.

Aphrodite shot her a breathless smile. "Sorry."

"Great minds."

On the ground, Hephaestus's fingers laced around his bad knee. Clara's leg still ached, a problem that she still wasn't sure how to address with their bond.

"I'm sorry," he blurted, struggling to sit up. "That one got me."

Clara knelt, momentarily safe as Aphrodite guarded them with her spinning chain and darting dagger. "I'm fine. Can you can stand?"

"Yes, yes." He forced himself to his feet, but certainly leaned into her assistance as he rose. "By Styx, why hasn't anyone gotten to Set yet and ended this…"

"He's surrounded by spectres," Clara said, eyes darting around as she spoke. "But it's mostly the big one that keeps getting in the way. It's taking out people left and right!"

Hephaestus untangled himself from her, supporting his weight back on his cane. "Their weapons do nothing. And good luck getting the Sword of Creation off of Set…"

Clara looked around the battlefield, which had become the definition of insanity. Sanctines made a leap for the massive creature, only to be batted way. Even when they tried to strategize, attacking at multiple angles, trying to distract it, the monster disposed of them like a dog shaking off water. One unfortunate soldier took a backhand to his entire body, and he limply flew off the edge of the jetty. His screams echoed for several seconds, all the way down the fall, until darkness claimed him.

That sound would probably never leave her nightmares. But from it, a spark. An idea.

"We don't have to kill it," she said. "We just have to get it to go over the edge."

Hephaestus sputtered a laugh. "Oh yes, we *just* have to do that. All our problems are clearly solved."

Aphrodite glanced over her shoulder, rolling her eyes. "Her idea is a good one. If you work together to lure it to the edge, I can push it over from behind."

Hephaestus steeled his fingers, clearly choosing his words carefully. "My dear wife, I adore you. But you may be underestimating how difficult it is to push that thing around."

Clara cocked her hip, shooting Aphrodite a smile. "She just threw a spectre like it was a frisbee. I think she can handle it."

"If I can't, someone else can. Either way, you two need to get to work."

And so, they did. Clara kept her steps slow to accommodate Hephaestus, which worked well enough since they could plan along the way.

"Basically," she said, "I'll hit it with the axes and lure it toward me. If you tease it with fire from its other side, but still in the direction of the cliff, we should be able to guide it in that direction."

Hephaestus nodded, filling one of his hands with fire. "I can start from here. If it gets too close to you, then you run. We'll contain it."

Maybe it was the Bishara blood running through her veins, but all she could think was *I'm not running. Not anymore.*

As Hephaestus sent his first burst of fire toward the lurching monster, Clara rounded its other side. One of the war gods gave her a funny look, but she shooed him away.

"Stand back! We're gonna try something! Make sure Set doesn't get in our way!"

The war god nodded and backed off, making a beeline for Set instead. Clara took a deep breath, steeling herself for the task at hand. They were nearly fifty feet from the edge of the cliff. Fifty feet to guide this creature without Set getting in the way or getting hit with an instantly fatal swipe of its hand.

Easy, right?

One of Hephaestus's fireballs hit the creature in the face. Along with his fire, Hephaestus threw out plenty of verbal taunts as well.

"Get over here you lumbering bastard!"

It roared, rushing toward him with speed that should not have been possible. His eyes widened. Clara's heart leapt into her throat— they were both so damn terrified, she couldn't be sure if it was from Hephaestus or herself—and she quickly threw an axe to land in the base of its throat.

The creature stopped in its tracks, swaying to regain its lopsided balance. Hephaestus shamelessly let out a relieved whimper as the hulk set its sights on Clara.

"Yeah, not him! Not him! Come and get *me*!"

Thirty more feet.

Clara braced herself for the rumble of the ground as the creature staggered toward her. She backtracked on the toes of her feet, tossing another axe into the monster's shoulder. It opened its jaw wide, revealing a mass of fangs and a pure void of blackness. She glanced back. She'd run so close to the edge that falling off herself was just as much of a risk as getting crushed by the monster.

That meant it was time.

Clara spied Aphrodite readying herself behind the creature, both her hands lifted. Clara raised her own palms, only to reclaim her axes before the creature met its fate.

"Now!"

Aphrodite pushed the air in front of her with a carnal scream. Time itself groaned with the force, and the air seemed to ripple like a soundwave. The force of moving air lifted the creature wholly off the ground, a leviathan of pure mass, and it hurtled directly toward Clara.

She rolled out of the way just in time, feeling the rush of falling mass brush by her. With her face buried in the stone, she couldn't see the monster succumb to the force of gravity, but she could hear it— the howl of its plummet and the unanimous cheer that echoed across the battlefield.

---

G*oddamn. I will never doubt you again, sis.*
This close to the edge of the jetty, wind rippled across Connor's shoulders and through his hair. As he watched the monster careen into the abyss, time seemed to slow.

While everyone else cheered and ogled the dying leviathan, Connor zoomed right to Set. The pariah's face was screwed up in anguish.

He recalled the duel with Michael, where Set had shed his mortality for a moment by taking off the ankh. Taking away his Icon was the only way to win. It was hanging around his neck, too close to his person to grab, but there were other ways of parting him from it...

Right after that same duel, Set had fled as soon as the odds were against him, only to find another sanctuary for himself and his army. Maybe if Connor had been faster, or better, it wouldn't have been that way. No way in hell would he let that happen again. His aim had sucked before, his focus torn between himself and Raphael's pain.

Today, his insides were calm as an ocean. Failure was not an option.

He jumped to his feet. "I've got an idea. Trust me, okay?"

"Don't go, Connor," Raphael's voice was barely audible over the wind. His hand sunk into Connor's jacket, pulling him back down. "I vowed to protect you."

"And I promised Michael I'd protect you."

It hit: the moment when Connor recognized something terrible and inevitable that could not be taken back. He saw the inside of his commander's office after Eric's death, and the guilty look on his roommate's face as Connor hauled his personal affects out of the barracks. The realization that his timeline was now fixed with only one outcome, only one choice, and the time to act was gradually eroding.

"Cover me."

"Wait!" Raphael cried, but his voice vanished beneath the roar of battle.

Connor was all fists and American muscle. With adrenaline glossing over the fatigue in his joints, he ran to Set, leaping over the fallen. His golden guns had never felt heavier. For the next twenty strides, nothing stood between him and Set. The bastard's back was turned, and oblivious to what was coming.

With ten feet between them, Connor shot three times at the base of Set's spine. The bullets barely dented his torso plate, but it was enough to get him to turn around.

That's when Connor took his real shot.

The bullet whizzed through the chain hanging around Set's throat, shattering metal fragments all around him. The ankh necklace flew from his neck in a fluttering somersault and landed near the edge of the cliff.

Their eyes met across the battlefield, Set's fingers clawing at his bare throat.

Before Set could make a move for it, Connor unloaded what would be an entire magazine in his direction. The god screeched, susceptible to all the pain without his Icon to numb it. Connor tried his best to make the bullets nonfatal, still determined to let this bastard survive long enough for Paradisan justice, but he wouldn't let Set get that Icon back.

Connor shoved aside a Sanctine in his way and slid across the stone, grabbing the fallen ankh as he passed. His body stopped inches before the cliff's edge, slowed by the friction of his jeans. His hand with the ankh flung out over the lip, and the chain dangled over a bottomless pit.

Set's Icon glinted in the faint light, swinging like a pendulum. He glanced back toward the Egyptian god, who was running at him in jackal-headed form, fangs bared. It was obvious what had to be done, and Connor anticipated those canines ripping him apart as soon as he let go. But at least Set would be mortal.

He opened his hand, watching the ankh slip from his fingers and plummet three hundred feet into the growling sea below. As Set roared in anguish above him, Connor curled inward in preparation for the inevitable.

Oblivion never came. There was only the warmth of twin fire swords, and the comfort of Raphael's proximity.

The angel and Lucifer stood on either side of Set. Their weapons crisscrossed his throat, casting a blend of blue and red across his skin. While Set transformed back into his human form rather immediately, the snarl took longer to fall.

"Now, now," Lucifer said, inching Michael's sword close enough to graze Set's skin. "The last thing you want is to die by my hand. I think that means it's time for you to surrender."

Connor stared up from the ground, creeping his free hand back under his arm. He rested his palm on the butt of Castor, waiting for Set to retort. To retaliate. To untangle from his current predicament. To have some kind of backup plan to thwart them yet again. But with his greatest creation crumpled at the bottom of a ravine, and the vast majority of his spectres destroyed for good, there was nothing to save him this time.

Set spat a curse and lowered himself to both knees. Athena and two Sanctines who Connor didn't recognize swooped upon Set. As one group, they dragged him to his feet with his arms restrained behind his back.

Raphael lowered his sword and de-manifested the blade. He hooked the hilt back onto his belt, smiling down at Connor with an expression of relief. *Cover me,* Connor had asked him. And so he had. He always would.

# 27

The Graveyard of Gods fell quiet, save for the hushed words and creaky movements of aftermath. The remaining Inquisitors dusted themselves off, checked each other for injury and dented armor. Hephaestus and Aphrodite had been around minutes before but since vanished from the jetty. Connor snorted to himself, wondering if they were making out like teenagers somewhere. Whatever had happened between them while he was away clearly did good for them.

In these post-adrenaline hazes, Connor always took a few moments of alone time, willing his mind and body to realign. So, he leaned against a statue of an old goddess, her pedestal covered in runes. She could have been as old as Phoenician. She towered over him, one hand outstretched, larger than life. At least, maybe she had been once. Now she was just stone. They all would be, one day, human and Sanctine alike. Seemed that Ascendants were the only creatures immune to such things, but if they had to look like nightmarish shadow creatures to do it...hard pass.

Footsteps drew nearer, and a swinging brown ponytail emerged from the scant crowd.

"Clara?"

She engulfed him, leaping into the bodily nook where she had so often curled as a child. Clara's long hair cascaded over her arms.

She pulled back, hands still grasping his elbows. "I think we managed to take down all the spectres. I guess without anyone leading them, they're not going to do much else…"

"Not gonna lie, you were pretty badass out there."

"No big deal. Just played a bit of Dark Souls before." She winked. "That, and always trying to figure out how to do things in the laziest way possible."

"The simplest answer is usually the right one."

Connor ran fingers over her hair. He missed the quiet moments— carpooling her to class on his way to work or sharing Chinese takeout on Friday nights. He used to feel like he learned so much about her during their quiet talks, about her emotions and her goals and the way she thought. In hindsight, he'd learned more about her in a few days of peril and adventure than in years of little chats.

"I can't believe it's only been a few days since we were in Tunis," he said. "Feels like a lifetime."

Clara snorted. "Yeah. I could go back to school before finals at this rate."

"Still going back to college after all this?" Connor smiled. "You know what? Good for you. Always wanted you to be the educated one."

"*Or*…we could get to Dublin from here. Just a hop through a portal. I think Raphael said one of them could drop us off at the Hill of Tara, and from there we can get a ride into town." Clara shrugged. "I imagine Mam and Dad are back there by now."

"Yeah. Guess we should check in with them. By now they'll know that we never made it back to the States."

Footsteps approached them, soft and crunchy. Connor didn't have to look into his bond to know who was drawing near. Clara bowed her head, hiding a grin as she untangled herself from Connor.

"I'll give you guys some time," she murmured under her smirk. Clara said nothing to Raphael as she slipped past him, but Connor spied the furtive pat she gave his arm.

Raphael moved closer, close enough to touch. His eyes were larger than usual, swollen. Connor's throat grew thick. What to say?

"See?" Connor broke the ice, laughing under his breath. "Told you to trust me."

One moment, the angel stood a few feet away. The next, Raphael was in his arms, his hands grasping Connor's face, his lips moving against Connor's in a crushing, desperate kiss.

When they finally parted, Connor could hardly breathe.

"Never do that again," Raphael whispered against his lips.

He swallowed. *Hngh, what are words again?*

"It, uh...it worked out. Besides, you don't need to worry about me."

"Of course I do. You're my ward."

"Just your ward?"

"No. Much more." Those three words burned through Connor's chest despite the simplicity of them. "But...perhaps we do need to talk about that."

Connor sighed. "Yeah. Look, you're gorgeous, and you could probably punch a hole through a comet, so I think it's probably obvious why I dig you. But...what the hell do you see in me? I'm just a hot second of your life. And even if I wasn't, I'm pretty surprised you'd put up with my paranoid ass."

"You're a lot more than that." Raphael laced their fingers together. "You make me wiser, braver. I could sense when you used to block me through the bond, but all I wanted to do was tear it down and see you properly."

Connor snorted, looking away. "And when you did?"

"I found a lovely heart, Connor."

Hard to believe that after so many years of doubt, so many years of preparing himself to be disappointed. But no, this was real. Tangible. Shared. Elation had flared mutually in their bond in the Claustrum, when he had slipped his fingers into Raphael's hair, pressed his lips against the angel's. Relief and longing filled their bond with the kiss Raphael had just given him. And judging from the barest hint of red on Raphael's pale face, he knew he'd be welcome to do it over and over again.

Across the jetty, Lucifer met Connor's eyes and smirked. The expression didn't match the rest of him. A burly Sanctine held his arms behind his back, and Hachiman stood guard over him, his lips a flat slash. About the first thing Hachiman did as soon as Set surrendered was to tackle Lucifer straight to the ground and prevent him from slithering away.

Raphael caught him watching the prince of darkness. "What is it?"

"Lucifer. What's going to happen to him?"

"He's kept his part of the deal, and I've kept mine. I spoke to Hachiman, along with leaders from the Guild of Law and Justice. I explained that Lucifer was a necessary ally to us, and that he did not make an attempt to run or betray us. They've agreed to let him reside in Cocytus now. He should be much happier there, but still far away from any harm he could cause."

"He's had so many opportunities to kill both of us and he didn't." Connor bumped his shoulder, lightly. "Maybe you are a good judge of character. I'm sorry I gave you shit about it."

"Maybe I'm not. Even if Lucifer redeems himself, I'm not sure my memories of Michael can ever be repaired…"

Raphael looked away. Connor could also feel the remorse and distress tugging at angelic heartstrings. Connor hadn't meant to reopen that wound, but it was pretty clear Michael wasn't the hero Raphael had worshipped for so many years. Regardless of whether his actions with Lucifer were justified, his Ascendant inquisition showed that not even angels were perfectly righteous.

Raphael looked to his feet, continuing. "He kept so much from all of us. The Ascendants were perhaps dangerous, but if he really felt justified in his actions, why cover it up? No one keeps a secret unless they feel guilt for it. I wish I could confront him about it, but…"

*But he's gone.* Through the bond, Raphael's gloominess overwhelmed him. Connor allowed the tide to wash over him, accepting it peacefully, and returned a sense of understanding. He reached for Raphael's hands, folding them between his own.

"Hey. My parents are probably in Ireland by now. It's a pretty nice place, if you're interested in joining me. Might be nice to get away for a while…get your mind off all this. And hell," he smiled, "it's almost Christmas."

Raphael's expression lightened substantially. "I'd be honored to meet your parents."

The more Connor considered it, the more it sounded like a terrible idea to bring gods home to Mam and Dad. But he couldn't deny the attractive image of Raphael sitting by Gran's fireplace, a 100-year-old Dickens novel spread across his lap, as Mam brought them evening tea, or the image of Raphael on the porch swing, immune to the chill of falling snow. Connor had once feared seeing Raphael in the mundane, like it was somehow defiling the sacred, but now he reveled in such fantasies.

"No idea how I'm gonna explain all this to them, but I guess we'll cross that bridge. So. Think your schedule's open?"

The light came fully back into Raphael's face, echoed in the invisible bond meandering toward Connor's heart. "For you? Always."

<hr />

It rained in Ireland with sweet, welcoming arms. Connor watched rivulets of water trickle down the bus's window and the hills of Tara pass beyond their streaks. Tara was home to a portal, due to its sacred history with the kingdom of Avalon. And at forty-five minutes outside of Dublin, it was the easiest path back to Mam and Dad.

Beside Connor, Raphael sat in stillness. The bond between them laid calm and comfortable. Emotions ebbed and flowed between them without conscious thought in a companionable silence Connor once thought gone forever.

In the opposite row, Clara slept mildly against the bus's window, head rocking back and forth with the rickety movement of the vehicle. Hephaestus and Aphrodite occupied the seats directly in front of her, chatting idly. The noise of the bus overwhelmed their voices, drowning out the specifics. To outside eyes, they could have been a couple on their honeymoon, their hands perpetually clasped with one another's.

The bus stopped at the entrance to Mam and Dad's neighborhood, a quaint street of identical row homes called Black Rock. Connor exited behind all the others and tightened his jacket around himself to fight off the wet Irish morning. Black Rock always smelled the same: damp, Earthy, mentholated. It tied his memories together from his years as a toddler through teenage Christmases and visits to his elderly grandparents.

He frowned at the identical houses. Despite having visited this place a dozen times, he still didn't remember which one was Gran's.

Clara's elbow hit his ribs. "Follow me."

He had to smirk. Of course that's why he never bothered remembering—Clara was always there to keep track of things.

They walked up the steps of a white-washed townhome. Moss grew between the stones in the sidewalk, scant splashes of color against the washed-out brick.

Connor shifted himself toward the front of the group and knocked on the door. The seconds ticked by, dense and long, then a slender hand slipped into his. In the corner of his vision, Raphael encouraged him with shy smile. Connor squeezed the hand, his cheeks growing warm.

Mam opened the door, her lips parting. She glanced between her children, reaching a hand toward each of them. "Connor? Clara?"

"Hi, Mam." He couldn't fight the grin broadening on his face. "How about we finish that vacation?"

# EPILOGUE

Cocytus: the prison of invisible bars. For miles and miles, islands made of ash floated in a sea of holy water beneath the cavernous Abyssus sky. On the edge of every island, marble crosses stood every six inches to lock their prisoners in. To touch any of it, or to attempt escape, would ignite the unwise prisoner in never-ending flames.

Lucifer sat cross-legged in the middle of his isle—his *cell*—silent, watching, fingers wrapped around his ankles. The water quaked with the rumblings of punishment below. Other wretched creatures, like the starved Judas Iscariot, whimpered nearby in their personal hells.

Ambient groans filled the air, along with the occasional ruffle of fire. A few prisoners had made escape attempts long ago, but the fires of punishment still used their flesh for kindling.

Lucifer wouldn't make the same mistake.

He stood, smirking, his bare feet sinking into white powder. He stared down the fence of crosses, power surging through his veins. All the power had laid dormant inside him, jailed within his bones for millennia while he sat in a prison made specifically for him. For someone of his kind.

Once he escaped, it would take days for anyone to realize he'd gone. And when they did, they would stand baffled by how he did it. They'd check every nook and cranny of their ancient prison for some point of failure but find nothing.

Their one mistake was trying to cage an Ascendant.

# ACKNOWLEDGMENTS

Paradisa was a seven year labor from first draft to publication, so many hands were involved in creating the book you see today. I probably had two dozen betas, too numerous to name individually, but I am grateful for all their feedback. I'm especially thankful for Greg Howard, who has always been curious and supportive of my writing since we were children together, and who gave me some of the best ideas for elevating this book in its earliest drafts.

I'm grateful for my husband and muse Austin, who always could get me out of a tough spot with enough conversation; for my mother Janet, who read at least two iterations of the book and gave me the very base concept for it - "what if all the gods teamed up?" - way back in 2009; for the team at Falstaff books for taking a chance on my cinematic gay myth book; for Leona Wisoker for providing an early developmental edit; and for all the folks who encouraged me and followed my progress back in my Wordpress days. Millie Ho and Thomas Reich, I'm looking at you.

Finally, the most significant person involved in the crafting of this book is Michelle Hazen, my mentor from Pitch Wars, who plucked this manuscript out of a field of sixty and spent the next three months of her life dedicated to making it publishable. The confidence and worldliness I gained from working with Michelle legitimately changed my life as an artist, and I'm so humbled that she still has kept tabs on what's going on with this book, even after all these years.

# ABOUT THE AUTHOR

Michelle Iannantuono is an award winning filmmaker, debut novelist, and online content creator, most primarily known for the found footage horror film Livescream, and her queer transformative fan films in the Detroit Become Human universe. Her work leans in the science fiction, fantasy, and horror directions, because before switching careers to follow her passion, she was an industrial chemist (which is equal parts scientific and horrifying). When she's not behind the camera or behind the pen, she's probably gaming, fangirling something, or politely asking Cthulhu to eat her chaos.

ALSO BY MICHELLE IANNANTUONO

Livescream

Available at all Video On Demand Services

Coming Soon

Detroit Evolution

# FALSTAFF BOOKS

**Want to know what's new
And coming soon from
Falstaff Books?**

**Try This Free Ebook Sampler**

https://www.instafreebie.com/free/bsZnl

**Follow the link.
Download the file.
Transfer to your e-reader, phone, tablet, watch, computer,
whatever.
Enjoy.**